Fidan Bagirova

I Am a Shoe ... And You?

Shoes fashion and the modern world of jet-setters

ISBN: 0985197307

ISBN-13: 9780985197308

Library of Congress Control Number: 2012909958

NADIF Publishing

Part One

Part Two

Part One

Chapter 1

Ellie *and* Bernie

Ellie and Bernie

They were twins. Their facial features and body sizes matched perfectly. Still young, the colour of the shining extravagant skin was angelic, and the purple outer skin was slightly scratched from the rough London streets. Vivacious in colour, they shimmered on their journey through the dull pavement filled with monochromatic shoes walking in all directions.

It was late January, and the cold breeze was a reminder of almost-forgotten wintry weather. They were newborn, not even a week old. High-postured and straight-backed, their elegance and beauty could be seen from meters away. They fit perfectly, enveloping neatly manicured feet that poked shyly out of the ends, just over the golden sole of the shoes. With an Egyptian feel, their ancestors dated from 7,000 BCE. These twins were very much from a certain background; their forebears were worn by Cleopatra. And unlike much of today's footwear, they were personally named and designed by Balthazar Bozzi, a legendary Italian shoe designer whose masterpieces were iconic fashion must-haves.

Peculiar beings, they at all times watched the rest of us, without our even perceiving them.

They protected feet and were a fashion accessory, a must-have in our urbanized world. These twins, however, were particularly keen on placing themselves in the global society, as they felt understated. They could not accept the treason of their fellow shoes.

A block of wood had been chiselled into a wooden last from the print that Balthazar had created of the sensual feet of Hollywood's newest star actress, Crystal Baron.

Marlon Gordon Wesley was an oil and real estate magnate from Denver. He had moved to Los Angeles along with his family and began investing in films. It took him little time to develop one of the most successful film production companies in the USA. He gave enormous importance to women's feet.

There were rumours that he chose his main actresses according to the neatness and beauty of their feet rather than their talent. In fact, according to a Hollywood news story, one actress complained that he never allowed her on the set because she had a foot injury.

Crystal was Marlon's newest star. She was strikingly beautiful in every way, and he cherished her beauty and that extra glow that made an actress a fabulous Hollywood star.

However, things were getting complicated at home for Marlon. His daughter found out about his affair with Crystal. Still upset by her mother's recent death, his daughter threatened to leave if he did not end the relationship immediately. A family man, Marlon chose to let go of his passionate love to avoid causing more pain to his loved ones.

Nonetheless, he decided to order the most exquisite pair of shoes for his lovely Crystal. It would be his very last present to her, and he wanted to make sure that it would be ideal, as though he were giving her a part of his heart in the shoes.

Balthazar Bozzi, an old friend and Hollywood's most wanted shoe designer, was the best choice to create Marlon's vision.

Balthazar worked very hard on the shoe prints. And when they were finished, they were still not the exact dimensions of Crystal's anatomical foot, which would be the closest to size 7.5. Instead, they seemed to be an abstract representation of some pop art *chef d'oeuvres*.

Balthazar personally clipped the wooden shoe prints he was choosing in the crocodile skin imported straight from Senegal's finest leather importer. The very same importer provided leather for Buckingham Palace and the British Royal family.

Balthazar was very careful with this particular shoe project, especially when the upper sections were shaped to the insole. Then he followed by bottoming, the key part in shoe making where the sole is attached to the upper. The process of bottoming was the hardest, yet it determined the fundamental structure of the shoe.

Balthazar had a special technique that he kept as a sacred secret even from his closest friends and family members. His shoes were somehow incredibly comfortable no matter the heel length. He had figured out how to mathematically balance out the feet, and he had created the dimensions of the sole and the heel in such a way that a woman could spend hours walking on eight-inch heels and not have foot ache or fatigue.

'I can't, he's tickling again,' giggled Ellie while Bernie tried to detach herself from her shoe body and not feel the tickles. But her sister interrupted her, and she burst into a loud laughter. 'My nose is itching. What a bizarre sensation. And you?' cried Ellie. 'Me too, he's been polishing the same spot over and over. But I have to admit, we look terribly cute!' said Bernie as she watched Ellie being polished. They were surrounded by spiky stilettos, thigh-high boots, intricately beaded lizard-skin moccasins, and feathered and jewelled evening shoes of all colours and materials. Here they were the most fine-looking, sophisticatedly sewed crocodile pumps.

'What do you think she'll look like?' asked Bernie.

'I think she will be blonde,' murmured Ellie, who enjoyed teasing her sister.

'I think brunette! Let's bet,' said Bernie. The twins laughed when two masculine hands picked them up to repaint their freshly sewed soles.

'It's so cold. Seriously, why do these humans have a heating system if they don't bother heating the paint before painting us?' said Bernie displeasingly.

'I wonder how they would feel if I painted their bums in cold purple paint,' Ellie said with irritation in her voice.

Then they were placed in a special heating machine to help the sole dry. 'Feels great! I love to be in the sauna in the middle of the day,' declared Bernie, who was enjoying the warm air from all sides.

Ellie was hugging a piece of rubber. She still had her baby reflex, and this was her teddy bear. Indeed, these gorgeous little pumps could talk. Human beings wouldn't hear them, but the rest of the shoe society and many other objects with souls could. Ellie and Bernie were privileged to be beautiful and they were a special order, which meant their creator used the best materials to create their body features. In addition, they also inherited the basic morals of Balthazar Bozzi, who often spoke to his shoes. The old man spent so many working hours on his special orders that he caught himself talking out loud to his shoe babies. Crazy or lonely, Balthazar was a genius who knew how to create beauty.

The twins had a great time at their shoe nursery, otherwise known as the shoe atelier of Balthazar Bozzi. Their time with Balthazar didn't last forever, however. Soon after their birth, they were sent to Upper East Side New York, where Crystal Baron, the Hollywood A-list actress, was to receive them as a gift from Marlon Gordon Wesley.

The door bell rang as the dazzling blonde Crystal rushed to open the door. She looked at the package and felt excited like a little girl who just received her present from Santa Claus.

'Ma'am I have a package for you' said a medium tall man in his early thirties with a Latino accent.

'Thank you' she gently took the beautifully presented black gift box package. Nervous with excitement she stood still for a moment. The brilliant sunlight sparkled from the precious box, beckoning her it seemed, begging to be opened. The inviting burgundy bow was very elegantly tied on the top of the box. Crystal wondered what the tempting package contained. Her imagination created intriguing scenarios, for the box was so beautiful on the outside, how could it not hold exquisite treasures inside?

Inside the box Ellie and Bernie were waiting anxiously.

She couldn't wait any longer and opened it hurriedly with her tender little fingers.

As she unwrapped the crimson packaging paper and removed the box top she suddenly saw two most delicate, cutest and sweetest little baby crocodile black pumps with shiny purple sole that gave them a special twinkle glow. Resplendent in all the finest shoes she had seen in her life, great amazement and wonder took hold of her, such was the effect of the Bozzi twin's beauty. They watched her with amazement. She was really gorgeous her face was like one of a fairy tale princess. Her eyes were one of a very genuine and affectionate lady.

'My babies!' she exclaimed and took them out one after the other hugging and smelling the newly painted leather.

'She's very touchy! I'm tickled Bernie!' giggled Ellie

'She's saying hello to us, what a warm hearted woman!' happily admitted Bernie.

There was a little envelope with Marlon Gordon Wesley's initials. She opened the envelope with her silver plated envelope opener from Collet of rue du Rhone in Geneva. She had received it as a gift from her Swiss fans last month.

She took the letter gently and held it close to her eyes. In a matter of seconds her eyes were filled with tears.

A great wave of compassion swept over the twins who watched their stunning mistress heartbreak.

'How could he leave her?" asked Ellie.

'Balthazar told us we were her last goodbye gift, don't you remember?' said Bernie anxiously.

'I did not realise it was going to be like this' said Ellie saddened by what she was seeing. Crystal's tears were running down her pale cheek bones right on the marble floor where they lay still sparkling like diamonds. She rubbed her eyes put on a Barry White CD and slid her feet into the new crocodile pumps. The minute she had her feet in them she felt like a dancing angel. Her feet have never felt this comfortable.

She opened a bottle of Crystal Roederr Champagne, put the volume slightly louder and danced the day away like she were living a dream.

'It feels so awkward but I love it' Ellie exclaimed.

'I know I hardly feel my soles but I feel balanced and I am feeling the floors like I owe them' said Bernie in bliss.

'This place looks amazing!' said Bernie delightfully trying to change the topic and feel positive about their first day in a human apartment.

Crystal's apartment was soft, feminine and grand by NY standard, with a soft eclectic and Baroque touch. Furniture was mainly velvet light blue and pistachio with a small number of white and cream coloured details. She had many mirrors and the wild vanilla aroma of the apartment was blending wonderfully with the interior design that was very soft and smooth comfort oriented with a few antiques here and there.

Crystal fell in love with her new shoes; it was love at first sight.

She couldn't stop looking at them. Marlon's gifts were always very dear to her yet this last present was one of a kind. She gave up on all her other shoes and wore her new little ones everywhere.

'She's blonde! I won,' giggled Ellie.

'Blonde indeed,' Bernie smiled.

'If I were a human I would invite you out for a lunch or buy you a pair of shoes' giggled Bernie 'Instead I offer you this gorgeous actress our dear Crystal. Isn't it ironic how human think they owe us when in reality they cannot live without us they all need to have us to embellish their legs and feet' Bernie chuckled. She was in a very jokey and happy mood where life seemed like an entertaining and amusing playground.

'Aren't we the luckiest?! Bernie, dear, we are carrying around the most famous actress in Hollywood! I mean, could it get any better?' she demanded jokingly. They were astonished. They had never envisaged such a life. Carrying around a Hollywood star meant they were going to be in the centre of attention as well.

The twins enjoyed the view of Manhattan from Crystal's magnificent apartment and were overwhelmed with cheerfulness. Ellie and Bernie glanced at Crystal who was getting ready to walk towards the beautifully decorated dessert tray filled with an assortment of luxury handmade Belgium chocolates. It was still early yet the meeting with the Crystal their mistress and the trip until her apartment tired the twins and shortly after she placed them back in their box where they napped for a few days.

Vogue USA, 1996

An Italian-born fashion guru, Balthazar Bozzi is famous for his daring and sometimes shocking designs. This season he revamps the classic black pump with bright-purple leather sole. The black crocodile looks fiercely elegant for day and evening; these are some pretty amazing shoes! And as if the eight-inch heel isn't fabulous enough, there's also a hidden one-inch platform! Where can we buy it? 'This was a special order for Crystal Barron; however, my new season will be concentrated on daily pumps in a similar style as these are the one-and-only private order.'

The twins noticed the brightness of the daylight and the fresh gentle wind in Union Square in late February. They were still virgin-like with plenty of hopes and expectations for their very first walk on genuine streets. Indeed, the sensation felt rather bizarre to them, although they were simply enclosing little harmless human feet. They were indistinguishable, just like the twins. They had enjoyed an unforgettable tickling when Crystal slid her feet into them for the very first time. Shortly after they adjusted to fit the feet flawlessly, their texture made them the ultimate in perfection.

Their father was an exceptionally experienced shoemaker who had worked on shoe designs for decades. They were indeed proud to hold his name. In fact, they were the blue blood aristocracy of the so-called "shoe society."

Even though the shoe view of the world was from the lower perspective, and humans did seem as giants to them, they walked with dignity and offered individuals that extra touch of allure, style, confidence, and comfort.

Not only did they make women's legs look great, they influenced the speed and mood of their owner. When wearing uncomfortable shoes, women tended to walk less. But wearing comfortable shoes made women smile and generally feel happier about themselves.

On the left was Ellie, whose name in Italian, *Eleanora,* means "shining light". Bernie was on the right, whose name in Greek, *Bernice,* means "victory bringer." While they were identical on the outside, inwardly they were total opposites. Balthazar had felt their differences as he was curving, shaping, and bending the leather and fashioning the heel. Ellie gave of herself easily. She fully trusted Balthazar to make the best out of her. Bernie was a more disobedient creature who was bent and topped up only with difficulty.

Thus Balthazar named the twins, as Eleanora (Ellie) was open to change and was innocent and unquestioning, resembling dazzling sunlight, while Bernice (Bernie) was named after his own grandmother, a very strong-minded and stubborn lady.

While some might consider naming a shoe in memory of one's grandmother disrespectful, Balthazar considered his shoes his masterpieces, his newborn children. He was very attentive to their characteristics, and, having spent almost all his life making and working with shoes, he had developed a strong passion and love for them. They were living creatures in his eyes, which resulted in the twins getting souls, unlike many other shoes.

The two were nicknamed the baby twins, Ellie and Bernie. Only on rare occasions would they remember their full names, which were inscribed on the back of each heel: Eleanora and Bernice.

Bernie had a rather more masculine approach to life. She liked things to be her way. She cherished traditional British education where there were high values placed on manners, respect, and self-discipline. She wasn't fond of change and preferred to remain in one place, in quiet and peace.

She was a patient, steadfast, and reliable personality. Little Bernie was especially solid and enduring; continuing with dogged persistence long after everyone else had given up. However, she could be particularly resistant to change, unable to adapt to new and innovative ways of thinking.

Of course, she appreciated the social evenings at gallery openings and could never forget that wonderful night at the Metropolitan Opera opening in September. She very much enjoyed being surrounded by luxury, in elegant and what could often be referred to as snobbish circles. Bernie felt like an aristocrat, and she was convinced that her aim in life was to live up to her aristocratic shoe roots.

Bernie's downfall would be the way she often appeared stolid and phlegmatic. However, she had a strong fund of common sense. Furthermore, she was always very cautious, constructive, and stable.

Ellie was a free-spirited artist like who enjoyed life. She was open to novelty and spontaneity. She tended to collect shoe friends the way some people assembled an art collection. She felt a deep desire to be free, and she made many fellow shoes friends in her adventures. She had very few confidants, though. In fact, she had only one, her dear sister and best friend Bernie.

Ellie had a deep need to search for wisdom. If she were human, she would have been a great philosopher and explorer. Her appetite for learning and travel formed her openness to the exterior universe and not just the rigid shoe society. Ellie preferred to be footloose and fancy-free, and as a sister and a friend she promoted an enjoyable, happy, and fun atmosphere.

Ellie loved dramatic change and adventures. At one point she became rather close with the dirty, stinky grey Converses who belonged to the electrician who came to fix the lights a few times and left the shoes behind. Crystal felt bad to throw them away so she kept them by the door neatly on the floor. Converses told Ellie about their great adventures and stories of the street life. She was forced to keep that friendship secret, as Bernie didn't approve of it, calling the Converses 'uneducated, filthy kids who should learn better than to tell empty stories about streets.'

Ellie respected her sister, but she was filled with natural curiosity to get to know the Converses better. They had a history as well, as their family had survived for decades and still were seen everywhere. True, they were not handmade, but at least they felt free in their natural and simplistic design. They were all about comfort, fun, and free spirits. They were even considered to be more fashionable when they looked used. They were the new downtown New York trend, street funky style.

Ellie sometimes wished she had been made a Converse shoe, but then she thought that she might be the only limited edition Bozzi with such an open mind to new ideas and artistically free-spirited approach to life.

'Where are we off to?' asked Ellie.

'To our annual shoe society meeting,' said Bernie.

The International Shoe Society

In the Metropolitan museum in uptown Manhattan, they all gathered for the "Shoes of the world exhibition". They hadn't a clue that a major political coup could take place right under their dresses. Indeed, the shoes' revolutionary meetings occurred right under them. In its high-gloss epoxy

The International Shoe Society, ISS, was the real shoe name of the event. The previous year it occurred in the Guggenheim Museum, but this year The Met agreed to gather up the exhibition.

The shoes gathered from all over the world. Some flew in, others drove, and some just walked a few blocks. They were all excited to hear about great shoe inventions, new trends, and tips for longevity.

This year's main topics would be fashion and its advantages and disadvantages, high-maintenance shoes, humans and their feet, and the perfect size for heels.

They were all there—a sparkling stiletto, a leather knee boot with red-leather inset, a brocade dance shoe with rhinestone buckle from the 1930s, a stacked-heel Mary Jane with faux python trim from the 1970s, a suede zippered bootie with gold chain overlay on the heel, a green-leather pump with upturned toe and decorative topstitching, a tiger-striped snakeskin peep-toe platform, a silk pump with die-cut beaded vamp, a sculptural vertigo heel with wood and metal oversize wedge. And a silk court shoe with metal and silk floral embroidery of early 1700s watched over everyone on the top shelf. They were thousands flown from different countries and museums. Some young, some old, they were the world representatives of the ISS.

Today's speakers were a blue-suede, low-heeled platform blue pump with two-tone rosette ornaments named Miss Violet Love, a multi-leather stiletto sandal with metallic napa piping named Kitty, and a beaded handmade Spanish sandal named Denis Jose Ignasio Pinto. The special guest was a handmade, plastic-and-wire wings shoe prototype named Heather Paperstein.

Ellie and Bernie were seated at the first row, which meant grand respect but above all a lot of expectations. The hundreds of shoes were eyeing them, glazing at their stitching, their skin, and their slim heels. The chunky heels threw them jealous looks. Everyone wanted to be them—slim elegant, and smart.

'Dear ladies shoes and gentlemen shoes,' began one of the speakers with an ear-splitting voice with a Scandinavian accent that definitely made all the shoes listen to him.

'We are here today to celebrate the shoe society annual meeting. We have guests from all over the world to discuss the issues and progresses that we shoes have. Beforehand I would like to thank you all for assisting. Your presence here is immensely meaningful to shoes all over the world. Their future is in your hands.' The speaker was a plain, dark-blue suede Moccasin, but his voice was very sharp and shoe-persuasive.

'He should play the main role in Hamlet next month,' whispered Ellie in her sister's ear.

'I don't know about him but I want us one day to be up there and give grand speeches' dreamingly said Bernie

'Shush, listen. It's important,' pointed at Bernie a classic pink Lurex brocade pump dating 1950s. Ellie and Bernie both looked at her and didn't quite know what to say as Balthazar taught them to respect the elder human or shoes, they were brought up to be smooth with the elder shoe generation.

A voice came from the back 'Don't worry, she has temper issues these days, you know age doesn't make her happier' said a silky embroidered pansy motif slipper with velvet trim. He came from France in the 1860s and was beautifully conserved at a private shoe collector - who every year sent him to shoe museums and exhibitions around the world

'In my retirement years there's not too much walking but a lot of flying' he admitted

'You look very young,' said Ellie, analysing the shoes skin and the omnipresent wrinkles.

'And very happy' said Bernie.

The slipper looked at the twins and smiled 'I am quite old; in fact I lost count of my years. But you are right I look awfully young, didn't walk in centuries and have been pampered and re-painted too many times. Sometimes, I wish I had a piece of dust fall on me, the minute it does human hands quickly take it off me and place me into a glass capsule where I feel like a shoe trophy.' He inhaled and watched the twins. 'You are still young but you will see after having walked for a few seasons you will get tired and this is a great way to retire. One has to be lucky of course. Not easy to be the "chosen shoe" but hey why not give it a try my dear brother always says.' The shoes exchanged a few pleasant comments, Ellie and Bernie thanked the slipper for his insights and they continued watching the speeches of the shoes.

The gathering also included celebrities' shoes: Miranda Kerr and Orlando Bloom wore their wonderfully happy shoes, Jack Nicholson wore classic, dark-navy aristocratic shoes amongst others less famous yet still all beautiful and wonderful.

Violet, an electric-blue pump with bead-trimmed platform, began her speech.

She rattled a few facts while watching the lousy pink ballerina shoe that was half asleep from what seemed like her last night grand performance. Violet switched focus and watched the grand shoe audience that were eyeing her every move.

'Welcome, welcome, welcome! She said in her most dramatic Atlantic accent 'I am pleased to see such a variety of shoes everywhere. My shoe heart pumps faster from this excitement,' she said thrilled with joy. She looked around satisfied to see the numerous colourful shoes, her bead-trimmed platform shaked from all the shoe eyes on her and she continued after taking a deep breath.

'We are here today to discuss the impact of fashion on shoes. As you all know, we have been experiencing a high growth of our shoe population, and that is thanks to fashion. Women's shoe demand growing higher means shoes birthrate is increasing by day. Our value has also grown in price for unique shoes and it has lowered for factory-made ones. Indeed, our society is fighting against the shoe-soulless beings that have been fabricated without a soul. However, a new miraculous factor has begun. Human beings are becoming shoes. Every day we get letters, and our agents are interviewing shoes who were human beings and one day woke up as their favourite shoes. Nature is balancing out the quantity of shoe without a soul- shoes and humans with souls that are better suited to be shoes. Our dress code has become one of high variety and grand choices, thanks to designers' shoes becoming even more popular.' The blue pump Violet cleared her shoe voice and continued. 'I would like to present Kitty, the expert in shoe fashion.'

As Kitty was walking to the tribune she looked around to look at the hundreds of shoes around her. Kitty's shoe nose was nervous and at the same time thrilled to see the other shoes and feel the shoe power and the shoe presence in the world that often is being neglected and not taken seriously. They were tapping with their heels and shouting out 'Bravos'. She smiled and waved - she loved being a shoe.

A multi-leather stiletto sandal with metallic napa piping Kitty, had a warned out tired voice of a hardworking yet still impeccable looking female. She was a shoe who was determined to make it through the shoe life being a hero. As she looked at the audience she saw that everyone seemed happy to be there, they were friendly and talkative. Kitty began her speech

'I carry the editor of Vogue, and I must say that I see the fashion companies, designers, and journalists working day and night to always let the most competent shoes be the *"IT"* shoes. Of course they don't choose it by comfort, so dear feet have to suffer at times. However, I see that they are really looking for creativity and choose the shoes very democratically. Indeed, some designers seem to have lost their talent at creating shoes. I have talked to some major shoe designer shoes, and they explained that sometimes we should talk to the younger generation shoes, as the older we get the older our taste and preferences are as well. I cannot say that I disagree however I also told them that the younger generation should seek advice from the elder as we have more shoe experience than they do even if their ideas are more fit with the todays modern world' She waved at the audience and smiled like a true Hollywood star.

'We will prevail, dear fellow shoes!' She exclaimed in joy 'Our photos are in the shoe illustrative books, and some of us are in shoe museums. And most importantly, *Vogue, Elle, Bazaar*, and other fashion magazines always catch any newborn shoe with high potential. There is no need like in the past to be from a respected shoe brand name, in today's world any shoe can be the next shoe star.' She pointed her heel at a fuchsia Tory Burch pump that lay innocently next to her twin and was watching with her big gold medallion that illuminated her face and made it even more attractive.

'Yes you my dears! Before 1994 your name hasn't been known in the shoe society.' A gasp from all around the shoes begun whispering and pointing at the poor ballerinas who looked puzzled at the speaker.

'Despite their fairly new name in the shoe industry they are today one of the most favourites in the fashion world.'

The shoe face expressions of the shoes changed immediately with curiosity and interest in the Tory Burches.

The ballerinas smiled and the looks of revulsion faded into relief. Kitty winked in a friendly way and showed a high five shoe sign at the shoes to ease their discomfort of being talked about from the tribune. Kitty remembered her young days how awfully shy she used to be and sympathised the little ballerinas for their cooperation.

'In a very short time Tory Burch label was an immediate success and was even endorsed by Oprah Winfrey show.' Kitty clapped her heels in the name of Tory Burch ballerinas. They smiled in return and waved to the rest of the audience

'She really knows how to give a good speech' noted Bernie.

'I know one day you and me will as well' said Ellie in an optimistic tone.

Everyone was looking when Kitty talked; they listened like soldiers listening to their general.

They won't allow any gorgeous shoe to go unnoticed. As for the less glamorous, like Uggs, Crocs, and Havaianas, they are in fact the most wanted and bought shoes. They represent comfort, which is a holy word for the feet. Many of you fellows know how upset these feet can get when they are not comfortable. To that end I want to wish you a very healthy year filled with smooth walks and promenades on silky, velvety, flat grounds.' Kitty finished her speech and received many shoe heel claps.

The conference took a few hours. Ellie and Bernie, amongst all the other shoes, were very interested in the international and national shoe businesses and relations. They were still fairly young, yet they had a lot of will to learn more and more about their shoe history and issues.

'I can see you're new here' whispered a red napa ankle boot with textile inset and chevron striped heel.

'We are it's our very first time here' said Bernie like an A student replying to her teacher.

'I got bored of these meetings it is always the same shoes talking and we are dragged to listen to them, it's pathetic' she said displeasingly.

'Why don't you go up there and talk?' asked Bernie

'I wasn't chosen it is not that easy, this whole shoe society structure is all about connections. If you know the right shoes everything will be nice and smooth, if not then you will spend the rest of your lives watching them teach you lessons from that shoe tribune.' She said pointing at the tribune.

'How do you meet the influential shoes?' enquired Ellie

'The ankle boot looked around her and said quietly 'It is all about being at the right place at the right time, just like cars there are Ferraris and Aston Martins. If you don't meet Ferrari don't worry because Aston is around the corner somewhere.' She inhaled shook her chevron striped heel and said 'It is important to be active and help other shoes but I just cannot get myself to do all of that I just want to live a quiet life. But if you two decide to be shoe activists then I suggest you watch these shoe fellows and what they have to tell. I wish you to be the net speakers little twins' smiled the boot.

The twins nodded 'Thank you our new friend' they both said melodically. The boot smiled, and shoe waved and tottered out.

Ellie and Bernie continued watching the rest of the speeches.

Denis Jose Ignasio Pinto, the Spanish beaded sandal, was called to the shoe tribune. Shoes began clapping their heels and watched Denis jump up on the stage. He cleared his throat and begun talking in his deep Spanish accent that made his speech even more lovely to listen too.

'I just came from Dubai, and it is a wonderful place for shoes. We do not walk as much as you do in New York, where grounds are uneven and trash bags leak and at times you can step on something very unpleasant.' He smiled as he watched the public raise their shoe noses to look at him. 'UAE and Dubai's weather is so hot that we mainly spend the day in the car or at malls. Malls are gigantic and very well air-conditioned. Our life expectancy is long yet passive we don't have much fresh air promenades or even any walks at all. We are most of the time covered with the cloth of the long robe or we are worn at home which is not enough for frivolous shoes like ourselves. Nevertheless I feel the happiest to look as young and beautiful while my fellow relatives who stayed in Europe look like they went through third world war.' He giggled mischievously.

'Middle Eastern women are known for their vast choice of clothes and shoes, but they also have massive dressing rooms that are the size of a New York penthouse. Men are less into fashion, yet still there are a few who have major shoe collections.' He said enjoying the attention and curiosity that he felt in the back rows, teenage shoes dreamed to travel around the world for their 'gap year' and he had grabbed their attention with the stories about the sunny Arabic land of Dubai.

The shoe audience were taken with Denise's story about UAE and clapped a few times when he praised the shoe society. Many never travelled anywhere but New York, others have came in from Africa and had no clue about the magic Arabian culture. Flippant giggles could be heard in the back of the audience, those were the youngsters who were dragged here by the elder ones to be part of the shoe society to hear out the elders a sort of an educational session. Denis clapped his heels on the white stage floor and continued with his speech overjoyed with delight to tell more of his wonderful travels. He lifted his sole and pointed to the east where there was a large projector with the grand buildings of the United Emirates.

'In the Arabic culture, it is seen as culturally rude to cross an ankle over a knee and display the sole of the shoe while talking to another person. Just like us, humans understand that no shoe wants to show its worn-out sole to the other shoes or to another human. That is simply embarrassing and not proper. Humans don't go around showing their underwear to the whole world. Why should we? As a sandal representative of today's conference, I must say that booties and closed shoes shouldn't feel left out. In Dubai and UAE, shoes are also being purchased. Perhaps they are not worn that often, but they are the chosen ones for the multiple long trips that our masters take.' He shook his nose and continued with his ever present Spanish accent that made his speech sound even more pleasant to listen to.

'People say that those in Dubai wear shoes, whereas those in Abu Dhabi are sandal-wearers. I think in both places humans mostly wear sandals and pumps. Boots are rarely worn, yet they are still sold in the numerous malls around the city. Their national sandals are called Na-aal. These are essentially the sandals that most people wear. Nice fellows. I have had a few encounters with the Na-aal, and they were very friendly.

'With all the wars and conflicts in the Middle East, I felt a little shoe insight into the reality of things would be informative. I know how media and newspapers portray that part of the world. I prefer to ignore human politics and enjoy the smooth, polished, cream-marble floors of the many places in Dubai,' said Denis Jose Ignasio in the jolly voice of a happy sandal.

Violet Love returned to the stage. 'Now that was a beautiful speech! Thank you for this little insight into Dubai. I have never been, but I do hope that one day my mistress will decide to go there. And I hope I shall be on the plane with her,' she said as she giggled.

Ellie and Bernie watched the stage as music began and a beautiful shoe performance proceeded. The special guest handmade plastic-and-wire wings shoe prototype Heather Paperstein flew in the air and performed some acrobatic shoe movements. They found the setting to be startling and marvellous with dimmed light and the white, winged shoe flying around. Astonished shoes gazed at

Heather like she was a shoe angel or ballerina from the Bolshoy Theatre.

It was the end of the conference, shoes were expected to mingle around and chat. Unfortunately Crystal was late for a business meeting, and she dragged the twins out.

'I didn't have time to exchange our heel sizes' exclaimed Ellie

'Don't worry you saw how they all looked at us we are hand-made Bozzi's you don't need to give your heel sizes to other shoes first day you meet them' muttered Bernie

'I just hoped to get some friends' said Ellie.

'Honey, my dear sister, we are each other's best friends forever, no need to search far' said Bernie with a pinch.

'Ellie jumped up and they marched the streets carefully placing their soles and making sure no chewing gum or other garbage was on the roads.

They had loved every minute of the conference and hoped to come back the following year.

Shoe Confession: Bernie the pump

My name is Bernice, but Bernie is what my dear sister and my friends call me. I have been born as a shoe and am very proud to be the creation of Balthazar Bozzi, the most talented shoemaker of the twenty-first century. At least, that is what I believe, as I have observed many shoes in my young yet still experienced life.

You might think being a shoe is *weird*. That's the new word all teenagers use for something they are not familiar with.

I'll describe for you the incredible shoe journey of my life.

We shoes are born into this wonderful world. There are many of us, young and old, and we all are here to serve human beings and their feet. Yet fashion has given us a power to be the most wanted thing that makes a woman happy. Society needs us, and we are happy to be there for our masters and mistresses. We observe their lives through the ground perspective. We feel every little vibration of their feet, and we often support them throughout a tough walk or a stressful day.

Here we are, two sisters. We might look identical, but we have two separate minds and souls. We are always together, and we love each other tremendously.

We are proud to be shoes, and we love helping our mistresses and making them look beautiful. Even though we are young I had met many shoes who have shared their life experiences and stories to help me form my own perspective of the world. The twenty-first century seems to be a very progressive era in which technology and fashion have moved to another level, yet human beings remain the same. Their need for emotional stability, love, and reassurance is the same. Unfortunately, much more than before, in today's world some human beings place such a great importance on objects that they become those very objects.

I haven't met such shoes, but many jeweller pieces and cars are alive thanks to their former owners. Indeed, it is a great secret that no one in the human world knows. Unlike my sister and me, many objects are not born with souls—they are manufactured, beautiful pieces that find life later on. We don't understand exactly how it happens to be, but it seems that when human beings value material objects too highly, they in fact make the objects more important than themselves. Slowly, without realizing it, these humans pass their lives into these objects. There is a famous story about a young woman who was extremely attached to her seven-karat diamond ring. After a few years of living in fear of losing it, having made her life around the ring, she one day disappeared. It is said that her beloved ring shines more than ever, and she is believed to be the ring. Of course, no human will ever know it. But we hear these objects, and they all have very adventurous stories to tell. Surprisingly, they love their lives and don't miss being human.

Of course, some are not happy with their object reality, and it takes these folks years to get used to their new life. In our case, we love our life as shoes. We will never know how it feels to be human. They seem to love us, so it is very convenient to be us.

Here I am, all honest with you folks. Being a shoe is a great responsibility. Nevertheless, we somehow feel peaceful. Balthazar, our dear father, and the rest of the newborns gave us a feeling of a certain foundation, and we knew that we were something special. Balthazar kept whispering to us how special and gorgeous we were. Whoever said compliments and saying nice things are useless was completely wrong. In fact, we believe our shoe self-confidence was developed right at that moment we were born into this world.

We quickly learned about human beings, gender, ethics, and what was right and appropriate and what wasn't. In reality, it felt like we had already been alive, as if we had just been asleep for a long time and had finally awakened. But we had no previous memories, so life to us was all-new.

We realized that relationships between men and women are very important and that sometimes they don't work out well. We were actually made for a man to comfort a woman. That is not always true, of course, just in our case. Balthazar said out loud that we would comfort a woman the day we were being made. Oh, I can still remember the tickling of my freshly carved heel. Unlike humans, our birth can take many days if we're handmade. Machine-fabricated shoes take only an hour.

Going back to men and women, we thought that a relationship between a man and a woman could well be compared to that between a foot and a shoe. Buying a pair of shoes is sort of like beginning a relationship. The fit and comfort of the shoes make up the compatibility between them. Sometimes, however, it takes a few days of walking and getting to know each other to adjust to the feet and be more at ease with each other's presence. Wearing shoes for too long tends to irritate the feet, just like human beings need some space from each other in order for a relationship to work.

Humans might see the world from higher perspective, but we feel more of it. We sense every vibe of nature, every rush of the subway that makes the roads slightly shiver. It is all transmitted through shoes.

In the fashion world, we play a tremendous role. Let's face the fact that we are the most-needed and desired objects in people's wardrobes.

The love affair between ladies and shoes has a solid footing. Ladies love us shoes simply because the style of shoes gives women an instant magical change in appearance. Any new pairs of shoes can make old clothing feel like new again, granting women completely new looks. Shoes can also let ladies feel good about their bodies. By simply wearing a pair of high-heeled shoes, ladies can have slimmer, sleeker, and longer legs, making them appear instantly gorgeous. Enough of self-publicity. We are simply living creatures that like to observe and help the human race.

Shoes are quite telling, especially if you're a real fashion connoisseur.

One can look at people's shoes and tell a lot about them, their culture, and their background.

These days, people often choose us well. The importance of fashion keeps footwear in the spotlight, especially in an urban environment.

Historically speaking, we shoes reveal the host of tortures people have put themselves through in the name of fashion.

For one thing, shoes can mean permanent damage. They are an example of the way people will modify their bodies for fashion. It's like liposuction and other gory things people do for reasons of vanity. However, Bozzi's are all very comfortable. I love my life as a shoe. Just think about it—what can make a girl change from looking all right to looking absolutely stunning? The right shoe is the key to looking fabulous regardless of the fast-paced change of fashion. Beautiful classic shoes, especially exotic skins like ours, stay in forever. Not many handbags can say the same, perhaps the Birkin and the classic black Chanel, but that's about it.

Unlike other garments, we shoes are very noticeable. And in New York's pedestrian-oriented traffic, we are often the first thing people see.

It's not for nothing that they say the best way to make a woman happy is to put your feet into her shoes.

Men act, and women appear. Men look at women. Women watch themselves being looked at. This determines not only most relations between men and women, but also the relations between women. The surveyor of woman in herself is male: the surveyed female. Thus she turns herself into an object, and most particularly an object of vision: a sight.

Our importance and popularity has been enhanced just recently with Carrie Bradshaw from *Sex and the City*. Her character exaggerated the importance of shoes in a woman's life; glossy magazines resold this as a serious idea; girls started yearning for $500 footwear; and suddenly it's an old saw that the wife nicks the credit card and compensates for everything that's missing in her life by hurrying down Madison to lace designer ribbons up her calf. The show somehow became a cultural phenomenon of shoe mania.

Human society has gone shoe-crazy. Kids beat each other up for Nike trainers, and grown women are found licking the window of the Jimmy Choo boutique. Shoes have become investments in artwork. There is a relentless quest for new styles and designs to spark shoe-related debate. There is no colour that cannot be tried, no material that cannot be tested.

Whereas once we were limited to certain styles and couldn't be made differently, now we are more extravagant than ever. The sky is the limit, as a Valentino pump used to say to us. Just as humans have become freer in spirit and more open-minded, shoes have followed this artistic mood.

As the UN proclaims freedom of speech and human rights and equality, shoes have picked up on this, and now they can be both cheap and stylish, super high-heeled and awkward, yet unique.

Manolo Blahnik famously stated that he spent his childhood making shoes for lizards and now spends his time making lizards into shoes. No material costs too much to become a shoe anymore. Cinderella could have her glass slipper in today's shoe-friendly world. My sister Ellie gets upset at that comment as she dreamed to be a crystal shoe. But I keep telling her that being a baby crocodile pump is much more old-school and forever; crystal shoes can't live long if worn. Their life expectancy couldn't be longer than a few months if not a week. Girls in today's world are not as careful as they used to be; they have such a variety of shoes in their huge closets that they tend to be less careful and more in the, 'I'll get a new pair for next year anyway" vibe. I don't approve of such behaviour; I'm more of an old-school girl. I like to be respected and worn by a well-balanced and mannered lady who will wear me gently and with class.

There are good sides to today's world too, of course. I love it that shoes today are not simply footwear. They are pieces of art and beauty, as high up in fashion as designer jewellery. Fashion designers have created outstanding shoes that are in some cases just to be looked at or worn exclusively on the red carpet.

Shoe fetishism is now sold as a crucial part of the modern woman's armoury. Imelda Marcos's shoe collection was apparently worth a million dollars, but you'd need a very specific buyer since they all fit Mrs Marcos.

As women's shoes, we see how wearing high heels is one of the great joys of being a woman, just as wearing enormous basketball shoes and oversized jeans appears to be one of the great joys of life if you're a skinny teenage boy. They both exaggerate the qualities that differentiate the sexes: elegance, delicacy, and longer legs on the one hand; size, strength, and potential physical dominance on the other. That has no appeal to some people, but for others it can be one of the basic pleasures of a day. Offices are dull enough already, full of internal politics and dreary meetings, without also demanding that everyone in them turn up in practical, serviceable shoes and clothes.

Adults don't get many chances to play, but dressing up is a daily chance to do just that, especially if you're a woman. Men are not as fortunate as women in today's world, born in an era where the clothing codes for men are so limited and strict. How different could men's lives be if they lived in eighteenth century Versailles or Alhambra? As it is, they have to content themselves with ties, shirts, cufflinks, and the occasional flash of a pale beige silk lining inside a severe, dark-blue suit.

Heels in an office can also serve a very practical purpose. Height matters. It signals, 'Take me seriously!' Heels not only add inches for women, they're also part of a protective working uniform. They say, 'I'm not relaxed, I'm not lounging about, and I'm being a professional now.'

What makes us shoes so important?

Ever notice how people often glance down at your shoes when you are dressed nicely? Why is that? Why would they instantly start looking down when they can clearly see that you are well-dressed and impressive? It's because the shoes are the finishing piece. We shoes are the barometers as to whether you are truly well-dressed. A great pair can lift your outfit up, and a busted pair can drag your look down and cause you embarrassment.

Women's shoes are one of the most important aspects to a woman's wardrobe by far! One thing that makes women's shoes different in regards to every other item that a woman wears is that shoes are more easily damaged and need a higher level of upkeep. After all, they are usually touching the ground. Which of your other pieces can you say that about?

Yeah, it's easy to keep that blouse or pretty black skirt looking good for a long time, but you really show your class when your footwear is on point and well taken care of. It takes diligence and effort to have top-notch footwear on your feet at all times.

Think about how silly a man would look in a beautiful Brioni black tuxedo if he finished off his look with some rusty, dusty worn-out dress shoes. You would want to ask him, 'Why did you leave the house looking like that?' This shows you how vital footwear is. You would completely overlook everything else he was wearing, even if the rest of his attire were worth thousands of dollars. Never be the female version of that guy and have people questioning how you even left the house looking like such a hot mess! Keep it right, and keep it tight!

In ancient times, it was often very easy to tell the difference between the royal class and the normal folk because of their attire. While this was true for nearly all attire, it was especially true of their footwear. The royal class could afford to wear nice, expensive shoes, while the poor had to wear work shoes. These work shoes were strictly utilitarian in nature; they were not anything to be seen as fashionable. Shoes were strictly for lowly ones to use to finish their day's chores without tearing up their feet. You can imagine how quickly those shoes would get worn down and look a mess after working long, hard days.

In Europe the ruling class spent lavishly on footwear (as well as other clothing items) and even had shoes made specifically for themselves and their families. Some of these people would not even wear the same pair more than once. While this is ridiculous, it set a certain standard in the mindset of people about class and footwear. It became ingrained in the culture that the two things were interrelated. That sense still stands strong, but thankfully today men and women don't have to be royalty to enjoy a handsome pair of shoes.

Great women's footwear can also give you a great comfort in two very important ways. First, we shoes can feel the mental transition of a barefoot girl as she slides her feet into our high heels. The girl's expression changes; suddenly she feels fabulous! Indeed, the feeling you get when you strut through a room full of people and you know that you are dressed well from head to toe is something that will help you speak and behave more confidently. When you are assured that nothing about your look is out of place, it relaxes you and puts you in a confident mood that allows you to truly be at ease and enjoy yourself and enjoy the company of others without worry. This feeling in itself is worth the price you pay for an awesome pair of women's footwear.

Secondly, the physical comfort you get from a great pair of shoes cannot be overlooked. Nothing is worse than feeling pain in your little piggies because of bad shoes. It can actually make you a cranky woman. Many times people don't even realize that they are becoming accustomed to feeling uncomfortable until they happen to change what they wear. That is why it is always good to try out new shoes and just see how good they feel. It very well may brighten your whole day.

Comfort is something that no one should take for granted. Many things that you can do nothing about, that are out of your control, can make you uncomfortable. But when it comes to your footwear, you have full control of your comfort, and you should take advantage of it. Happy feet make us happy, not sore, moody ones.

We shoes are like friends. We are always there for our master or mistress, and we crave to be worn and walk as much as possible.

Sometimes humans keep certain shoes around because they are comfortable. Wey are with our masters in sickness and when they get up in the morning and go to bed at night. We are their best friends, the ones who see them as they really are. Then there are shoes that one can buy to go with certain outfits. To many, these are friends that fit you at certain times of your life's journey. But the shoes go out of fashion or don't serve one well or a heel falls off, so humans just don't want to wear them anymore. You may either relegate these shoes to the back of the shoe closet or give them away. And then there are shoes that you have for particular occasions, like your running shoes or flip-flops. These are friends with whom you do specific things and whom you enjoy being with.

Chapter 2
Shoes' Everyday Life

Back to the street: they moved fast, one after the other, like a royal guard march. Their delicate, eight-inch heels moved firmly and purposefully, marching through the obstacles of modern life: litter, dog mess, and the very worst, chewing gum.

Unlike promenade types, they preferred the indoor life. Their mistress guided them into the famous uptown Parisian café, Ladurée, filled with multicoloured and ornate desserts. They quietly searched their way onto the spacious, light marble floor. The waitress examined their mistress, smiled, and showed them to a petite corner table with a velvet chair. Finally resting by the table, they seemed peaceful, the chairs standing solidly by like the guards at Windsor castle, ensuring the security and tranquillity of their special twin guests.

The sophisticated Parisian atmosphere drew attention to the many chunky shoes thudding around, full of earth and dirt. An adolescent pair of Nikes moved aggressively towards the Bozzi's in their quiet corner.

'Can I take this chair?' requested a middle-aged Arabian-looking man with a strong foreign accent.

'Sure,' came the reply from above the table. As the chair was swiftly removed, the wooden legs almost hit the Bozzi's. They hadn't moved an inch behind the seat.

A drop of tea innocently spilled while the waitress was pouring jasmine tea into the cup. The other waiter brought a strawberry cream Saint-Honoree dessert, matching the dress Crystal was wearing above the Bozzis.

Next they were mingling their way along the streets through a blushing group of girls. Their owner looked at the windows of the most luxurious stores of Madison Avenue and continued her afternoon promenade *a la francaise*.

As they entered their birthplace, the Balthazar Bozzi Boutique, hundreds of their siblings lay in wait for their turn to venture into the outside world, finally to be worn and shown off! They sparkled with grace and stylishness. Their sophistication made them appear as royal as one could imagine, all mini-princesses waiting to greet the world. The twins slowly approached their sisters as they let their mistress cuddle their siblings. They lay naked without her feet; one lost her balance and fell next to the right foot. A call for attention?

The salesgirl picked one up and said, 'They are absolutely gorgeous! They are a limited edition. My God, it's one of the only pairs made by the Maestro Bozzi personally!'

'They're a present from someone very special to me. Ever since I received them I cannot spend a day without them!' Crystal said wistfully.

'They are gorgeous on you!' said the salesgirl as she smiled, and the two girls giggled while their mistress reserved another pair of less colourful, more discreet, yet classic shoes to match. 'Of course we are,' said Bernie, laughing.

'We are definitely more beautiful on Crystal's feet. We wouldn't want to be your shoes,' said Bernie deliberately. She did not like the way the sales girl was walking, rubbing her shoes on the wooden floor like a lazy teenager who doesn't bother to lift his feet to walk properly.

'She can't hear us. That is pretty amusing, I must say. We get to laugh at them and say whatever we want. And all they can do is look at us,' said Ellie as she chuckled.

It was only 4:00 p.m. as they strolled to the San Regis Hotel, which served the best cheesecake in New York. They overheard the mistress say as much on the phone. As she entered, all eyes were on her feet. They made one of their many entries in the most glorious, majestic manner. As their mistress sat on the central perennial tartan couch, they gently wiped themselves against the Scottish kilt material, making them glimmer even more than before.

Twins in mythology are often cast as two halves of the same whole, sharing a special bond unlike other siblings. In Greek mythology, Apollo the sun god and Artemis the moon goddess are twins. Unlike Apollo and Artemis, these Bozzis were taken care of by one mistress who enjoyed their company more than anyone else's, complimenting them constantly. With her slim silhouette, she was their perfect match, a third twin.

Their day was strenuous, and they needed to rest, to lie peacefully in their cosy red box where their mistress so tenderly placed them every night. They felt loved and secure, covered with a soft dark cover. They lay close to each other, watching the room filled with clothing, bags, and a range of garments, until they finally fell asleep.

* * *

Shoe social meetings

The morning was busy. They walked a few blocks to finally arrive at Mercer Hotel in Soho. When they first arrived, the refreshing scent of candles filled the lobby and the reception desk. The vibe was very chic and swanky as they went into the Mercer kitchen where their mistress was meeting her giant friend.

Crystal's friend Patricia was wearing a massive red coat signed by Valentino and pair of elegant Ferragamos that looked as though they could have witnessed the Second World War They were scratched yet still stood very straight and proud. Lola and Lila were almost twenty years old. The restaurant was loud, space was small, and floors were cold, but in a way all this created a sense of cosiness.

As the two friends sat for a midday lunch, Ellie and Bernie were left to converse with the two classic red patent ballet flats with grosgrain trim and bows. Lunch passed quickly in conversation mostly about shoe history, as their mistresses dined on grilled sea bass and discussed Cristal's c experimental cartoon movie proposal before diving into small chit chat about mutual friends.

'Hey girls! I'm Lola, and here's my sister Lila!' said the red patent ballet flat.

'We're Bernie and Ellie! Pleased to meet you!' both Ellie and Bernie said happily.

They exchanged a few remarks on the pavements in Soho which need to be rebuilt as they cause rash to the outside soles of the shoe bodies and is somewhat uncomfortable. Lola and Lila told a little about their lives and they explained that thanks to their mistress they spent much times in the libraries and picked up on a lot of shoe history and facts that many shoes ignore of.

'What a wonderful day' said Ellie.

'Indeed wonderful except an arrogant hairy stiletto had walked all over my face before we got in here, it was an awful experience.' Lola said in aghast with her face down.

'That's very unfortunate Lola dear, did she not see you?' inquired Bernie compassionately.

'Oh no she most probably did that on purpose, because when I screamed she didn't even look back nor did she even apologise. I really don't like these new skeletal, skinniest on Earth shoes, who think just because they have a tiniest slim heel they can be arrogant and step on other respectable shoes' declared Lola angrily.

'What about her twin?' asked Bernie.

'Oh her twin was totally under her heel, she was mute and completely under her sister's influence' Lila added.

'Now I wouldn't be surprised if she did something to her poor sister to mute her so she would feel like the queen stiletto' said Lola

'These stilettos will not go far in life, it is not by stepping on others that one achieves anything in life' said Bernie thoughtfully.

After brief small talk Ellie couldn't contain herself and asked, 'Lola, you seem like you know a lot about shoe existence and history. Can you tell us about your views?' asked Ellie.

Lola giggled as Lila caressed her bruised nose tip. 'Lola has always been an adventurer. That's why she looks like she went through a harder life than me. However, I was always there.' Lila said, laughing.

Before they knew it, Lola began a true shoe history lecture.

'We are all well aware of any woman's foremost fashion indulgence. It is simply us, *shoes*. This passion unites all women and is an equal opportunity infatuation that transcends age, size, and shape and offers an object of desire for every budget and every style.' She took a deep breath and watched the three shoes sitting motionless and waiting for her to continue. Lola loved the attention, and this feeling of importance boosted her vocabulary memory. She continued with even more confidence. The restaurant was now full yet the with Lola's beautifully melodic voice all the outside noise was neutralised and all they could hear was her smooth talk.

'I have observed fashion advisors often say that shoes are the easiest way to spice up an old outfit, test out a daring colour, or try a new trend. More than practicality, shoes represent potential: a new look or even a new outlook on life. No other item of clothing has quite the same power to convey the human state of mind or sense of self. Shoes, it seems, have big personalities. We are just ambassadors of many more shoes with different life stories to tell.' She smiled as she looked at her scratched nose tip.

'What about in world history? How did we come to be?' asked Ellie curiously. Bernie added, 'Ferragamo played an important role in the social life of shoes. I'm sure Lola and Lila will know more about that.'

'Indeed, we hold the name of Ferragamo very dear. And even though we haven't met him personally, he is a renowned figure and an important shoe name. But let me come to this in a bit,' said Lola, who continued her big speech about shoes with a lot of enthusiasm.

Lila, Bernie, and Ellie hoped their mistresses weren't going to want to leave yet as all three loved shoe history. Even though Lola had heard it a few times, she couldn't remember the last time anyone had asked Lola about shoe history. It felt like all fellow shoes could talk about was the red carpet Grammy awards shoes and latest vogue trends and fashion tips. It seemed that for most shoes, fashion has been more important than shoe history. Lola felt that many shoes only knew their brand names and a little about their designer, like he was their God. Ironically, none ever realized that fashion was their creator but could also be their killer. For example, one day platform wedges were in, the next day they were out and had to wait decades to become vintage and come back. In most cases shoes never came back into style.

Ellie banged her heel and curiously asked, 'What about the so-called shoe maniacs?'

Lola looked up at the motionless legs of her mistress and whispered, 'Shoe maniacs is a fairly recent phenomenon. For most of history, shoes were practical necessities. When only the elite had the means and the circumstance to own fabulous footwear, court culture provided the stage for statement shoes.

'One interesting historical fact about shoes is that millions of pilgrims have worn down the feet of the statue of Saint Paul in Rome with the loving pressure of their lips. At the beginning of the Holy Roman Empire it was the custom for the faithful to kiss the right hand of the Papal Father. In the eighth century, a rather passionate woman took liberties. According to legend, the pope cut off his hand in disgust. The custom of kissing the pope's right foot was adopted as more appropriate. Pope Innocent, who lived from 1198 to 1216, had kings and churchmen kiss his feet. . Lips are aimed at the cross, which is depicted on the shoe, and the act is either taken as a tribute to his authority or a simulation of servitude.'

Lola stopped to take a deep breath while Lila, Bernie, and Ellie remained mesmerized by all the fascinating history that Lola was sharing with them. 'I read it in a book and it I loved the thought of people kissing me, it wouldn't do them harm you know?' She giggled 'Sometimes it's nice for human beings to see us in close proximity and show us some affection, we are always there but the only ones who get attention are the red carpet shoes and really it is a one chance in a million that we will be on the red carpet' she exhaled and paused as she felt sudden energy and tapped with her tip.

Lola, adrenalized by these facts herself, was ready to start a war for shoe rights. She literally felt like Napoleon, just a horse was missing. Instead, she had the big foot of her mistress, still motionless but warm. 'Free heating!' Lola and Lila sometimes jokingly called feet.

'What about Anne of Bohemia? You forgot to mention her,' reminded her sister.

Lola looked around as if worried others would hear her secret information and said, 'The arrival of Anne of Bohemia in the English court of King Richard II seems to have launched the vogue of shoes with extended toes. They were called *poulaines* or *crakows* in honour of their supposed Polish origins. Crafted of soft leather or substantial but sumptuous fabric, the shoe featured an elongated vamp culminating in a pointed tip.

Most daring ones were male garments - by the mid-fifteenth century they displayed most of the leg - quite ironic that these were worn mostly by men. She tittered.

'What about sixteenth century?' demanded Lila.

'The towering shoes of the sixteenth and seventeenth century aristocratic circles proclaimed status through stature meaning shoes were the tool to look higher ranked. Near the end of the fifteenth century, female courtiers in Venice began to wear *chopines*: very high platform shoes constructed out of a carved cork base crowned with a mule. Lila and I have met a few at the shoe exhibition last month in Paris. Very interesting creatures' Lola paused as Lila continued excitingly.

'They were wonderful she exclaimed!' 'Originally worn by stage performers, courtly chopines were covered with such luxury fabrics as velvet or tanned kid and ornamented with tacked patterns I felt naked next to them even though they were old and their colours faded. Lila looked at her red simple elegant shoe body and said 'I wish I were a Chopines living in those days in Venice' she looked at Ellie and Bernie who laughed together at the honest wish of a NYC shoe.

'I don't know about Venice but I surely wouldn't want to be the shoe of the Pope and be kissed all day long by strangers, that would be really too much for me' laughed Ellie.

'Indeed, being worn out and having to say it were because of too many kisses just sounds bad, no proper shoe would be fine with that' she said, relieved that she was not being kissed by human beings.

A piece of grilled sea bass fell on Lola who was reminded of her shoe reality and nor a history professor how she begun to feel since her lectures. She turned to the shoes and said 'Did you know that Platform shoes were invented by the Qing Dynasty in China?' 'You see, royal edicts forbade foot binding among women in the Manchurian court, but the imperial wives and daughters simulated the appearance of tiny feet, , by wearing shoes with high platforms of two to four inches, perched on bases no more than three or four inches long. When seen peeking out beneath voluminous robes, the ornamented bases of the *shoes* looked just like the perfect lotus shoe of a fashionable Han beauty. The separate high heel, forcing the weight forward to the toe, became a non-gendered feature of footwear in European courts as well. Louis XIV liked his heels painted red, and others were allowed to emulate his striking style only with his majesty's permission.'

'So the red heel was invented by Louis XIV? That's probably where Louboutins got the idea to use the red sole and who thought that it were Louis XVI?,' Ellie declared knocking her little heel on the ground.

'I guess we know whom Louis the XIV would be wearing if he were alive' giggled Bernie.

'Who?' asked Ellie.

'Oh you are slow my dear sister' laughed Bernie.

Ellie looked at Lola and Lila confused.

'Well, of course Christian Louboutins, since they have red soles and that is what the French king liked' said Lila.

The four shoes giggled and smiled at each other in pure shoe happy feeling.

'Lola you are absolutely the smartest shoe I have ever met. It seems like you have a PhD in shoe history,' Ellie said with excitement. She was overwhelmed with new information and history and didn't know how to thank Lola for the beautiful lunch.

'Oh, thank you, girls. I have always loved history, so I've been getting information from here and there over the years,' Lola answered shyly.

Lila rushed to ask Lola about their creator. 'And Salvatore Ferragamo. You didn't mention him yet,' she added impatiently.

'I will come to it right away, Lila dear!' Lola answered her impatient sister.

'By the twentieth century, celebrity had replaced royalty as the inspiration for fantastic footwear. And in terms of daring, no designer surpassed Salvatore Ferragamo. A cobbling prodigy, our creator, he made his sister's confirmation shoes at the age of nine. By the 1920s, Ferragamo was making shoes in Hollywood for the stars,' said Lola proudly to be holding his name on her inner soles.

'What were his most innovative designs?' asked Bernie.

'Of course, the wedge, created for Peggy Guggenheim in 1937, combined a traditional *ghillie* in sharp black and white suede with a high, sharply tilted cork wedge. Then a shoe called "The Rainbow" lofted a gold kidskin sandal with a cork wedge on a chucky heel and a rocker platform sole,' said Lola.

'That's fantastic! I love humans who dedicate their lives to shoes,' said Ellie.

'What exactly did he do with cork?' asked Bernie.

'Ferragamo crafted the spectacular support out of cork slabs covered in multicoloured suede as a tribute to Judy Garland and her signature song "Over the Rainbow,"' explained Lola. 'He was only one among many who took shoe design to a fantastical level. The towering heights achieved by shoe designers over the last decades have shaped not only fashion from the bottom up, historically speaking, comfort has not been of primary concern when it comes to statement shoes,' said Lola.

'Did you know that the term "well-heeled" goes back to the nineteenth century? It was used to describe members of the upperclass whose preference for carriage transport meant that they could wear fashionable, highly uncomfortable shoes not meant for walking treacherous city streets,' said Lila. Indeed, she knew what she was talking about. The two sisters were very informed on the shoe matters and its history.

Lola looked at her friends who were looking back at her, mesmerized.

'This was wonderful!' Bernie congratulated Lola and Lila on their mini speech and thanked them for a great lunch.

'For a second I forgot I was a shoe. I felt like I was a student in a university. It was really a great experience and so much information. Thank you, Lola, for this incredibly interesting conversation,' said Ellie.

The twins sent air kisses to Lila and Lola as they moved slowly out from under the table and approached the door. They came out into the fresh air feeling extremely fulfilled by this lunch and this very informative encounter.

* * *

The smell of coffee is something that united shoes and humans. The two twins, unlike their beloved Crystal, had to be cajoled from sleep with tenderness and coffee smell.

'Come on, my little beauties. It's time for us to start a beautiful day! I won't let anyone break my heart today,' Crystal said in a semi-melancholic way. Her loved one had left her, and here she was talking to the last present he had given her. She watched them for hours only to feel better. They were her best friends, except she never knew what was going in their minds. She loved them and cared for them, but she never imagined that they possessed high intellect and were truly alive.

The room was filled with aroma by Crystal's Guerlain Allegri lime and basilica perfume, a combination that wouldn't suit all but went wonderfully with her allure.

Bernie watched the cartoonish skyline; it had impressed her ever since her first promenade at her first birthday. Ellie was by her side, scratching her sole on the newly built pavement of Park Avenue. They were heading to Nello's, a little Italian restaurant known for its tasty food and high prices. They were headed to a lunch hosted there by Pamela and Dottie Goldenberg. The two sisters were very active in philanthropy and loved famous faces such as Crystal. Thanks to such prominent friends, their events were sought-after. Everyone wanted to see the top Hollywood star, and they were ready to donate thousands to any cause just to be at her table. The Goldenberg sisters were happy with the end results. As for Crystal, it was another way to get away from her gloomy nostalgia of Marlon. Being surrounded with joyful people was the best cure for heartache.

While the Goldenbergs, Crystal, and the five guest donors were ordering their dishes, under the table was another gathering of many different shoes.

On one side of the table, Ellie and Bernie saw a pair of red suede minimalist platform ankle booties, orange ikat-print ankle boots with rhinestone tassels and stiletto heels, a leather-stacked heel oxford with fringed decorative tongue and buckles that danced around like sweet, juvenile tresses flying over a thoughtful-professor-looking shoe face. On the other side of the table, they saw green snakeskin shoes with sculpted polyester heel and scalloped topline signed by Renate Volleberg. They seemed less social than the others, yet were the most different-looking shoes.

Ellie and Bernie were the simplest ones. They weren't spiky stilettos or exotic feathered evening shoes; they were the most comfortable as sleek, black, timeless crocodile pumps.

'How do you do?' the orange booties started the dinner conversation.

'Wonderful day,' replied the oxfords, making small talk.

'Why are human beings so superstitious about us shoes?' suddenly asked one of the green shoes with sculpted polyester heel. The shoe looked very artistic, but must not have been comfortable as the mistress kept taking the shoe off and airing her right foot.

Bernie shook her head to get the breadcrumbs off, always a restaurant issue. She often wondered why they don't use bigger plates for the bread to catch the crumbs before they fall.

Kitty, the multi-leather stiletto sandal with metallic napa piping, the same one who gave a speech at the ISS conference at The Met, was surprisingly here.

'Loved your speech,' Bernie nodded.

'You were there? asked Kitty. 'Thank you! I was very nervous. My heel was shaking. All these shoes watching me felt scary.…You must remember Violet Love. She also spoke at the ISS, and she's right there.' Kitty pointed with her little shoe nose.

'Hey there, girls, the Bozzi twins. I remember you two,' said Violet Love with a smile. 'Young but determined, that's what I have written about you girls,' she said.

'You were wonderful,' the two Bozzis said rhythmically.

'Do you have something written about each shoe in the world?' enquired Bernie.

'Don't worry, no one is speculating anything about you two. You are the only handmade Bozzis made by Balthazar personally from A to Z, and above all you are with Hollywood's most sought after actress.' She smiled. Violet had very aristocratic shoe elegance to herself, her manners were like she just came from Madame de Rotschild's finishing school. She invited the twins to meet the rest of the under-the-table gathering.

'So you know everything about every shoe?' asked Ellie.

'I know everything about every shoe that is part of ISS,' Violet replied. 'There are still many lost souls that I hope will all join us soon. We are the American society. Imagine the billions of other shoes that are all around the globe.' She took a deep shoe breath.

'You see, we shoes are more organized than other objects. Look at all the jewellery that has souls, and the hand bags, and even cars!' she exclaimed.

'All are unorganized with no sense of life, no community get-togethers. The ISS is the key to our shoe education, the place where we can share, solve problems, and discuss the shoe world.' Violet Love was a determined and very active shoe. She and her sister Allegri were great shoe ambassadors; they even spoke French and German.

The other shoes under the table agreed with her before continuing to chat about their everyday lives.

Over the course of the conversation, Ellie and Bernie learned the rest of the shoe names. Kitty's sister Kate, pink leather pumps

Candy and Candy-Pinkie, Violet and Allegri, Bee and Banu, Nora and Nola were all given names at their birth. All the shoes in this great shoe society had birth certificates from the world's most sought-after shoe designers.

'Many people feel very nervous about the thirteenth of any month falling on a Friday, and shoes seem to have been given some magical powers on this particular day. Humans think that if they wear old pairs of shoes on this unlucky day, they will ward off any bad luck that may cross their paths,' said Candy-Pinkie.

Allegri, who initiated this conversation, listened carefully and seemed to like this piece of information.

'Did you know that shoelaces have also been connected to humans' love lives? Some women believe that if shoelaces suddenly come undone, the man they are destined to marry is thinking about them at that very moment,' Bee the oxford shoe said excitedly.

Banu added, 'I once heard our mistress say that some humans believe that if they leave a pair of shoes on the front porch when they leave for a trip, they will return from the trip with a smile on their face.' She giggled.

Violet, being an activist of "shoeism," angrily in a smug-sounding voice spoke out, 'That's great for the human. But what about us? They just leave us on the porch and expect us to sit, wait, and bring them luck? What if the weather is cold, burglars steal us, cats tear us apart, or little kids pick us up and play football with us? These humans—all they think about is themselves, and want us to play along. I think we should start a shoe revolution!' she exclaimed.

Allegri started laughing right away, and soon all the shoes were rolling on the floor with hysterical laughter. Ellie and Bernie watched the tiny and ferocious shoes cackling like the rattle of a machine gun. Allegri, Violet, Nora, and Nola started singing in fluently in Italian. The Bozzi twins weren't into shoe revolutions they loved their life and amused themselves with the other shoes companies. They noticed the snake skin shoes deep green colour like palm tree leaves. The colour reminded them of the lively and bright island advertisements that arrived in Crystal's post box, enticing her to jump onto a plane and fly away to paradise. The shoes were joking and enjoying their time Ellie and Bernie were happiest to be part of the shoe social gatherings, something they always cherished.

The red suede ankle booties sisters were quieter and more reserved than the rest, yet they really knew everything about the shoe society and history.

Ellie decided to chat with the rest of the shoes. And before Bernie knew it, her sister was the centre of attention under the table.

'I once heard our mistress say that in many small-town weddings, shoes are tied to the wedding car to bring good luck for the couple. But I found that this superstition goes even further. Apparently, the bridesmaid who tied the shoe to the car had her own fortune in mind, for, as with catching the bridal bouquet, it means she will be the next to marry.' She chuckled at the thought.

Bernie then couldn't help but add in an older-sister touch to Ellie's first big speech. 'Well, that would certainly explain the multiple shoes that I have seen tied to the backs of cars. Each bridesmaid was out to catch herself a man!' Bernie finished with a nervous laugh. She wasn't used to being the centre of attention.

'Poor thing! That's vandalism!' exclaimed Kitty as Katy hugged her for comfort. 'Indeed, let's hope it was a sole-less one.'

'It wasn't one of our kind. It was just a plastic shoe, a clone that had no soul,' said Bernie.

'Still, somewhere deep inside it might have been living. Maybe we just don't see some of them, who know,' said Banu while her sister patted Kitty, who was still saddened by the story.

'And how many times I was worn to a funeral just because of my age!' cried out Candy-Pinkie. 'I'm worn just because someone said that funeral outfits should never be new, especially the shoes. So humans save one outfit and a pair of shoes at the back of their wardrobe for that unfortunate occasion. I would so much more prefer going to weddings and happy events. Funerals are really sad, especially for the shoes that obediently go down into the earth with their master like their life is over.' She had tears in her eyes.

Candy grabbed her sister and shook her. 'Sweetheart, we can sit here all say and talk about all the unfortunate things in our shoe worlds. But I think it's pretty amazing to be here and finally interacting with other shoes!' A huge smile came from her suede face. 'The father of our mistress always said, "If you wish to become wealthy, you should never throw out a pair of shoes until you have worn a hole in them."'

Over the course of the meal, the shoes became friends. They talked a little bit about everything: politics, society issues, their mistresses, and each other. Ellie and Bernie felt a slight tickle, and it was time to go. As their mistress stood straight up, they marched out from under the table and sent kisses to the shoe girls who stayed behind.

Life with Crystal was full of events, constant travelling for the never ending receptions, movie premieres and meetings with many kinds of shoes. The Bozzi twins met shoes from all over the world. Most were very nice, though some were unpleasant. Overall, the little Bozzis' life was quite fun and jolly. As the months passed and there were weeks that Crystal wouldn't wear the twins, they enjoyed calm, restful time in her closet room.

It wasn't long before the Bozzis found themselves in Paris with their mistress. One day they watched Crystal step out of her Avenue de la Montaigne apartment. Both Ellie and Bernie looked up out of the window, their leather faces squashed against the ice-cold glass. She waved, and in her wave she tried to convey everything she knew of love. Swallowing hard, Ellie and Bernie sat down, and an awkward feeling came across their minds that nothing would be the same after this. Crystal had never waved at them before. This was rather worrisome.

It wasn't long before the twins found out that their life was going to change forever.

Chapter 3
New Life

> *At the age of forty-six, famous Hollywood actress Crystal Baron died at her home in Paris, surrounded by loved ones, on November 5, 1999.*
>
> *The actress received wide recognition for her work in films, including* Love Me Forever, *for which she won an award at the Cannes Film Festival in 1990,* The Fabulous Queen, Great Game, *and others. She was nominated for a Golden Globe, BAFTA, and an Oscar.*
> *Baron was born in New York City, the daughter of Julia and Peter Baron, famous theatre actors in the late 1960s. She attended Sarah Lawrence College, where she studied acting. Baron married screenwriter and playwright Wyatt Green. However, their marriage lasted only a year. She was later rumoured to be involved with famous oil tycoon and movie producer Marlon Wesley. —*New York Times, *1999*

The two sisters didn't have time to realize what had happened. They were placed in a carton box until someone finally lifted them out. All they could think of was that they had misbehaved and now were going to be punished.

After weeks of uncertainty, and trillions of questions, Ellie and Bernie found themselves in a dark space, which they discovered to be an attic in New York. Crystal's sister had been left with Crystal's belongings and couldn't bear the thought of leaving them all behind.

It took time for the twins to realize they were not going to see Crystal again. After a while they even persuaded each other that perhaps they would never be worn again and they would spend the rest of their lives passively in the dark corner of an attic.

Ellie and Bernie never forgot the first night spent in the attic. During its passing, they lived through a wild, mature woe of which they never spoke to anyone about. There was no one around who could help them. As they lay awake in the darkness, their little shoe minds were forcibly distracted, now and then, by the strangeness of their surroundings. It was, perhaps, well for them that they had time to mature, as the persistent darkness and silence were not going anywhere. All they had was each other and their numerous question marks.

'Why did this happen to us, Bernie?' Ellie kept whispering. She had also developed a dust allergy and sneezed every now and then.

'Patience is the only way to happiness,' Bernie said as she tried to keep her twin sister calm. She felt a certain responsibility for her more emotional twin shoe.

The stiffness of their carton box and the darkness seemed more intense than any they had ever known.

As the darkness wore on, Ellie and Bernie developed a very mature character where patience prevailed. 'Remember how we went on the red carpet and all the cameras were flashing?' asked Ellie.

'Of course. I'll never forget it. And Crystal's mini-dress that gave us all the attention we could possible get.' She giggled, and the two shoes began to laugh at their present miserable situation.

The wind howled over the roof among the chimneys like something that was alive. During the dark nights the twins heard rain scuffling and a squeaking in the walls and behind the skirting boards. The two shoes sung to the noises they heard as though they were Christmas carols. They played with the sounds and made each other laugh.

'Ellie, we had a harsh past. I mean, who said it would be easy to be a celebrity shoe? For one, we got as addicted to the attention as our celebrity owner, and we got used to all those eyes gazing at us and what we carried, our mistress,' said Bernie.

'You're right. We got very attached to Crystal in those years. Her feet were the very first feet that slipped into our inner soles, and we matched them perfectly. She had a graceful allure, and her walking was light and absolutely not painful. It was actually quite sensual. Oh, God, I really miss our angel-faced Crystal. Remember how she waved at us?' Ellie was saddened by what had happened to their life.

And then came the dark days.

Not only did the Bozzi sisters lose Crystal, who had abandoned her career and life and moved to Paris, where she had died eventually of a disease the twins never managed to recall the name of. But they also lost their active life.

'I'll never forget how we were shipped to Crystal's sister's house in New York,' said Bernie looking in the darkness at Ellie. The twins got used to the darkness of the attic and somehow learned to enjoy their calm days of passivity.

'She greeted us by throwing us savagely into a carton box, all dusty, and we were left in the dark attic with not a glimpse of light, not a glimpse of anything.' Ellie remembered with shivers running through her gently curved heel.

'Now when I think of those days it feels more like a dream, like a pause, a time when we should have been sleeping instead of developing our philosophies. See, we only had each other. No one else was there for us, no other object was to be seen anywhere, just lots of garbage, old textbooks, books, and unnecessary objects that simply were thrown there and forgotten,' Ellie said thoughtfully.

Bernie couldn't help but hug her sister and whisper to her that everything will be great. 'We are Bozzis. Our life will never end. Remember, he made us forever,' Bernie said very confidently while observing her figure in the mirror that lay innocently on the dusty floor of the attic. Thankfully there was a little glimpse of light. 'We still look pretty awesome,' she said.

The two sisters smiled at each other as they started the day jumping up and down to get rid of the past energies and start the stay all fresh and happy.

As shoes, they really wanted to be worn so they could observe life. They wished to experience the bumps on the roads and the cold winter breeze. All those things that may harm their sole also made them feel alive and experience life! What was there to life if shoes weren't worn, but were kept inside a box?

* * *

Meeting Fay

After several long years of solitude, one early April morning the two sisters were awakened when two hands took them out of their box, shook the dust off, and threw them in a plastic bag. After a few hours, the still-drowsy twins found themselves in a store full of objects. It was an uptown Vintage store called "Joan's." They felt like zombies and thought it was just a dream. The second day they were pampered until they looked brand-new. After a little more time, their enthusiasm and genuine happiness from the bottom of their soles was back in the game.

The vintage clothing store contained a mixture of whimsical shoes, all coloured with sexy, shiny elegance. The twins felt so new, so dreamlike, as though they were in a fantasy world more than reality. The store owner placed shoe stands out on a bustling West Village street in New York.

'Just a few days ago we were in that little dusty box, motionless, with no hope left, no prospective thoughts. I was so used to that silence that this buzz of the street noise feels almost intrusive to my now-sensitive ears,' said Bernie happily.

'It feels good really good. I feel alive again to finally be out on the street with other shoes after all these years.' Tears ran through Ellie's newly polished cheeks.

'Do you feel what I feel?' Ellie asked still shaking from happiness and disbelief at the new chapter of their life. 'I feel like an alien,' Bernie responded.

'I feel old. Look at them. They are so young and sexy. I feel dull,' she said in disappointment.

'Well, just take a look up. This nice-looking lady has picked us out of all the others. We are Genuine Balthazar's, for God's sake! We can never be dull,' Ellie pointed out.

'Ellie, I really have difficulties understanding you sometimes. How can you make such pitiful comments? How can you even compare us to any other shoes? I don't want to sound cocky, but we are simply unique,' said Bernie bitterly, like a proud, true Bozzi.

'I want someone with a sweet personality. I hope she's funny witty, friendly and polite to everyone, smart and eager to learn new things, basically perfect.' Ellie took a deep breath and continued, 'I want one who could love us and take great care of us and carry on thoughtful conversations about life and current events. In other words, I hope we end up with a smart, ambitious girl who doesn't talk negatively about other people, especially friends or family members. I'd like one that doesn't swear and doesn't wear extreme clothing, tattoos, or excessive piercings. She holds herself to a higher moral standard than everyone else, and she doesn't succumb to peer pressure. She is at least moderately athletic and likes to bike, hike, run, or something like that. I don't want someone who is necessarily competitive. Maybe she just does something active to stay in shape.' Ellie hoped this perfect girl was somewhere close by.

Bernie nodded and then said, 'I don't care so much about her physical attractiveness. I'm not one to say one characteristic is better than another. For example, some girls are gorgeous brunettes, others are gorgeous blondes, but neither should dye their hair. Leave the details alone, I say. It's more about the girl and what she brings as a total package. I think God knew what he was doing most of the time. I am simply looking for someone who isn't obsessed over herself and is generally nice, but not afraid to stick up for herself. I'd like a girl with class and grace: that is all I am really looking for. I want someone like Crystal, at least little bit,' she said concerned about their new mistress to be. The twins wished their mistress was as pure and genuine as Crystal was. They hoped she would be an easy piece to carry and a warm hearted one to take a good care of her shoes.

A middle-aged lady with interesting facial features but rather gigantic feet, at least size 9, was picking them up. What was she thinking? The two sisters wondered as the lady watched them in pure satisfaction. She paid for them, and the salesman wrapped the twins up. The lady seemed bright and aware of shoe fashion according to her sleek and elegant Loro Piana beige and brown colour combination style, with Donna Karan shirt a Balenciaga purse and a pair of empty simple brown flat shoes.

In a matter of minutes before the twins had time to say goodbye to their friends they were being wrapped in soft paper and placed into the white bag where they could only see the light from the open roof of the bag.

'That's it I think we're on our way to our new home' Elle whispered confusingly yet with a slight feeling of joy.

'It's nice to change atmospheres, the store was getting a little monotone for me' murmured Bernie.

In the car, the twins overheard the lady on the phone. 'I have found real Bozzis from the 1990s for Fay. She will be extremely happy. I believe it's the best Christmas present!' she exclaimed in joy.

'It is Christmas,' Bernie whispered to Ellie.

'Do you have a good feeling?' asked Ellie.

'Let's wait and see,' replied Bernie.

'I really hope her daughter will be like her and not like the father,' responded Bernie.

'How do you know who the father is?' asked Ellie.

'I have no idea! I'm just joking with you, Ells!' said Bernie, laughing.

'You really got me there, Bernie.' Ellie smiled.

Humour was at all times present with the two twins. It kept them going in hard times, and they made pranks and jokes at every possible situation life offered them.

In the Gramercy apartment, Ellie and Bernie met a few pieces of clothing that offered them insight into their future mistress. They observed her through the box.

She seemed to know exactly what was going on and where things were at all times. She also enjoyed helping others, like when she picked up the old lady's napkin when it fell on the floor. The twins knew such things meant that she took pride in her many abilities.

Like a magician, she juggled multiple tasks with ease, and as they later found out from her umbrella, she was known for her skill and dexterity. Fay was practical, yet mercurial. She needed movement, communication, and travel. She was used to moving around since she was a child, so staying in one place was a hard one for her.

Fay Amanda Waltensen was currently working on a bachelor's degree in acting at the New York Film Academy. Like many other girls, she dreamed of being an actress. It was too early to say if she was going to achieve success, but she could transform herself on stage. She was learning and gaining life experience, trying to figure out what she really wanted to do. A unique child, she had all the support of the family and was a very positive and happy girl. Quite spoilt, she loved fashion and clothes. Her apartment seemed more like a luxury outlet with Oscar de la Renta, Balenciaga, Gucci, YSL, Jimmy Choo, Louboutins, Missoni scarves, Chanel handbags, Balmain jeans, and the little Bozzis, the newcomers and her very favourites.

For the shoes, the getting-to-know-Fay process would take a very short time. She was one of those girls who were genuine and honest, and you could read her emotions and mood by her eyes.

They were also excited by the fact that Fay loved travelling and that she had been looking for Bozzi black crocodile pumps for ages.

'I feel great to be alive again!' exclaimed Ellie.

'It's wonderful, isn't it? The dark days are over, my lively sister!' said Bernie happily.

'She will love us! I really hope she will!' Ellie crawled slowly over to her sister while Bernie was watching the excessive amount off scarves that Fay placed on the hanger.

'She is a good girl the Converses that hang out by the entrance mentioned it to me while u were sleeping. I just hope no one will upset her like Marlon upset Crystal,' Bernie thought out loud. Crystal was a very kind woman and treated them like little princesses her sympathy and consideration would always be cherished in the memories of the twins.

'Oh, Berns, I can't go through another sad love story. We better make sure Fay doesn't fall for the wrong man.' Ellie felt like she suddenly found a nice strong purpose—a certain mission to accomplish.

The twins were jumping and dancing of joy. It felt really good to have a new real home with caressing gentle feet and things to observe and to talk about.

Fay Amanda Waltensen was a young girl in her twenties of international origin: her mother was half-Italian and half-Swiss, her father was half-American and half-Turkish with a French great-grandmother. She was a US citizen, but she did her schooling in Switzerland, finally ending up in New York to be an actress. Like many others, she dreamed of one day winning the Oscar, walking down the red carpet holding the golden trophy, and smiling with a huge Hollywood white, sparkly smile like they do in movies.

Young and full of dreams, she was eager to work hard and yet enjoy life's experiences. She had deep passion for fashion and footwear. She loved shoes as her beloved mother had, and like her mother she had beautiful feet always cradled in very elegant and fine-looking footwear. Her parents were retired. She had her family's support to pay for her rent and schooling, yet she had no support in her acting career. Alone, she was pursuing a dream in a very harsh and competitive industry. At times her sweet character was upset by the cruel environment and criticism.

A hopeless romantic ever since childhood, she looked for true love. However, she hadn't met it yet and mostly concentrated on her acting and her friends. She was a happy girl, full of life and joy. She loved her shoes and Ellie and Bernie were excited to meet their new mistress.

Bernie opened her eyes and hopped out of her carton box bed excitedly. She gently shook still-sleepy Ellie awake. Green glass Dyptique candles wild-fig aroma had warmed the atmosphere of their new home with its exotic smells. The two shoes dashed down the corridor to the main room of the apartment.

The cat's eyes sparkled as she gazed at the walking shoes and at all the presents that lay under the fashionably decorated Christmas tree which even had an artlessly placed Chanel box on its right side. Bernie squealed and dashed back to Fay's room. They hopped back inside the box while one of the Hermes pantoufle helped tie ribbons around the box. Before they knew it they were lifted high up. All they could hear was excited female voices, and they sensed enthusiasm in the air.

The lights flickered as the morning alarm started to scream.

Fay groggily opened her eyes and glared at her alarm clock. '*I thought I left it off this morning*', she mused, looking at the box where Ellie and Bernie stood motionless by her bedside. She yawned and turned the alarm off.

Fay smiled as she crawled out of bed.

'My lovely little oldies, you are the most gorgeous pantoufles in the world!' she cried, as if she knew they could hear her.

Both Hermes pantoufles smiled and remained still on the soft, warm, Swiss-chalet-style wooden floors.

'She sounds like a sweetheart!' Bernie said.

Both little *principessas,* Ellie and Bernie were flattered by Fay's genuine warmth and care over her old pantoufles. Their father Balthazar taught them while he was manufacturing them that everything starts with respect towards the elder generation.

The old Hermes pantoufle winked wearily at Ellie, who now sat on the shoe couch where Fay's mother had placed the box to make sure they didn't pick up dust from the wooden floors.

'Don't look at me like that. I am just an old shoe,' the pantoufle cooed in a cranky voice.

Bernie shot him a strict look and commanded Ellie to behave.

'May you have a long and healthy shoe life,' she said.

He nodded thankfully, surprised at the level of refined politeness he hadn't come across for a very long time.

Bernie thought back to the day Fay's mother had decided to surprise her.

'I have something that will make you very happy!' the older woman's voice came across the room. It was Fay's mother, who had come in from Washington to spend the holiday with her daughter.

'Surprise! Oh, Mommy, you shouldn't have.' Fay picked up the present that had a big, pink ribbon on it that read, *Joan's Vintage, New York*. She tore off the wrapper while her mother trembled with excitement next to her.

'Wow! Look at this, Mom!' Fay triumphantly held up the pair of vintage baby crock black matte Balthazar Bozzis in perfect condition.

'Bernie, she's tickling me! Help!' Ellie bawled.

'I can't even talk! Um…her fingers are so tiny that she can barely hold on to me! I think I'm falling!' Bernie yelled.

Before she knew it, she landed on the soft-cream Frette bed covers, and the whole fall didn't seem anything but great fun.

'Bernie, are you alright?' Ellie helplessly tried to help her sister from the air.

'I think I'm perfectly fine, actually,' replied Bernie, looking up at her worried little sister, who had big human faces checking every inch of her shoe body.

A giant hand picked Bernie up, and both Ellie and Bernie were now very close to Fay's beautiful little face. She was a Preppy-bohemian and her clothes were luxurious yet easy going, she had a "laissez-faire" hair style and her eyes were very warm and glowing.

'This is so pretty! Thank you, Mommy! Thank you so much!' Fay hugged her mother and then her new shoes with pure sincerity and joy. Bernie and Ellie could feel her heartbeat.

'Oh, my God! These are the most beautiful pumps I have ever seen! Baby crocodile black Bozzis! Mother, I really don't know how to thank you! And they are my size! And incredibly comfortable too!'

Her little feet rubbed the inner soles of the twins, sending a tingle up their spine which caused them a delightful tickle.

'What a perfect fit!' amusingly cried Ellie.

'I never thought any other feet would feel so perfect in our inner soles I feel full again! 'Blissfully spoke out Bernie.

Ever since Fay wore them the first time, she couldn't bear to go a day without them.

The twins were surprised to see her attractive face and sparkling joyful eyes. She smelled the vintage leather and caressed them with special shoe polish for baby crocodile skin, and it felt really right to the Bozzis. Her touch was gentle and caring, unlike many others who had grabbed them and tried to fit them to their oversized feet. Her feet slid in perfectly, just like Crystal's had.

It was an unforgettable *déjà vu* moment, the happiest feeling that no human could understand. The feeling of the right feet in the shoes is crucial for the shoes to walk perfectly, to look beautiful, and simply to be the best!

That is how Ellie and Bernie met their new mistress, a beautiful brunette with big, warm, glowing eyes who loved them as much as a mother loved and cared for her baby twins. She was relaxed and easy-going, and her natural beauty shone through her ever-smiling face.

Fay was physically the opposite of blonde, blue-eyed, six-foot-tall Crystal, yet she had the same foot shape, which was really impressive. She was rather petite brunette with a few blonde highlights and big brown eyes.

'Do you think we'll be happy here?' Ellie asked Bernie.

Bernie smiled. 'I think this apartment looks marvellous, and by the neatness of the place, I wouldn't worry for our maintenance.'

'She seems good-hearted and happy,' Ellie responded.

From the back, the lonely, once alluring Hermes pantoufle cleared his old, cranky voice. 'She's a shy girl. Don't get fooled by her appearance. She's very social and has plenty of friends, but there's no boyfriend. She is really missing the young-love experience. I can see her sometimes watching romantic movies and dreaming of her own romance.'

His words had such a profound effect that Ellie had tears in her eyes.

'We will surely help this young lady to shape up and find her true love,' Bernie said. Then she revealed a small portion of their past to the old pantoufle, who happened to be a great listener and their first friend in the new home.

'I cannot believe we are once again in a love-problem situation. This time I will not let this girl lose herself. I don't know how yet, but I will do everything in my shoe power to make it right,' declared glorious Bernie as Ellie jumped up in excitement.

Ellie looked at Fay and said, 'Bernie, it doesn't have to be so problematic. Not all love stories are as tragic as what we experienced with Crystal.'

'Thanks for the summary of the situation here. You are a truly good shoe, and a welcoming one, too. What is your name?' Ellie asked the pantoufle.

'I don't really have a name. Ever since I was born, they called me by my brand name, Hermes, and so I remain Hermes to this day.'

'Hermes is a pretty nice name. It sounds like Greek mythology,' said Ellie, observing the pantoufle.

Bernie took a deep breath. 'Hermes is derived from *Hermeneus*, which means "the interpreter." So you have a very nice name, my friend,' concluded Bernie.

Hermes lay back and observed the twins. 'I think I can be a good interpreter. I like my name. Thanks girls!' He smiled.

* * *

'Feet are of paramount importance for us, as they are for any other shoe in the world. The right foot is a guaranteed fun life,' declared Ellie.

'Right feet are more important than left feet,' said Bernie, teasing Ellie. Being the right shoe, she wanted to pinch Ellie. Nevertheless, Ellie exploded into a big laughter, and both sisters' rolled on the Carrara marble floor of the Four Seasons hotel lobby bathroom with mirth.

The weather was sunny and fresh; Fay was walking confidently to a new shoe store that she had been dreaming about for a long time.

Walking into a René Caovilla store was like entering a walk-in jewellery box. Ellie and Bernie's hearts were pumping when they saw all the glittery, sparkly, gorgeous shoes; they were goddesses, and each one was prettier than the other. Not resembling any other shoes, they were like jewellery pieces.

Fay's eyes lit up at the sight of exquisite evening shoes, and she was terrified to touch them, just in case she tarnished its beauty with a fingerprint. But then all resistance crumbled, and she seized the opportunity to have a pair of these jewels grace on her feet.

'She's slipping out to slip into them!' grudgingly said Ellie.

'She's just trying them on. Besides, they are unwearable,' replied Bernie.

'And why would you say something like that?' came a voice from the top shelf. It was a lady dragon sling back with Swarovski crystal trim.

Both Ellie and Bernie were speechless. They had been sure that behind all these sparkles there was no life, let alone ears.

Ellie tried to change subject from the embarrassment. She said, 'She meant that you are so beautiful that it would be unfair for anyone to wear you. On the contrary, you should be placed somewhere so people can watch you like a stunning trophy.' She finished with a diplomatic smile

Lady Dragon replied. 'It's not that great to be full of stones like a Christmas tree. I sometimes wish I were a sneaker. Then I could see the world instead of waiting on this shelve until I'm bought by an old lady who'll wear me on two or three occasions and then keep me in a box all closed and wrapped up as a piece of wood,' she said in bitter despair.

'Why couldn't it be a young girl full of life who will take you on her incredible life journey?' asked Ellie. Bernie preferred to say nothing, as she understood what Lady Dragon meant.

'Young ones rarely have the financing to purchase us, unless it's sale season. Even then the old clients reserve us, and by the time the youngsters get here, pieces like me are long in the hands of the others. I have seen the destiny of my fellow sisters. And, yes, there have been a few lucky ones that have been worn by some celebrities and then became famous and loved and photographed. But, let's face it, it's a one-in-a-million chance. Mostly we end up in countries like Saudi Arabia or Russia where women don't hesitate to grab us, sale or not. They like the shining and try to squeeze in their often not-so-delicate feet.'

A middle-aged oriental lady all in black with a bulky gold Rolex filled with massive diamonds and earnings to go with it picked up Lady Dragon. The woman's perfume was so strong that it neutralized the store's vanilla and orange aroma. Lady Dragon was right, the lady didn't even try her and her sister on. She simply requested the salesgirl to have them ready because she was going to purchase them right away. Her phone rang, and she talked in Arabic. Ellie and Bernie didn't have time to say their good-byes to Lady Dragon. She was gone, and the two twins couldn't help but wonder how her life would be in the Far East Arabian lands.

Fay slipped back into the twins and made her way out of the store. As they were leaving, the twins reflected on all they had learned about the brand during this shopping session.

The father of the brand, Eduardo Caovilla, chose to explore traditional Venetian shoe making. But it was his son, Rene Fernando, who combined art and couture to sculpt beautiful evening shoes, which would ensure that the simplest of women be mistaken for royalty or Hollywood screen sirens.

The shoes were adorned with Swarovski crystals, pearls, flowers, and genuine leather of every conceivable hue. And many women, like the one who purchased Lady Dragon, happily sacrificed an entire paycheck just so that they could rest in the knowledge that they actually own a pair of these exclusive stilettos.

Ellie was deeply touched by the encounter with Lady Dragon, and she couldn't help but reflect on the shoe-and-foot relationship.

'Ellie! Bernie? Is that you I see?' exclaimed a voice from behind them.

'It is them! Of course it's them!' said another voice.

'Wonderful shoes, dear' came another voice of an aged lady. She was dressed all in black. It suited her beautifully with her little baby crocodile Birkin bag that completed her stylishly gracious look.

Fay turned immediately to thank the old lady. 'Thank you,' she said and smiled.

Ellie and Bernie looked at the two green pumps and could not believe their eyes. It was Candy and Candy-Pinkie. They looked a little older but in perfect condition.

'You are alive! We wondered where you were after we heard about Crystal's death!' cried Candy.

'Indeed, we asked everyone about you. Even Lola and Lila haven't heard. And Kitty and Kate said the last time they saw you was at the lunch at Nello's where we were all together, like, almost a decade ago!' cried out Candy-Pinkie.

Ellie and Bernie tried to hug their old friends, but they couldn't reach; they had little time. Fay was going to leave the store.

'We missed you! It is such a pleasure to see some familiar shoes!' exclaimed Ellie.

'And you girls haven't changed a bit,' said Bernie, flattering her friends

'How is everything with the others? Is it going well for them?' asked Ellie.

'Nora and Nola have been exiled to India. Their mistress moved there and gave up her shoes there to become a non-materialistic human being. Although, she still travelled first-class on her return journey to New York, and she still shops. You might bump into her. She wears Uggs all day long,' said Candy.

Candy-Pinkie reached her nose to Ellie and Bernie, and they said their good-byes.

After shopping, Fay hailed a yellow cab and went straight down to Soho.

The two sisters strolled down Soho streets to Broome street and West Broadway. Their mistress stopped into Cipriani Downtown for an early Bellini and vanilla cake with her girlfriends. Cipriani Bellinis are known as nectar from heaven and an absolute must for drink lovers and social mingles. This was the place to see and to be seen.

It was a really terrific scene of fashionistas, tourists, and artists. Set in Soho, this restaurant oozed the dolce vita.

Fay sat with a few girlfriends. Shoes were very artistic in this scene. People sipped on their drinks, watching and enjoying.

Fay's friends were all aspiring artists and fashion designers. But mostly they were all over-privileged socialites on the international level. Some were young jet-setters. Others liked to refer to themselves as artists, but they didn't really know much about art other than the few Andy Warhol paintings they saw at their parents' homes and a few Roy Lichtensteins, and Damien Hirsts here and there.

They were hyper-social, always out and about. These were social butterflies who knew everything about social events and what was in or out. Cipriani Downtown was the *in* place, so they constantly met there for follow-ups and catch-ups on the social happenings. Their shoes were all brand-new yet bizarrely soulless. Ellie and Bernie remembered their conversations with Lola and Lila about the shoe history. They missed them dearly.

Suddenly, a voice came from the table next door.

'Hey, I think I saw you pumps at the ISS a few years ago. I remember that you were said to be very smart by other shoes. See, my mistress is a very famous actress, and also a very intellectual one. She knows a great amount of history, so I now feel close, too.' Ellie and Bernie looked over at a gorgeous sleepy leather bootie with a pointed nose.

'Sharon Stone!' exclaimed Fay. 'I am such a big fan!' she cried out.

'Thank you, dear!' said Sharon, smiling with her strikingly gorgeous teeth. Fay blushed from excitement and wished a 'Bon appétit' to Sharon. Still amazed at her idol actresses' presence in the same restaurant as her, she stood up and got ready to go.

'Sharon Stone's boots oh my,' said Bernie still astonished.

'I love this city. All the celebrities are just around the corner,' fanatically Ellie said as she hugged her sister.

'They were very hot. I must admit, high heels always look nicer than flats,' confessed Bernie.

'Indeed, but our length is the best,' said Ellie, joyfully battering her heel on the wooden Josephine armchair.

Ellie's Confession about Feet and Shoes

Eleanora is my full name, but my father and sister call me Ellie. So I am Ellie for you all. Today was a very interesting day. I met a wonderful shoe by the name of Lady Dragon. She was forceful and strong-minded. She knew the problems shoes like she faced, and she wasn't scared to speak out about it. She refused to sit quietly and wait dully like her other siblings. She talked about a crucial problem: uncared-for feet. Human feet are terribly neglected and often horribly abused. I don't know why feet have been relegated to second-class status, especially when they can be so attractive and even sexy!

Often, women only think about their feet when summer rolls around and they start thinking about wearing sandals. Sometimes women think of their feet only after years of abuse have resulted in chronic foot pain.

As far as toe length goes, I pretty much think anything is good enough. My personal favourite is Roman toes, where the second toe is longer than the big toe.

We all have a relationship with our feet. If the feet are not happy with us, it is usually a very bad sign. We risk not being worn again, since they somehow manipulate the woman's mind with pity and put all the fault of their misery on us.

Nevertheless, I truly admire feet. For me, seeing them without nail polish makes them even more natural and beautiful. It allows me to appreciate every tiny curve and subtle change of skin tone without having a red flashing light distracting me from the subtle beauty. And when there is nail polish, it's never applied perfectly, so my eyes immediately go to the over-sprayed areas where the paint is on the cuticles or on the sides of the nail bed, or I notice the chips and other imperfections in the paint-job. See, we are in the closest proximity with the toes, so no pedicurist can fill us with a second layer of nail polish over the imperfect first one.

As to dark colours of nail polish, even though Chanel came up with a black polish, I find that it does nothing but emphasize the deformed nail shape. And that's not a pretty sight.

Once, when we were at the beauty salon with Crystal, women were discussing an article in *Cosmopolitan* about men and what colours they prefer on women's toes. I can recall hearing that about 80 per cent of men strongly preferred clear, beige-coloured nail polish or no polish at all. Only about 10 per cent of men strongly preferred red. About 2 per cent liked black. So if women are doing this to get positive attention from men, they're not succeeding.

I think many women get pedicures because it *does* attract attention to their feet. The problem, in my opinion, is that it is a kind of blind attention. I've noticed that it's often the women who have really trashed feet who are the ones who most often wear toenail polish, and they often wear the most attention-getting colours. Why draw attention to feet that are in such sad shape, that are so hard to look at?

I think some women feel that toenail polish dresses up their feet. I think they just don't realize that women's feet are subtle, natural, and amazingly beautiful things *already*, and painting their toes overwhelms the delicate beauty they already possess.

The sad irony is that when women discover that many men just love their feet, they think, "Oh! I had better pay some attention to my feet then!" And instead of giving their feet the attention their feet really need, they start trying out flashy colours.

I guess what I'm saying, in all of this, is that women's feet are stunningly beautiful just the way they are naturally. I appreciate the natural beauty of a woman's foot, the more natural and un-abused the better.

And here they were: all-natural, lightly French manicured, Egyptian-formed.

Let me tell you that Egyptian feet are like goddesses of all feet. Crystal had Egyptian feet, and so does Fay.

According to anatomists, three quarters of the population have a so-called Egyptian foot, which is characterized by a great toe longer than the second toe, one-sixth of the population have a Greek foot, where the big toe is shorter than the second toe, while the rest of the population have a square foot, where the great toe has the same length as the second.

The reference to Egypt is due to the fact that in Egyptian paintings the great toe appears longer than the second toe. The reference to Greece has to do with the fact that Greek statues showed feet having the second toe longer than the big toe.

Notwithstanding the prevailing anatomy, nearly all the Roman statues, often copies of Greek originals, have Greek feet. It is not easy to find a statue with an evident Egyptian foot, because even Egyptian statues have Greek feet. Anyhow, maybe by chance, maybe on purpose, the colossal statue of the Nile in the *Piazza del Campidoglio* was restored by replacing its lost foot with a distinctly Egyptian foot. Neoclassic artists had such an admiration for Greece that their statues have Greek feet exaggerated to the point of bordering on deformity.

It is quite ironic that in ancient times Roman Emperors promoted themselves as having a divine nature by being portrayed barefoot. However, today's western viewer associates being barefoot with being uncivilized.

If I could, I would ask human beings to take a better care of their feet. Uncared-for feet mean our deformation, and it's hurtful too. Our bodies ache from those who purposefully refuse to take care of their feet but decide to hide them in shoes.

Chapter 4
Fay Meets Adam

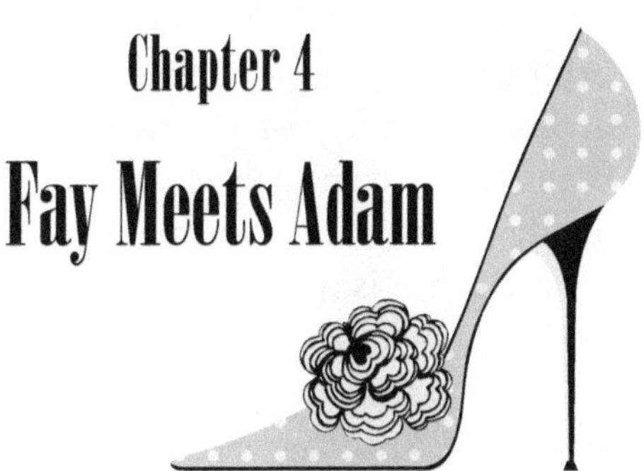

The twins strolled down Park Avenue heading to Barney's. Their mistress was going for a quick meeting with her manager in Fred's restaurant located on the last floor of Barney's.

As they were walking through yet another shoe department, the twins observed the hundreds of other brand-new shoes of all colours and materials. They were all beautifully presented on the decorative tables and lit shelves, and all were waiting to be picked.

'There are so many wannabe shoes,' Bernie said briskly, glancing at her heel.

'Wasn't it the same back in the days we were born?' asked Ellie.

'These so-called shoes come from nowhere, striving nevertheless to place themselves high up. As a matter of fact, some even make it to the top-ten shoes of the season, since they're trained to seduce young celebrities and fashionistas who rush out and purchase them. Furthermore, slowly but steadily, they achieve high authority and almost immediately dictate to the fashion industry. From harmless trendy newcomers, they turn into ruthless commanders,' cried out Bernie, who was sweating from the stressful facts she'd been analysing for a while.

'Oh, Bernie, my lovely sister, you're not jealous, I hope.' Ellie asked and then regretted she'd ever said it.

'Fashion dictatorship is awfully slippery. One day you're in, right on the top of the fashion hierarchy; the next thing you know, you're old and out. No, I'm not jealous. I just want us to be prepared. We are older, and there are so many shoes around us. We must be careful and keep our eyes open.' Bernie breathed in relief. In the middle of their conversation she whacked her heel and was in pain, but she felt more pain when she watched her sister. She worried about Ellie, who was much too open and honest with all the shoes she'd meet. She was not aware of evil, which made her full of positivity and made her glow. However, Bernie felt she needed to inform her sister of all the negativity that also exists in the shoe world.

'You're right. Many of our friends disappeared shortly after their birth,' said Ellie sadly as she half-hugged Bernie. They suddenly missed Lola and Lila, who taught them about shoe history and Candie and Candie-Pinkie from the lunch at Nello's.

Ellie and Bernie had seen it all. Many of their friends and relatives sold all across the country fulfilled the dreams of many girls. Not long after being sold, the shoes were ripped up and worn out while their soles were stacked with cigarette ash and broken glass from the nightclubs. Not needed any longer, they were forgotten and thrown in the garbage can, lost and replaced by a newer, trendier pair.

Was it karma or unfairness? Ellie and Bernie felt that it was a complete disrespect to their nature, which is one of a piece of art. "My little newborn *cheuf d'ouevres!*" their father had exclaimed at them with a gigantic smile on his face. His eyes glowed with pride and admiration at his own creation.

The twins, being fairly intellectual, often reflected on this matter and concluded that every creation is a piece of art. The track of fashion was at times too fast to follow. Nevertheless, it did not mean that their fellow shoes were to be maltreated and disrespected, as if they were nothing more than junk.

The twins had inherited the patience and good manners of their creator Balthazar, but they often felt a certain irritation as they observed the new, so-called trendy shoes. At times, Bernie especially felt insulted at the thought that all those fellow shoes were produced in massive shoe factories somewhere far away and surely not by humans but by soulless robots. Cloned, they were not alive. They were bodies with no mind or soul. They were nothing more than pieces of leather, wood, and synthetics shaped, twisted, glued, and finally sent out for sale.

These clones appeared in all colours and styles, yet they were all created with no soul, only empty soles.

Lunch in Fred's went well; Fay had a Caesar salad while her agent, who had Jimmy Choos for men, was just sipping on a freshly squeezed orange juice. The Jimmy Choos banged their heels and greeted the twins in a very festive mood.

'Did you hear about what happened?' they asked the twins, who seemed rather confused.

'What happened?' both Ellie and Bernie replied, puzzled.

'We just flew in from Paris. When we were at the airport a gorgeous crocodile light-blue Birkin bag was savagely torn into pieces! It was the most awful massacre we'd ever seen, and it was live!' exclaimed the right boot.

'Why would anyone massacre a Birkin?' asked Bernie.

'The security at customs claimed it was a fake one! The girl holding it refused to turn it over to customs, so due to all the pulling and pushing the poor thing tore into two halves. It was very heartbreaking to hear her scream,' the boot said gloomily.

'Was it real?' asked Bernie and Ellie.

'We never found out. Our master went through customs without stopping. But, fake or real, the poor thing was alive, and now it is probably still stuck at customs and is being questioned for its papers and birth certificates,' said the right boot.

Ellie and Bernie were very moved by this distressing story. They asked whether there was a chance the bag could get better, or would it stay handicapped for life?

'Unfortunately, there is a chance it will be burned alive,' said the left boot with a heartbreak look in her eyes.

'But she's still alive that is just awful!' cried Ellie in despair

'You see, French government is very strict about replicas. And if that bag was a fake then it will see a harsh death penalty. If it is not, it will be returned, and after surgical bag stitching, the Birkin will look itself again,' said the boot with hope.

All four shoes banged their heels in distress and prayed for the Birkin to survive the cruel French customs.

The twins were not pro-imitation purses; however, they pitied the bag. Fake or not, it did not deserve such a treatment. Even if at some point in its life the bag wanted to be someone it was not, it was still a living bag and should be questioned like a respectful bag and not bruised and beaten, especially on such official grounds as the customs of Charles de Gaulle airport.

The twins were very upset at the French for this attack on the innocent bag; they didn't sleep well that day. They wondered if they should share this story with their friend, Hermeneus, the Hermes pantoufle at Fay's apartment.

* * *

At the Rose Bar

While Ellie and Bernie had to walk the rainy, muddy streets, other shoes had the privilege of hanging out in New York's hip downtown Rose Bar. Those who weren't allowed in the Rose were in Jade Bar, which was open to the public. Of course this unfairness didn't last long, and soon the twins would also be part of the glamorous shoe get together.

Ellie and Bernie had found that people and their shoes could be quite similar, with time even becoming the same. The twins noticed a Miu Miu boot who couldn't stop expressing her annoyance because her mistress had to step out into the main lobby every time she wanted to text or call since there was no network with T-Mobile in the Rose Bar. Both boots and mistress were annoyed and frustrated that they had to walk outside. The boots seemed to forget that footwear is made for walking, not just sitting around, even if it is made of the very best quality of pale pink suede.

Ellie and Bernie had a long day and didn't expect to come to Rose Bar, yet Fay had a meeting with friends planned.

The twins observed many funky fashionable hip and stylishly artistic people who complained about how they paid a lot of money for a room at the hotel just to be able to get a glimpse of the Rosebar but didn't get into the bar: they thought to themselves, what would happen if everyone who stayed at a hotel were let into an exclusive venue that happened to be part of the hotel? What if everyone staying at the Standard was admitted to the Boom Boom Room, or everyone at Gansevoort got into Provocateur? The exclusive venues would go downhill. They would lose all their regular clients and become just another average place.

Rose Bar clearly stated that people needed a reservation. It was not a surprise. Fay knew the bouncer dressed all in black, he was standing by the scarlet velvet robes that determinably set the territories and were reminding of the tough immigration officers at the JFK. The bouncer was strict with Fay as well, but as soon as he realised that she practically knew everyone inside - which meant she was herself the crowd's glowing star-to-be. He eventually added her on the email list that made her entrance "sans probleme". Ellie and Bernie wondered if these people who were complaining would walk into Minetta or Waverly and demand a table at primetime unless they were very close with the owner? They were faced by a purple stiletto on a tall blond models foot, she glanced at them and said 'I have watched several guys argue with security about how they put up tons of clients there, and that they deserve better treatment. That may be true, but doormen hear that story countless times a day—not to mention the fact that they probably couldn't care less,' whispered the purple stiletto in a wispy, worn-out vintage style shoe dress. She was outside along with her Scandinavian skeletal-looking model smoking Marlboro lights like they were her survival medicine.

'If you truly are a major corporate client who puts up a lot people at the Gramercy Park Hotel, I'd suggest contacting the sales manager and explaining how your company spends X dollars and you'd like a reservation at the Rose Bar. I'm pretty sure they'd be happy to comply. Arguing with the doorman is not only ineffective. If you ever return, he will remember you as being a troublemaker, and that's never a good thing,' she continued.

'For those complaining that they went there at 7:00 p.m. and nothing was going on: what exactly do you think would be going on? It's a hotspot at night. That's why you don't need a reservation during the day!' she laughed sarcastically, turning one hundred eighty degrees towards the twins.

'You really know a lot about this place,' said Ellie still mesmerized by the stilettos' confidence and ease. Ellie always wanted to be a confident and cool shoe. She loved this I-am-the-star attitude, yet she wasn't exactly like that. Her manners at times wouldn't let her to act that way.

'Oh, trust me, I have been around for the past four years almost every freaking day! The place is cool and hip, but I just want some vacation, I know I'm so messed up!' she said, giggling. 'I'm Alexandra, by the way. And my sister is mute, poor little thing. She's been that way since Scott Lipps had a concert here. She stood right by the speaker, and *bam*, it hit her fragile ears.' She patted her sister and looked at Ellie and Bernie.

'I am Bernie. Pleased to meet you, Alexandra' said Bernie.

'I am Ellie. It is very nice to meet you,' said Ellie happily.

Alexandra stepped on the cigarette her mistress threw on the ground. While turning on it, she laughed. 'You girls are funny. I like your style, but you gotta drink a few cocktails when you get in. They drop on you whether you want it or not since everyone is moving around with their glasses.' She tottered towards the twins.

'The Rose Bar Bellinis are the best I've had in the city. I also love the Vanilla Passion and Maracuya Mosquito with passion fruit. But practically all the drinks are worth trying. This is one of few places I could easily have ten or more drinks in a sitting, and there is also a bar menu. Service is very professional, friendly, and discreet, and the managers are really nice. Note that the cocktail options on the rooftop are a condensed list of the menu inside. Generally, it's a good mix of people and shoes.' Alexandra shivered from the cold and turned to the door. Then she turned back and yelled out from the door, 'See you inside, gals! I gotta go. Gisele is there with pumps.'

'Which Gisele?' asked Ellie.

'Umm…There is only one, and only Gisele Bündchen, of course!' she laughed teasingly.

'You shoes are hilarious!' she exclaimed and ran inside.

As soon as Fay saw the doorman, he had let her in. Thanks to her social skills she could open any doors.

The twins toddled in the chic environment with a palatial, Spanish air. As they marched on the red-and-white tile floor, still not sure of the new grounds, they looked around. Indeed, Gisele Bündchen was at the corner table with her gorgeous pumps. A little further sat Jennifer Aniston, looking gorgeous. Her silver python platform sandal with tiered design winked at the twins, as if they felt that Fay was dreaming to be like their mistress. It was a place full of celebrities. And all the other people were looking like someone famous, yet it was hard to differentiate them.

Rose bar was great and Ellie and Bernie begun watching the confident, relaxed shoe stars.

A well-placed pop art painting over a gigantic wood-burning fireplace—the twins observed a similar set of riches at play on the oak-leaf-shaped shelves that towered over each bar and were stocked with aged scotches and exotic liquors.

Ellie and Bernie loved the place. It had a wonderful aroma of burned wood and cinnamon and something else that made it so cosy, like a little chateau!

Here they were, the Bozzis and Fay at the Rose Bar at the Gramercy Park Hotel, a swanky, hot hotel bar in New York City that was extremely hard to get into unless you were an actor or model. They felt quite at home with the edgy and eclectic decor with enormous artwork adorning the walls.

Fay's best friend was in town and also was a big fan of Bozzis, which was great for the twins as they had some company. Thankfully, Fay wore them tonight to match styles with her Italian friend, Anna.

Anna was Fay's friend since school. After Fay went to New York, Anna came from Rome to hang out for a few weeks. Anna had just arrived from Milan and was very excited about her first night out in New York. Her Italian lizard skin shoes were much younger than Ellie and Bernie. Ellie thought they looked sweet but boring. Ellie kept looking for Alexandra, who was all over the place. One minute she was at the pool table, the next she was by the big table across the bar, and then she was heading outside again. Bernie watched the surroundings and enjoyed the clean and neat floors. Above the table Fay and Anna were entering into some deep conversation.

'He's super-hot. It's Adam!' Anna squealed.

'Who's Adam?' Fay asked.

'Adam Heimman! He's, like, the 'it' guy in the US. Everyone is going crazy about him because he dated all these actresses and supermodels and now he's BFFs with...guess who?'

'Who?' Fay asked.

'Jo Starov!' Anna announced.

'The little Jo? That's impressive that anyone takes him seriously. That kid is, like, nineteen, but somehow manages to act like he's thirty!' said Fay, laughing.

'Well, the point is Adam is with him, and they came to Rose Bar! Can we go sit with them? They are waiting for us. I think it's them by the fireplace, at that big table,' said Anna excitedly.

'What's happening up there?' demanded Ellie.

Bernie looked up and felt how suddenly they were lifted. 'It's time to go, Ellie,' she said even though she was lost as well.

The two baby shoes kept yawning and sleeping on each other like little angels who should be at home in their comfy Fennel shoe bag instead of out on the town. Yet the agitated movement of their mistress awakened the two.

In addition to her best shoes, Fay wore her favourite plunge-neck, black Herve Leger dress and her silverfish Chanel bag. Anna put on her black tight mini, her ever-present white tank top, and bunch of crazy accessories that she had accumulated throughout the years from YSL and Chanel. The two friends went towards their friends. Ellie and Bernie didn't approve of such sudden movement; they didn't have time to dust themselves off, but they marched obediently.

Anna was nervous about seeing Adam. For every European girl, an American celebrity was like a God, since being famous in America meant being world famous. And Anna of all people loved US gossips and celebrity stuff. She had it all except fame, so it quite impressed her.

Fay, on the other hand, was not too familiar with the local celebrities. She only knew the A-listers, not the local society stars.

As she walked through the velvet ropes into the bar and passed the massive pool table, Anna jumped onto Jo, who was sitting on the main table with a bunch of other people. She dragged Fay to his friend, whom Fay assumed to be Adam. She politely said, 'Hi.'

'Girls, it's wonderful you came! Please take a seat! Jo happily said and made the girls sit.

The twins were watching the people and their shoes, none of which had a soul. They were all just plain shoes.

'You know, Ellie, at times I prefer that all shoes are not like us. I mean, it's nice to know that we were the chosen ones,' Bernie said.

'I wish Alexandra was with us here. She really seemed like a fun shoe with lots of fun stories to tell.' Ellie said, expressing her adoration of Alexandra the Scandinavian model's stiletto.

The girl next to Fay was in her late thirties. She seemed slightly drunk and eager to find a good listener. She started spilling out her love problems. And Fay, who was usually a good listener, didn't want to be rude, so she listened to the half-drunk woman. However, after twenty minutes she started losing her concentration, and while the woman continued to tell her about how she was once again dumped by the guy of her dreams, Fay realized that Adam was watching her.

She blushed and looked away, and then she peeked once again. His eyes didn't move. He was looking at her with a certain charm and warmth, but also some mystery. She smiled, and he smiled back.

'She's nervous,' Bernie suddenly said, observing Fay's foot vibration.

'I can feel it too! Her feet are restless,' Ellie confirmed.

The twins giggled and continued to watch the surroundings. Somehow the whole table seemed intrigued by the new European girls. There was a blonde model dressed all in black and white and a model agency owner, who seemed very busy discussing some fashion show.

Jo was, as usual, talking big-boy style as though he owned the world. Adam at first seemed snobbish, and Fay thought of him like the usual pseudo-celebrity who thought he was really hot stuff. But soon she realized he was different. There was a certain mystery to his eyes, something she was very intrigued by.

Ellie and Bernie fixated on a pair of Berlutis under the table. They were very handsome but didn't say a word. The twins wondered if they were asleep or simply soulless, yet they felt them vibrate as well. Peculiar, they thought. Both the man carried by a pair of Berlutis and Fay were nervous, yet nothing seemed to reflect this nervousness in their conversations.

For Fay, time had stopped, though the half-drunk woman was still talking, Jo was still making jokes about the last deal where he had made millions, and Anna was excitedly chatting about her first-class trip to New York that seemed like forever and was extremely tiring and how she wished Concorde's were back in the airplane industry. Fay tried acting like she was listening, but she was far away with Adam. They were watching each other for at least half an hour. He hadn't said a word. He simply watched her like she was something for which he had been waiting for years, like he knew her, like he didn't know how to approach her without scaring her off, like he had recognized something in her.'Come on, guys. Let's go to One Oak!' exclaimed Jo.

One Oak was a new hip nightclub that all the fashion and music people went to.

They all stood up. She automatically said her good-byes and reassured the still-talking woman that the right guy would appear eventually.

Anna grabbed Fay and whispered, 'I saw how he looked at you. He liked you! You can start dating, Fay. And I am kind of into Jo! I know, I know, it's like a joke, but I find him funny!'

Fay and Anna giggled.

Ellie and Bernie were now sure their mistress liked the Berluti man. Her feet still trembled from the love-at-first-sight feelings. Ellie and Bernie made her walk smoother and made her legs look even more fabulous.

As they left the club, Adam suddenly took Fay into his arms in a dramatic twirl.

'What is happening?' screamed Bernie. 'I don't feel the ground!'

'We're being lifted! Oh, my, I think I am falling, Bernie! Are you there, Bernie?' Ellie looked around, scared of flying. She saw Anna and Jo laughing. She felt so much higher than she'd ever felt in her shoe life. The air whooshed around here like a breeze.

Fay was pleasantly surprised that Adam lifted her up so high. She smiled, thinking his childlike behaviour was extremely sweet and cute.

As the twins hit the ground, they looked at each other. Both slightly traumatized by the unexpected lift, they giggled nervously as they continued to stroll the streets with the Berlutis by their side.

They arrived at a teak doorway on an unremarkable stretch of far-West 17th Street. Inside, the hallway was faintly aglow. Lines of nearly indecipherable script were carved into the black ceiling and walls. Each word was painted with gold leaf, forming an excerpt from Darwin's *Origin of the Species*. At the hallway's end, curvy leather banquettes outlined a fanciful room where light fixtures fashioned from recycled bicycle tires evoked wizard's caps, walls were upholstered in ostrich leather, and mirrored open-air decks beckoned from behind a fireplace.

Ben, the toughest bouncer in the city, allowed his face to stretch into a huge smile when he saw Adam. He smiled even more as he saw Adam taking Fay's hand. She shyly followed Adam into the club, yet she was annoyed at the demonstrative nature of his actions.

'Oh, my God, did you see that Bernie?' asked Ellie as she pointed at Fay and Adam's hands.

'I think there is certain chemistry between these two,' nodded Bernie with worry on her face.

'From now on, Ben will always let us in!' Anna whispered to Fay.

'What a great beginning in New York City!' Fay reassured her.

Ellie and Bernie were contemplating the black-and-white floors of the fresh club that even Bernie liked.

'Love this song' exclaimed Bernie

'It is really fun here, Balthazar forgot to mention the party scene in NY' giggled Ellie

The two shoes watched the other shoes that were all ecstatically dancing to the rhythms. The energy was high and Ellie and Bernie loved every second of it.

Jay-Z's "Empire State of Mind" pulsed through the walls. 'Here we are in New York,' whispered Fay in Anna's ear.

Adam was all over Fay. He was sweet, yet not pushy. He kept watching her and her dance moves, copying them, and they giggled and laughed like kids. Anna was in some deeply hilarious conversation with Jo, who wouldn't stop with his legendary business affairs and his poker techniques. According to him, he had won them all. In fact, he shouldn't be allowed into any casino in the world. And the Brunei sheikh should kill him, since he, according to Jo, lost his castle to Jo but never compensated him and now has therefore disappeared from the scene.

Anna was so drunk she didn't care about casinos. She was happy to be in this magical city and to dance. And she kept hugging Fay and telling her how much she loved her and how she was her sister from another mother, a concept they had come up with back in college.

The twins danced joyfully. They were having a great time jumping up and sliding sideways. They completely forgot who they were. All they knew was that this was a magical place.

New York's aroma was amazing, or perhaps it was Adam's perfume. He handed Fay another Vodka soda and then took her to dance. She felt like she was living in a movie.

As the Berlutis shoes approached, Ellie and Bernie blushed. The gorgeous shoes were dancing. The twins found them to be very handsome but not very talkative. Ellie and Bernie continued dancing and again felt lifted. This time, the twins were not surprised. Adam obviously liked to lift Fay in perhaps a new technique or a new dance that the twins weren't aware of. The Berlutis shoes kept eyeing Leonardo DiCaprio's shoes that were the centre of the clubs attention. Adam knew the actor, so they chatted for a bit. Leonardo's dark black sneakers were throwing jokes about and declared with a laugh, 'This floor is so lame, we're gonna keep sitting on the couch.' They said in a cool celebrity bass tone.

Bernie couldn't help but comment, 'They are so fake, these Berlutis. I wonder where they were purchased from? Which market?' she enquired rather seriously

'You think they are fake?' asked Ellie. Ellie couldn't believe that such gorgeous shoes could be a not genuine.

'Replica I'm telling you' Bernie assured

Ellie confusingly watched the Berlutis who were almost motionless on the dance floor.

'Look at them. They are looking up to those sneakers just because they belong to Leonardo DiCaprio!' claimed Bernie. 'A real, proper shoe wouldn't behave this way, especially a Berluti,' she insisted.

'I guess we'll never know. They don't even talk to us,' said Ellie, turning away from them so they couldn't see her talking about them.

'Why be an actress in a movie when simply living in this town is a movie by itself?' Fay wondered.

'Let's get out of here,' Adam said. 'Let's show the girls Bungalow 8. Jessica is waiting for us!' Adam excitedly pulled Fay and the others along with him.

They jumped into a cab. Both Ellie and Bernie were confused by where they were going and how they had ended up there.

They soon arrived at their third destination, which the owner was known to keep very intimate and private. Bernie and Ellie had seen her a few times out about town. The twins had seen a few celebrities with her, such as Blink-182, Scarlett Johansson, Paris Hilton, Leelee Sobieski, P. Diddy, the Wayans Brothers, and athletes from time to time. The club touted a very ritzy and beachy-keen atmosphere with a stylish bar and seating. Palm trees, zebra stripes, and a very strong South Beach interior made an ultimate presence inside the club.

Of course Ellie had to flirt with P. Diddy's Tod's loafers, who were acting like they were the star and not him. Scarlett Johansson's leopard pumps were nice. They complimented the twins on their 'beautiful allure.'

They were escorted to the VIP lounge, where close friends were seated with the group. About fifty people were attending the private event.

There were open bottles of Clos Du Mesnil 1995, Veuve Clicquot, and of course Cristal. The wait staff served hors d'oeuvres. Caterers had provided abundant trays of seafood ceviche, lobster, mango rice paper salad rolls, tuna tartar, Moroccan Chicken skewers, creamy caviar spread, and crostini with herbed goat cheese.

"Your Love," by The Outfield, was playing loudly, and Anna was having a blast. It was her song, and she knew the lyrics well: *'Josie's on a vacation far away.…So many things that I want to say.'*

She was dancing on the couch with her glass of Dom. Nearby, Adam tried to impress Fay with his Blackberry messenger list, which included the whole of the red carpet crowd and Hollywood. She didn't want to show her shock at a few of the names that she got a glimpse of. In fact, she didn't appreciate his showing off. So she said, 'Yeah, cool.'

'Don't be arrogant,' he said with a smile that made her heart melt in a wink of an eye.

As "Give It Away" by Deepest Blue came on she smiled at him and said, 'Let's dance!'

'He thinks he's smart. What kind of a man shows off his Blackberry messenger list?' asked Bernie. She was infuriated by how the men Fay hung out with were nothing close to the ones she had observed around Crystal back in the days of Hollywood parties.

'He's trying to make her interested. Isn't it sweet?' Ellie, a hopeless romantic, looked with her angelic shoe eyes at the two dancing. At the same time, she tried to make her mistress's legs comfortable and most stunning.

Adam poured Fay a glass of champagne, and they cheered. He went to the bathroom, and when he came back, she was in a trance with the music. She was by now crazy about him, but she had to hide it. There was no way he should find out about it at this point.

Thanks to Anna's summary of his love life, she knew how easily Adam charmed all the girls, so that kept Fay on her guard.

As she stood up to look for Anna, who had disappeared into the crowd, Adam was suddenly in front of her. She smelled his cologne as he gently removed a tiny piece of leaf from her hair. She could only gaze into his utterly striking eyes. They had the most masculine and strong look, and she just couldn't resist as he tried kissing her.

'I don't really know you,' she managed to say, moving away.

'I just wanted to give you a kiss on your cheek. Don't be such a scary-cat!' he mumbled.

'I see,' she said calmly.

'Honey bunny, you're too sweet!' He smiled at her.

Many people had called her 'sweet' since her teenage years so she was used to the term. She was looking more for 'hot,' but sweet was the deal.

As very interesting-looking fashionable shoes were dancing around, Fay felt her feet were very light, like the floor was floating!

Ellie and Bernie felt her girly insecurities and decided to help her, at least from their shoe perspective.

'She's in love!' exclaimed Ellie.

'I know, I know, but there is nothing good in that,' replied Bernie.

'Love is always good,' said Ellie.

'No, look where it brought Crystal. There's nothing good in it when it involves people who can't handle it with care and gentlemanliness. And he just doesn't seem the right one for Fay. She's way too fragile.' Bernie assumed all women were like Crystal, tough on the outside yet fragile inside.

Ellie loved the impossible-love concept, so she was now even more excited for Fay's feelings. But she opted to nod in response to her sister instead of arguing.

Fay and Adam were by now dancing to the beat. She was quite petite, and he was rather tall. From outside it seemed very sweet, and he was handling her with protectiveness and care. His style was like some sort of rock star. She was like a typical European girl, dressed in brand names from head to toe, trying to look New York, but with the European details showing. She even tried making her hair look messy, but her hair looked perfectly curled after a one hour blow drying session at the hairdressers.' And her black and skinny Herve Leger dress and the ever-present Chanel purse added classiness to her look.

Fay was tipsy and enjoying herself. She felt good with him. There were no more kisses, just glimpses. Nevertheless, she felt like they had lived a whole love story with countless chapters in just this one night. She started wondering if it were the drink or if she had by mistake swallowed something that gave her this effect. But, no, she was simply feeling the air of newness and exciting adventure.

'Let's go to my place,' Adam said. 'Let's have an after at mine! Yo, Jo. Let's go!' he commanded. Jo was chatting with Anna and the other bunch of people who had been following them since One Oak.

Before Fay had a chance to say anything, they were all walking towards the exit. They didn't even pay the bill, as apparently his presence was publicity for the club, and so all drinks were on the house.

They hailed a cab, and they all piled in: Jo, Anna, Casey the model, Adam, and Fay. The rest waited for a second cab.

As they arrived at Adam's Mercer Street one-floor loft, Fay saw that his shelves were filled with thousands of DVDs. A ladder allowed access to those up high.

Adam took out a bottle of Grey Goose and managed to spill half of it while handing the glasses to everyone. Fay refused and helped herself to a can of Coke.

Ellie and Bernie examined what felt like new, beautiful hardwood floors from Wood Timber Flooring. Shoes knew very well the incredible choices available for wood floors: blonde pine, black walnut, red mahogany, and grey ironbark were just a few. Wood timbers are available in planks and laminates, and there's a type for every loft. Wood timbers lie upon the subflooring and fit tongue and groove or by click locking. The twins preferred dark walnut, as it was the most soothing to step on and somehow felt friendlier than old-fashioned blonde pine.

Fay sat on the meticulously modelled version of Rodolfo Dordoni's Hamilton Island lavish sofa for Minotti. It was the same sofa Fay had at her place, highly detailed with individually modelled folds and stitches in a deep brown. Hers was cream, but she liked the masculine brown in Adam's flat.

She sat there while the group watched *Mission Impossible II*. As Tom Cruise and Dougray Scott shot at each other from the backs of motorcycles, all Fay could do was examine her newly born feelings towards Adam.

Ellie and Bernie were also lying on the brown sofa. Fay refused to remove them, so they lay peacefully watching what seemed like a lot of punching and kicking and flipping.

Fay was engrossed in an action scene when Adam laid his head on her upper leg and looked at her. She was startled by such an unexpected move and half-giggled, half-watched if he was going to move or stay.

She then politely asked him, 'Can you move, please? It's a little heavy.'

Without warning, he screamed at her, 'I don't want to have my head on your hairy legs! It's giving me a freaking headache!' He suddenly stood up.

Fay was shocked, Ellie and Bernie were speechless, and Anna seemed not to have understood what had just happened.

In a matter seconds, Adam started saying awful things and fighting with Jo, who was making fun of him. He called Anna horrible names for having drunk from the bottles. And he pushed Casey, who had simply been just sitting there all night and nodding at whatever anyone said.

Fay had to think fast. She couldn't bear another second of hearing insults, and because of her strict education she couldn't make herself answer in the same manner. It was hurtful, and though he was drunk, she couldn't understand him. She quickly wondered if she had been rude to tell him to move his head. But she said it softly and nicely. 'Why on Earth would anyone react this way?' she wondered.

It was now 7:00 a.m., and she didn't know how such a positive atmosphere had turned into this. She pulled Anna, who was quite drunk, waved to Jo, and got out of the apartment. Ellie and Bernie followed obediently and marched right out.

Adam didn't even look at her as she left. Anna was angry and talking out her confusion. Fay was perfectly sober and still trying to digest the situation.

'Fay, he was drunk,' Anna said. 'People do stupid stuff. He will probably forget all about it tomorrow!'

Maybe he would, but Fay doubted she would. It just really felt like someone had just slapped her for no reason.

She had finally fallen asleep in her apartment. When the 8:30 alarm went off, she couldn't pull herself up to attend her class. She wasn't prepared for *Hamlet*, and she was supposed to have learned a piece. She was still quite sad from the previous night. She hit snooze and continued sleeping.

Ellie and Bernie were by the bed. They couldn't sleep after a night like that. They hadn't ever been out to so many different places with so many shoes that were not alive. It comforted them in a way, feeling like the only survivors of the shoe world. But it also made them sad.

'Shoes like us don't go out to nightclubs, Bernie,' reassured Ellie. 'I wish she would get another pair like us, so we could have at least another Bozzi to talk to,' Ellie dreamed out loud.

'I doubt that will be happening any time soon. Bozzis are extremely rare these days. We are like the jewels of the shoe world, according to something I saw in one magazine,' Bernie said.

For a long time, neither spoke.

'Why are you so silent?' Bernie asked.

'I'm just thoughtful,' Ellie replied.

'About?' Bernie demanded.

'Well, Adam. Why would he get so upset with her?' Ellie wondered.

'He was drunk, and she was sober. Typical.' Bernie concluded.

'I think he actually tried showing some warmth to her, and he perceived her reaction as cold and unloving,' Ellie argued.

'Then he's an imbecile. She acted like any proper lady would. If he can't understand that, then he has a problem,' Bernie replied.

'I just feel that he is like a teddy bear that is in deep need of love, and he saw potential in her. He felt her warm nature, but then he got upset that she didn't trust him enough to share her warmth with him,' Ellie protested. She somehow felt pity for clumsy Adam who seemed like someone with a lot of warmth to give yet no one to give it to.

'To me it looked more like a drunken human being trying to get in bed with a girl, and then he got mad because she indirectly refused,' Bernie persisted.

'Come on! There was nothing of that kind. He was seriously gentle and polite with her. He knew she was not the type, like his friend Casey whom he kicked with his legs, remember?' Ellie said, hoping her sister would agree.

'I don't know,' Bernie said. 'I just know this: she did the right thing when she left his apartment and all those people. She should concentrate on her career and not on some drunk who gets mad like a maniac!' Bernie said, feeling protective of their mistress.

Ellie herself was falling for Adam. If she were a human, she would have totally run after him. There was something very special about him.

She loved dreaming about how she would look if she were a girl. Would she be tall or short, thin or chubby, blonde or brunette? With all these thoughts, she slowly fell asleep with a piece of the white, soft cotton sheets slightly covering her nose and Bernie's heel. It soothed them right into a deep, comforting sleep.

Confession: Imelda Marcos's Shoes

"I did not have three thousand pairs of shoes; I had one thousand and sixty." —Imelda Marcos

My name is Arabella, and my sister is Anabella. We are Salvatore Ferragamo handmade shoes. Inside our inner soles is inscribed, *For Imelda Marcos, first lady, by Salvatore Ferragamo.*

Indeed, I am a vintage shoe who has been left behind along with thousands of other fascinating shoes. About 2,700 pairs were discovered in Imelda's rooms at the Malacanang presidential palace after the couple fled to the US following the 'people power' protests in 1986. We will never forget the number of people all suddenly breaking into our ever-quiet shoe gallery.

We were all aligned royally, all colourful and elegant on the massive wooden shelves. There were so many of us, each similar yet different, irresistible and alluring, graceful and entrancing: black, white, red, pink, mauve, purple, brown, silk, alligator, snake, lamb-skin, flats, high heels, platforms, stone-engraved frivolous pallets, amusing bows of sharp-nosed, irresistibly slim-heeled, massive-heeled. We made up a shoe dynasty of the era!

Many of these were incarnated fans of Imelda's, little girls who grew up wanting to be a part of Imelda's life. Those who placed the material factor higher than life were awoken into the shoe dynasty reality. Many enjoyed it more than their previous lives, until they were exposed in the Marikina Shoe Museum in Manila.

In 2009, there was a major flood. Marikina was one of the areas worst hit by Typhoon Ketsana, which killed more than three hundred people in the Philippines. Despite this tragic event, staff at the Marikina Shoe Museum moved hundreds of pairs just before water swamped the building's ground floor. Imelda's shoes are very secure, enjoying a kind of shoe status that many shoes could only dream of. With full-time security and care, they are not worn anymore, just preserved. In the Philippines, Imelda's shoes are very much respected.

She loved shoes with ostentatious extravagance. Ferdinand and Imelda ruled the Philippines, and Imelda was often referred to as the "Iron Butterfly." She was all about beauty. She believed that everything had to be beautiful, especially her shoes.

The many objects inside the mansion and her private rooms gave her an image she deeply wanted people to believe about her: that she was a woman with aristocratic origins who was destined to lead. She had many titles: The Rose of Tacloban; The Muse of Manila; the Compassionate First Lady from the Philippines who brought love and so many other beautiful things to her people and to the world; Iron Butterfly; the mythical Maganda (Beauty); the first Filipina; Mother Philippines herself; the Goddess of Beauty who rose from the sea. In my opinion, she wanted to show an image of herself just like the ancient Filipino Babaylan—narrator of the people's story, healer of physical and social ills, spiritual leader of the people. She wanted to be the bearer of *ginhawa*—Lady Bountiful.

Despite the deliberate attempt to hide the painful past and personality of the first lady, the Santo Niño Shrine is still a reminder of a dark truth. The mansion is a reflection of the megalomania that is actually in all of us: the grandiose dream of power and wealth for ourselves. The mansion also reminds us of the danger of being able to fulfil these grandiose dreams.

Whatever representation a personality or an institution would desire to ingrain in the national memory through text and concrete, and however great is the power used to establish this representation, in the end, it is the experience and socialization of the individual that will determine her image. The individual has the prerogative not to believe in such a fabricated image, especially if it doesn't square with one's experience of history.

To each his own Imelda. For my part, I remember her differently. She was very careful when picking the next pair of shoes for her outfit. She spent hours with us, smiling at each and every pair. She made sure the temperature in the shoe room was a little cold so that we could be kept in our best shapes. When wearing us, she would never step hard. She was more like a flowing angel, she moved so royally. Indeed, we felt she was living in dream world, but she enjoyed it and was always smiling.

There were a few lucky ones that were worn more than once. Unfortunately, I was only worn once, but that one time was the most memorable and cherished moment of my life. It was a dinner during the official trip to Libya.

In late 1976, Mrs Marcos made a historic visit to Libya and successfully secured a commitment from Libyan President Muammar Al Qaddafi, top financial supporter of the MNLF, to resolve the Moro problem in Mindanao. That was the Tripoli Agreement.

She wore me on her second day, and it was a great experience to see how a beautiful woman could manage to solve political issues, how at her smile all men were ready to collapse. Of course watching everything from the shoe angle is much more exciting. Thrills of excitement were running through us when we were stepping out into the Libyan parliament building to meet the colonel. All the male shoes were lumpish and grotesque. Imelda's dress was rather long, but as we placed our steps, we saw the politically intriguing scene in perfect vision.

We were never the hapless victims of the man versus shoe exploitation.

I feel certain nostalgia for those days. What can be better than being assembled with all the most beautiful shoes? And even after the revolution, we were left to age together in a museum, until an English lady, a true shoe lover, purchased us, and now we're isolated in a glass box overlooking her massive dressing area. It's very different from what we were used to. This room is modern and high-tech. She was an architect herself with a deep interest in shoe structures. We're not complaining; we're just getting used to the new environment.

After what I've observed in the human world, true progress is not and should not be confined to the satisfaction of the material needs of individuals. It must extend to the development of minds as well as to the fulfilment of spirits. True progress fills people with knowledge and wisdom, and it must enrich the quality of human life. Those who fulfil their lives with material needs are very vulnerable to the loss of those materials, but an educated mind is forever.

No matter how much people lose in material, they can always pursue more intellectually.

Confession of the John Lobb Shoes

As you turn off Sunset Boulevard and onto Stone Canyon Drive, you enter one of the most gorgeous enclaves in the entire Los Angeles area. A short drive down this road takes you to one of the most private, luxurious retreats on the entire west coast. The Hotel Bel-Air is by far the most unassuming and tranquil of destinations. A man needs some time to himself. That's what our grandmother used to tell us when our grandfather used to be deep in thought.

From the moment we pulled into the hotel, we were greeted with a smile by the valet service. These weren't your typical stoner types that peeled out in your car as you walked away, but were more like ambassadors for the hotel. They were neat from head to toe, and you have probably heard that the way to judge a man is by his shoes. For that matter, we have closely analysed the valet's shoes, and I must admit they were very decent, perhaps not handmade, but those of very well-educated gentlemen.

By the way, have you ever heard of us? We are Jo and Smith. John Lobb was our creator, and we were born in London on Jermyn Street in Mayfair, right by the renowned British members-only nightclub, Tramp.

Our creator's name is that of our brand, as much as I hate to call myself a brand. I guess *brand* could mean "nationality" in human language. I advise you to start remembering our brand name, since it is the ultimate must-have for any gentleman. Of course, there are other brands, but we are unique. And if you don't have one of us, I suggest you purchase one pair. It is a classic that you will use at some point in your life. Trust me on that one. If you don't trust a shoe recommending a shoe, then whom can you trust?

John Lobb started off with a store in London, and that is where we come from. We were handmade and measured to fit our owner's feet. John Lobb manufactures readymade shoes as well, which is part of the Hermes group nowadays. Our siblings are all around the world. There is a John Lobb boutique in most capital cities, and I even heard that they were on sale for Christmas at Saks in New York.

We are often criticized as being slightly stuck up and conservative. Our kilties over our shiny black leather vamp is somewhat disturbing to some, but I say the world should appreciate us, and the shoe society should be grateful that in this modern world there are still handmade shoes like us. For example, as much as our owner, we like to spend our free afternoons in the Hotel Bel-Air's bar. It is simple with elegance—a great piano bar with an incredible selection of elixirs from an '82 Rothschild or thirty-year Macallan to a Captain and Coke. Men and women sip on such drinks throughout the day. It is all about the atmosphere. And if you had a pair of us, you would fit perfectly in any classic gentleman place.

Now when you consider all that a shoemaker does, first measuring your foot, then creating an outline of your foot, then hand-carving a form of your foot, cutting the leather, stitching the shoes, and adding the soles—and remember, you have two feet, and they are not identical, no matter what your mother told you—then the cost seems, well, completely worth it. And the same shoemaker that made your shoes can maintain and repair them as you stroll through life in comfort and style.

Perhaps men have fewer choices of styles of shoes than women do, but at least our owners keep us for an extended period of time. Often they keep us their whole lives.

A theory came to my mind the other day that perhaps men run contrary to what is commonly believed by society and are, in fact, more faithful than women. Just look at them. They keep the same pairs of shoes for years. They take great care of them, and, apart from the fashionistas, they tend to have fewer pairs than women: one for the office, one for the night, a pair of loafers for the day, and sports shoes, and maybe a few more.

Women, however, have trillions of shoes, and they never stop buying them, especially when it's sale season. They simply go wild, like the world is approaching the end and even the universe is coming to an end and the sun is freezing along with all possible world disasters one can think up. They have to grab as much as they can, and, trust me, their expressions change. They aren't sensitive angels anymore; they are more like daunting tigers that grab everything in their way, full of greed and hatred towards all other female competitors.

A life or death mission, I call it. When you see it, your perception of the female gender will change. I got very scared, along with my brother, who was brutally stepped on by a very unmannered, big-headed yellow stiletto. She practically acted like the whole store belonged to her, like it was her father who built the floor we were standing on and that all shoes were her ground to step on so cruelly.

When men buy shoes it is not necessarily an expense, it's more like an investment. Women often go for anything that sparkles and is, "So cute!" No wonder the big brand names picked up on the "So cute!" expression, and now two-thousand-dollar shoes are "So cute!" too. Crocodile skin is painted in bright pink and marshmallow tones, when just a few years ago it would have been out of the question to colour such expensive and exclusive skins in such frivolous colours. But women always get it their own way, so that even important designers become their slaves, and our owner's fellow men work days and nights so that their ladies can go out and spend thousands on pink crocodile shoes that they will wear a maximum of five times! And then they go out to look for more shoes, something "different" this time.

Sometimes I simply don't understand ladies, or their shoes, for that matter. They are incredibly confusing for one reason: they never say things the way they mean them. They want us to figure it out. And when we don't, they get upset and claim that we have hurt them. And that is another whole case, since that distress stays for a few hours at least, no matter how hard we try to make them feel better. And when we feel completely out of words and fully devastated to the deepest part of our soles, they suddenly seem better. They flourish right there at the image of our feeling miserable. But even then they never admit their wrongdoings. It's always the man's fault.

Unacceptable, just because women are weaker by nature and have those little slinky heels and satin-beaded tops and super-sensitive gentle leather that can literally be worn only indoors and on carpet floors so it won't get absolutely ruined....All these factors make them feel like little princesses, and everyone around them, including us, are just servants. It is unfair, and just you think about all the attention they get, from those glossy fashion magazines to human compliments. They even made their way into the movie industry with such films as *In her Shoes, The Devil Wears Prada,* and *Ballet Shoes.*

Female shoes play a very important role in actresses' outfits, but not so much for men's. When you look closely at most movies, men just have those same uniform-looking black leather shoes, and no one seems to care what brand they are. Couldn't they focus the camera on them to flatter them at least a tiny little bit?

Indeed, I can't say that I don't enjoy the company of new, young, beautiful, fresh, female shoes, but all that was fun before. I mean, it was fantastic living like this while we were really young still at the atelier, but now that we are hitting late shoe-twenties soon (our second year), we are facing a crossroads. We are trying to live at a level of moderate fun, not all-out the way like we used to.

You know, as people say, we try to eat the finest food, exercise a little every day, enjoy the sun moderately with good sunscreen. We can still enjoy with bit of care, right? Our main characteristic is our shoe physique. If we look worn out and old, unless we have sentimental value to our owner, he will not hesitate to throw us out. Mike and Pete, my old friends, were given to their owner's daughter for her new art experiment, and she painted them bright red and glued them to a piece of wood. They are hanging in the house like a *chef d'oeuvre*, but they are saddened by the thought that they will never walk again. And, truly, what could be worse for shoes than not being able to walk? Especially for male shoes: that is how we show our authority, strength, and masculinity.

It is shame to see some beautiful girls' shoes, and some male shoes too, destroy themselves. I would love to see them age well, you know. That would be a very beautiful world with beautiful shoes.

The lady shoes around here are all way too conservative. Perhaps they think the same of us, but a woman needs a little something feminine to her, perhaps not to the extent of beads, but perhaps a high-heeled, graceful allure would do it.

The surroundings in this hotel are like something from the Garden of Eden. There are so many trees, flowers, and ponds all around; we tend to instantly forget about the concrete and smog-filled city outside.

It's so quiet most of the time, that sometimes we tend to feel like we are the only shoes here. The little lounge restaurant is perfect for a small afternoon respite to sit and read a newspaper, as we shoes have some peaceful time in comfort. Rumour has it that many stars and Hollywood producers come to the restaurant for deal-making, and I can see why because it's so private and the staff treats you like royalty. For a second I felt as though I were Steven Spielberg's shoe.

Just a few feet away the staff surprised a couple at the bar with a dessert with *Congratulations* written on the plate in chocolate sauce. Our waiter's shoes told us that their table was the one Ronald and Nancy Reagan always booked. Must have been interesting to meet their shoes. I bet they knew a lot of inside information about the White House and all those political conflicts.

Speaking of which, I was thinking to myself the other day that it is quite unfair how the world has turned away from male shoes. I would like to remind you of an important date in world shoe history: October 12, 1960. During the 902nd Plenary Meeting of the UN General Assembly held in New York, Soviet Premier Nikita Khrushchev took offense at the words of a delegate from the Philippines who claimed that Eastern Europe had been 'deprived of political and civil rights' and had effectively been 'swallowed up by the Soviet Union.' He was infuriated with rage.

What happened next has marked world history. After banging a table with both his fists, the Soviet leader took off his right shoe—a loafer, because he hated tying laces. He then waved it and banged it on the table, louder and louder, until everyone in the hall was watching and buzzing. Indeed he showed the whole world authority not with his voice, not with his arms, but with his right shoe!"

What I hear from fellow shoes who work at the UN is that nowadays visitors often ask, 'Where was Khrushchev sitting when he slammed the shoe?'

Indeed, a third world war could have started because of Khrushchev's shoe! Now, that is what I call important!

The Bush shoe attack in Baghdad, Iraq, when an Iraqi reporter hurled his shoes at President Bush, made world news headlines too. Sometimes our owners lose control, and next thing you know we are flying around like crazy spaceships.

Jokes have been made by the press that, 'The Americans have asked the UN Security Council to pass a resolution considering Iraqi shoes weapons of mass destruction.'

All that is to say that we have a say in politics and history, and our presence is significant not only for human feet. No matter how much you all try to put us down and wear us off, we deserve a little appreciation in important matters too.

Chapter 5

Adam and Fay
three months later

'Most women prefer to trip to hell in high heels than to walk flat-heeled to heaven,' Ellie read aloud from a *Harper's Bazaar* that had been lying on the floor for the past week.

'I guess women prefer to look elegant until the end of their life rather than be comfortable and not glam. However, flats these days can be glam too!' insisted Bernie.

'Thanks for that. I heard everything!' said voice from the back of the closet. It was the newly purchased Chanel ballerinas that Fay had yet not worn. 'I mean, don't forget that the whole concept of feminine glam was greatly influenced by Coco Chanel and not just Bozzi,' she said confidently.

'There's no need to take everything so literally. Let's face it. We have a nice posture. I mean, sorry, we have a posture unlike yours. But, indeed, you may be more comfortable to walk on. However, that is not for me to judge. That is a question for our fellow feet,' said Ellie.

'Before you start talking about glam, learn some manners from your sister!' snapped the Chanel flat pump before shutting herself in her box.

Shoes, just like humans, had tempers. High-heeled ones some-how felt more feminine.

The door to the room slammed wide open, and in marched Fay. She rushed into the room faster than Michael Schumacher races on the Grand Prix Formula One track in Monaco. She undressed, washed her face, ran into the dressing room, and grabbed the Dolce & Gabbana black silk top that looked like sexy nightwear, put on a pair of black shiny leggings from American Apparel, and donned a pair of fuchsia Louboutins from the Barbie Collection. Ellie and Bernie both were devastated at the thought of missing out on what looked like an exciting night for Fay.

Fay ran to the bathroom, where she applied makeup hastily. She used a bit of NARS bronzer along with some Mac pink blush; some Bobby Brown lip-gloss finished off the look. And there was the ever-messy hair, with her smoky eyes and long eyelashes thanks to Yves Saint Laurent Faux Cils mascara. She came back to the dressing area holding a bright green Nancy Gonzales clutch and a similarly coloured massive ring from Harvey Nichols that she had acquired earlier that year. The shoes all watched her, quite confused about whether she was trying to win the prize for the least tasteful outfit. Barbie pink pumps and a *Shrek*-green purse? Thought Bernie and Ellie.

She threw down her pink pumps and grabbed Ellie and Bernie. Before they knew it, they felt her slightly cold little feet, and it felt great! They were truly happy and excited to come out of the dressing area. It had been a few days since Fay had worn them. She went jogging in running shoes, of course. And she had been shopping in sandals. Somehow black crocodile leather seemed to be too heavy for her in early March. But now as she noticed the March breeze on her face, she felt absolutely happy and comfy wearing her true little starlets.

'I almost felt like she forgot us,' said Ellie.

'Never. We are her favourites; no other shoe can make her feet this comfortable,' declared Bernie fervently.

Fay pushed her way out, leaving her apartment a total mess. But what could she do? New York made even the most organized and neat people become this way at certain times; life just went too fast.

She hailed a cab, and as she rode towards 17th Street between 9th and 19th avenue, she sprayed herself with one of those little travelling tubes of Union Square Bond, and she felt so New York again. As "Lemon Tree" was playing in the background, Ellie and Bernie observed their mistress's sleekly toned legs and her delicately placed tip of a nose and magnificent eyelashes. From their perspective, she looked great. There was no doubt she would impress whoever she was going to meet, thought the shoes.

Ellie indeed felt little nervous. After all, it had been more than a month since she had made an appearance. She felt like an actress who hadn't been in a movie for a long time might feel.

Bernie whispered with a grin, 'I know what you are feeling, but there's no need. We will rock it!'

Ellie was quite surprised to hear Bernie use such expressions, but she loved it when her sister left her aristocratic values by the side to be closer to the streets.

They arrived at One Oak at 1:00 a.m., and people were standing around outside like the doorman was the Red Cross giving out alms to the poor after a catastrophe. The people desperately sought his eye contact, and they would have given him anything just to get in.

One Oak, they say, stands for the best. If you make it past the tough door, you're almost sure to spot a celebrity or two sipping Dom Perignon at one of the few tables. As one of the city's glittering clubs du jour, One Oak is stuffed to the gills with models, fashionistas, and bespoken bankers. If one is a mere mortal, she should make her way into the expansive room beneath the raw oak-lined ceiling, not forgetting to make her way down to the pimped-out bathrooms. The pitch-black stalls feature gold basins and an oversized image of a gold gun on the wall.

Fay stepped out of the cab and was heading confidently towards the entrance when someone called her name. She turned around and saw it was her old friend from college.

'Oh, my God! Fay, what the hell are you doing in New York?' The man didn't even try to stop himself from looking at her from head to toe, analysing her New-York-hip-chic style.

'Frederick! Yes, I live here now. What are you up to?'

'Oh, I was great until that total douche bag didn't let me in because of my glasses and shoes! Can you believe it?'

'Oh, God. I'm so sorry. Yes, they can be cruel, these bouncers.' Fay patted his shoulder.

Ellie was winking at the right Converse who didn't seem to react. Bernie pushed her. 'Can you stop shoving me?' cried Ellie. 'I'm just winking. What's wrong to it?' she demanded.

'Not proper behaviour for a lady,' said Bernie.

'Oh, Bernie, give me a break', ordered Ellie.

'You girls don't look like anything we've ever seen before,' said the left Converse.

'Where are you two from?' asked Ellie.

'Brooklyn,' replied the right Converse.

He didn't seem to be interested in Ellie. He tucked his head under the Frederick's pants that were way too long for him and were sweeping the ground.

'That explains it,' replied Bernie. 'We are from Uptown Manhattan,' she said.

'How's Brooklyn?' asked Ellie.

'It's cool. Rent is much cheaper. At least, that's what Frederick keeps saying. But generally, the same streets as Manhattan look-wise, it is not much different. You girls should check it out,' he said.

'They're too uptight for Brooklyn,' claimed the left Converse.

'Don't you dare speak to me like that, you filthy impolite shoe!' furiously commanded Bernie.

The left Converse laughed. 'Sorry, he likes to be mean,' said his brother.

'No worries, happens to all of us,' said Ellie.

'You should sign him up for traumatized-shoe therapy. Only a shoe shrink could help him with that attitude. In fact, he needs a good harsh walking—that should clear his system up,' said Bernie. She turned away and started to move. Fay resisted, and they only managed to move a few inches away.

Frederick was complaining about the bouncer to Fay. 'He is just so…so…scrawny, chicken-chest, greasy-looking, scraggly haired!' he cried out in despair. 'And he's a skinny-jean-and-little-league-baseball-jacket-wearing door twerp who wishes he were Vincent Gallo. He told me I couldn't come in with my sunglasses on. How can someone so utterly tasteless veto my accessories? I know it's night time, but I wear shades to avoid seeing douche bags like him clearly.' Frederick spit out his words as though to uplift his own ego.

'Actually, I wear shades twenty-four/seven to protect my eyes, because my job strains my eyes. What an asshole. I could've taken my shades off to get in. I wasn't actually wearing them. They were on top of my head. But I didn't want to at that point. He moved nervously, his face expression showing "upset" written all over his face. His hands moving dramatically like he was leading the national orchestra. The twins were watching him worriedly that he may with his long thin arms push their mistress, his emotions were clearly taking over him.

'Don't worry nightclubs and bars are always a pain' Fay said trying to calm her friend down

He looked at the door watching the bouncer and continued

'What next? He wouldn't like my shoes, and I'd have to take them off? What a shallow piece of shit. I'm sure if I showed up with one of my celebrity friends, he'd be tripping all over himself to let us in—shades or no shades. Meanwhile, wearing a jacket of any kind in the summer when it's extremely hot out is much more of a fashion faux pas than wearing glasses. And this little slime ball is wearing a polyester, league-looking bomber jacket in the twenty-degree heat. One Oak will be trendy for another five minutes.' Frederick barely took in any breath as he spewed out his speech. Fay was a lovely listener, yet Ellie and Bernie pushed her to move.

Fay placed her arm around Frederick, and with this motherly gesture he calmed down.

'I can get you in if you like,' she suggested.

'No way. Never will I step in that place, never until this idiot is out!' he announced. He puffed his chest out and seemed to be trying to make himself bigger and prouder. Even a bulldozer wouldn't sustain his fury. Ellie and Bernie glanced at his face and saw the rage slowly smooth away. He seemed to suddenly deflate again. 'I'll go home and have a bath. I need a bath. Yes, a good warm bath,' he mumbled.

'All right, then. Have a good night. It was great seeing you!' Fay said.

'You too. You look fabulous. We'll keep in touch on Facebook or Smallworld or wherever you are these days!' He made some weird-looking sign with his hand.

Fay looked relieved and pushed into the crowd.

'What a complainer, Bernie,' Ellie said.

'Humans, it's their nature to complain all day long. If he need-ed a bath, then why tell his life story to Fay? Just go home and have a bath,' wondered Bernie.

'You're not angry with me, are you?' eagerly to know the truth asked Ellie, who hated to disappoint her sister.

'For the Converses? No, not at all. I know you have a weakness for them. I just don't want you falling in love with such silly, im-mature shoes, that's all,' said Bernie. Then she took a deep breath of polluted Manhattan air and continued to stroll. 'I know you disapprove of my sympathy for all kinds of shoes but I feel that you too could be a little more open to new shoes even if they have a dif-ferent outlook on life and the shoe society,' passionately said Ellie. Bernie nodded agreeing.

Ellie and Bernie saw so many different kinds of shoes that they each ended up with a slight headache. The club was so crowded that the twins even stepped on some other shoes by accident. 'A battlefield! My God!' complained Bernie as she coughed from all the pollution.

Ellie and Bernie enjoyed the fact that none of the human be-ings knew that they were being observed, analysed, and talked about by their shoes. None of the humans had a clue that these incredible little shoe twins been very much involved in their lives. The shoes saw which humans were genuinely pure and honest and which humans were superficial and shallow.

'We are alive, Bernie! I feel so alive. I love it. I just walked on a pair of Louboutins. I literally stepped on their face and walked on them like they were the floor!' Ellie giggled to herself.

'Hey Ben!' Fay waved with such confidence that the whole crowd turned to see who it was.

'Come on in, darling!' He smiled and gently opened the velvet rope.

Fay thought he was the same old Ben, rude and tough on the exterior, but on the inside a nice kid who was just doing his job, playing the tough boy. The time since she last went out with Adam felt like an eternity. She hadn't seen or heard from him since that night. He'd probably been out and about, but she was busy with her studies.

She rushed in. Ellie and Bernie led her confidently into the club, and suddenly Adam was right in front of her, sipping on a vodka tonic. His sharp eyes met hers. She blushed a little, but after all this time she had learned to be a woman and not a little girly-girl.

'What's up?' she managed to say as he placed his big arm in his ever-present leather jacket around her shoulder. She was afraid that he could feel her pulse, as it was beating faster every minute. She couldn't help but gaze into his deep, black eyes that had taken her away from the first moment she'd seen them back in Rose Bar.

He pointed to the table on the left side where his groupies sat. Surrounding them were the always present, skeletal-looking top models that all looked the same and wore black patent Louboutins. The models were always interchangeable, and they never wore any other shoes.

'What would you like to drink, honey-bunny?' he asked in his charming tone.

'I'll have the same.' She pointed to his glass.

He handed the glass to her, and she quickly sipped to feel a little more comfortable.

The models each had the same wasted expression and could only laugh or stare blankly. And they didn't really make a girl feel at ease. Fay knew she was expected to act just the same, to act like a snobbish queen who simply loathed the place. The blank models loved people who complained, and they hated people who adored. Somehow those who complained seemed cooler because they gave the impression that they knew everything, whereas the models seemed to think those who were happy seemed weak and stupid.

Ellie and Bernie found that none of the shoes present were alive. They were just pieces of plastic combined together and seemed to have no sparkle in them.

Adam, like usual, had his five packs of Marlboro Reds tucked tightly in his hand.

Kid Cudi's "Day 'n' Nite" was playing so loudly that all the floors vibrated, giving the twins a peculiar massage. Little did Fay know that, even though Adam barely moved his head towards her to demonstrate he wasn't feeling anything towards her, the twins felt his feet approaching in a rather uncomfortable manner.

'He almost stepped on me!' Ellie screamed.

'He's such a child!' His patent sneakers, Prada or not, were not Bernie's style. She preferred manlier, classy, aristocratic John Lobbs.

Dom Perignon kept coming to the table like cans of Coke.

After a few glasses, Fay was moving to the rhythms, even chit-chatting with the models, and had begun some physical moves on Adam. Adam was like a big teddy bear; he had invented his own moves to the music that looked more like the comic moves of a fake tae kwon do. However, just because it was Adam, all the people around watched in amazement and even copied him.

Anna was by Fay's side. She wanted to make sure her friend became the new diva in the New York social scene.

Adam was now on his tenth glass, and his eyes still seemed as sharp and piercing as before.

He suddenly grabbed Fay by her right arm. Bernie felt a certain shake as she ran into Adam's shoes. Ellie complained of the filth Fay was making them stand in.

'What's going on?' Fay asked flirtatiously.

'It's time to rock! You look dope, by the way!' he managed to say even though he was rather drunk.

'It's boring here,' he yelled. 'There's this party uptown. Wanna come?' he asked.

'Hmm…um…sure!' she replied.

The next thing she knew, they were sitting in his limo heading to some producer's penthouse, who was Adam's older sister's ex-boyfriend.

Adam didn't stop looking at her, and she was quite comfortable with his eyes all over her. Indeed, she was looking right back, and there was a deep energy going on, almost playful yet strong.

'What's going on? Why is she going with him?' Bernie asked Ellie worriedly.

'Because she loves him,' Ellie replied.

There was a pause and they heard Fay's voice.

'Actually, I need to head home. I have an early-morning meeting. Can you please drop me at home?' she asked politely.

'Come on,' Adam insisted.

'I really need to go, Adam,' she said sharply.

He was obviously annoyed. He turned away at first, then back, then away, and then back. And then he managed to kiss her on the lips. Then he ordered his driver to take her home.

'Bye, honey-bunny,' he managed to say. He turned away as she got out of his car. Fay blushed, she could still feel the smell of his Tom Ford perfume that hasn't even came out yet, he explained her how he gets all the sample perfumes from his niece who is working at Tom Ford. Fay was worried, happy yet confused at the new feelings that were slowly yet steadily developing. She could feel her lower stomach worry and the butterflies of the first love were appearing and she somehow enjoyed the feeling and smiled to herself as she watched her beautiful shoes who were innocently glancing at her.

Ellie and Bernie jumped out of the car with their eyes on Adam. Fay was hardly able to walk. She had never come across such a deep attraction towards anyone.

Back home she slipped out of the twins and went to the changing room.

'If that isn't the beginning of something beautiful, then I don't know what this is,' said Ellie, smiling.

'I cannot believe my own twin sister is so gullible and naïve,' Bernie said angrily. 'Out of all the shoes I expected you to have learned that men cannot be trusted. Did you forget Crystal and Marlon?' she asked impatiently.

'I did not forget them. But it is a whole different story. He was married to someone else. This is a young boy who is obviously interested in Fay,' insisted Ellie.

'He's a young boy who is a semi-celebrity, drunk, and is all the time out and about, meaning unworthy of trust. And he is sloppy.' Bernie had a point. She didn't want Fay hurt like Crystal was at the end of her relationship. Yet Bernie did not realize that Fay was already head over heels with Adam.

Fay was a workaholic, and this was the only boy she had flirted with since she had moved to New York.

Chapter 6
Fay Out and About in LA

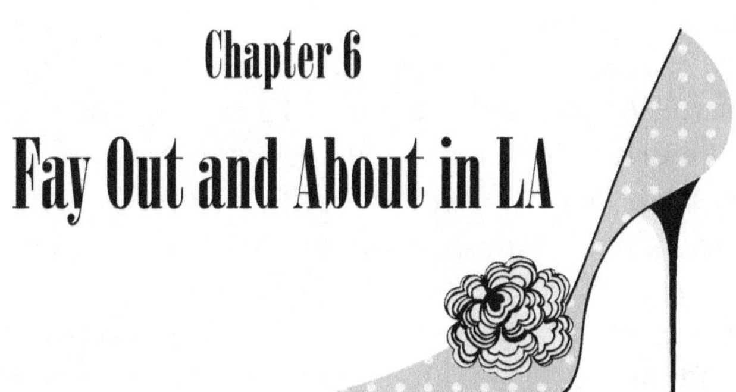

Months went by, and the Bozzis continued to live their everyday life with Fay. They were busy at rehearsals and group meeting classes, and they didn't go out and didn't see Adam. He hadn't contacted Fay since that night when he dropped her off at home. And then the day came when the twins went to the city of Angels—Los Angeles.

The flight with Virgin Airlines was beautiful. Ellie and Bernie enjoyed every minute of it.

Shortly after arriving in the city, Fay went to an Angel Hearts Charity Event. She wore a black-lace, bra-baring top, and she paired it with skinny black pants. She kept things neutral with beige patent pumps and a matching clutch. Today she didn't wear her favourite Bozzi pumps. Her mother had criticized her for wearing the same pair over and over. But Fay couldn't explain the special comfort and positive feeling she got while wearing the Bozzis. It was an almost magical energy boost. While every time she took them off it was like she had swallowed a Xanax, and she was sleepy and tired all over again.

As an energetic character, Fay loved everything that made her feel full of life, and she enjoyed her favourite pieces of clothing immensely. Shoes, especially her Bozzis, were of a special value to her, since they were almost a collection piece. They were probably worth much more than her mother had paid for them. Luck is what Fay believed in.

The event bored her, so she managed to escape with a few girlfriends and stop by the Thompson Hotel in Beverly Hills, where she checked in and changed her outfit.

The walls of the club pulsed with dance music. The crowd wove in and out between the bars and the dance floor. Adam was there. He spent most of his time dancing with different women, but when Fay arrived his attention was distracted. He couldn't have said why, and he did not spend much time considering it, but Fay had been coming to mind often lately. He would not approach her, at least not for some time. He first wanted to show himself off. In fear of rejection, he nervously sipped his Jack Daniels on the rocks while he looked at her in her vivacious, creamy white, Valentino dentelle trim lace dress.

'Love this energy. This place is fabulous,' said Ellie enthusiastically.

'It's nice. And people and their shoes look very different out here,' Bernie whispered. Bernie pointed at the leopard print wedges that seemed more like an art piece than a shoe.

'Is that Adam?' Bernie pointed at the tall young man.

'Adam! What? It is! It's him!' screamed out Ellie. She was happy to see him. She felt more than anyone how much Fay needed a man in her life.

The Tea Room was the new Hollywood hotspot. There was something very Hollywood, very arty and hip, in the air, from the peculiar hairstyles to the trendiest Boho-style shirts and the vintage strapless padded dresses. Bright-coloured YSL and Louboutin wedges and pumps sparkled from all angles, and artistic-looking guys gathered outside to smoke their Marlboro lights and exchange the latest gossip, mostly about each other.

Adam's head was exploding from the empty talk. He couldn't hold himself any longer. He feared that if he were to wait a minute longer Fay might disappear, and then he would have to wait another week to bump into her, or maybe even longer.

He ordered another glass as he stood by the bar, having carefully chosen to position himself opposite Fay. She was like the sunshine of the club, always smiling and giggling with her friends, her beautiful features and ever-happy energy making her even more special.

He watched her carefully, hesitated for a few moments, and then as soon as he caught her eyes, he held his arms high up and called to her with an innocent smile. She smiled back, surprised to see him. She soon came up to say hello. They were happy to see each other, and they chatted. Before she knew it, she was dancing the salsa with him.

They had danced together a few times in New York, but Fay had never really considered seriously dating Adam. She assumed he was the sort of guy who simply wanted to get a taste of all the good-looking girls, and she refused to be one of them. So, in her mind, she classified him as friend material, like the other player types she had placed on that list. They were all her brotherly friends, but never would she let them come closer.

Fay and Adam spent most of the night mixing with their friends and acquaintances, both hoping that it wasn't obvious they were keeping tabs on one another. Fay danced mostly free-style with her girlfriends and the occasional guy that broke into their loosely knit sanctum. As the night wore on and Adam consumed a little more alcohol, he felt less cautious about Fay. He watched her more intently, and after a few false starts in her direction that created knots in his stomach, he reached a high that swept away any remaining inhibitions. When she stopped dancing to grab a drink, he made his way over to her. He laughed, took her by the hand, and, over her weakly voiced objection, simply said, 'Come on, dance with me,' as he led her to the dance floor.

The image of the two of them together on the dance floor begged attention. Fay's beauty was in full bloom. Cascading brunette hair with blonde highlights framed her face and flashing brown eyes. Her white skin glowed softly. Her short, creamy white, dress highlighted the symmetry of her perfectly shaped legs. The straps of the halter-top decorated her alluring shoulders and the curve of her neck. High-heeled Ellie and Bernie completed the picture.

Adam's dark, athletically muscular body, was clothed in a form-fitting, short-sleeved, light-blue, open-collared knit shirt. He wore a gleaming gold short necklace and perfectly tailored dress pants over light-grey Tods. His dark, naturally curled hair framed his flashing smile.

The start of the dance was, admittedly, a little awkward. But as they both warmed to the music, he drew her close to him, holding both of her hands fully down to her sides. They slowly gyrated to the music, his brown eyes peering deeply into her bright hazel. As they continued to move to the music, he slowly raised their clasped hands, and their arms fully extended in a smooth arc out to the sides and fully up over their heads. Their syncopating bodies added the heat of friction to each other. He held their hands high above their heads for a long moment as they peered into each other's eyes, their minds and undulating bodies no longer aware of the surrounding onlookers.

The other times they had danced had been good, very good, but tonight…tonight was different. Tonight was special. Adam's eyes had never before bored into hers the way they did tonight, and she had never been as susceptible to their message as she was now.

'I love it' exclaimed Ellie. The twins were slipped into dance floor, jamming their noses against the bar then Adam's shoes and turned in circles like it were their happiest dance.

Bernie danced and loved this bizarrely new appreciation of electro tunes.

The music, the moment, and the movement drove Adam to transmit his extreme desire for Fay. She returned the feelings of yearning. As she let her guard down, she almost began to trust him. He slowly arched their arms back down. Then, moving her away slightly, he spontaneously placed a light kiss on the graceful curve of her neck. And, in one smooth motion, he spun her out and away from him, skilfully leading her into an empty space between other dancing couples on the crowded floor.

Adam spun into the space in a series of rapid three-point turns, with Fay dancing to the rhythm of the music just behind and to her right side. Catching one of her hands, he slowed his own steps, allowing her to pull out of her spin at the end of their extended arms. Then he reeled her back to him, wrapping her smoothly into a full embrace as their steps continued in time with the music. She tucked herself tightly to him, running her fingers enticingly along the contours of his chest and up to a position behind his neck.

'You're so beautiful,' he mouthed as they looked into each other's faces. The twins blushed at his words he really touched all hearts with his deep manly handsome voice.

Adam felt like he was part of the music, entirely in control of Fay now, leading, commanding, as he should be. He masterfully blended their movements in a fascinating display.

Most of the club's crowd had little choice but to notice them. Once they got past their initial envy, with some difficulty, the people appreciated Adam and Fay's presence on the dance floor. Some others complimented them about their dancing as the music ended and the club closed for the night.

The air outside the club was refreshing, and the clear night sky was inviting. Adam took the initiative. 'It looks like a great night for a walk on the ocean front. Will you keep me company?'

Fay hesitated for only an instant. She had been alone with Adam a few times before as friends, but tonight was different. Tonight there was a strong energy that had overtaken her. She preferred not to think, just to take it as it came. She wanted to live in the moment and detach herself from the rules of society.

The clear, starlit night, the watch of a full moon, and the sound of leisurely ocean waves making their way to the beach created their own romance on the now-empty boardwalk. In the nearly surreal view of the beach, the ever-changing, ragged white foam edge of the water rolled back and forth, up over the sand, and then smoothly receding. They walked hand in hand for a few quiet moments, enjoying the ambience.

'I told you, she is in love,' whispered Ellie.

Bernie still had a slight headache from all the spinning in the club, and she tried to focus on what was happening with her mistress.

Fay knew that it was Adam's nature to avoid complicated relationships. She thought he bordered on freedom-loving irresponsibility that seemed to attract many women. But strangely enough, she was not put off by her thoughts. Was she drawn to Adam's magnetism? Or was she merely curious about him?

Whatever the reason, the alcohol, the moon, the stars, and the view of the water's edge all helped Fay to continue to go with the flow of the night.

To his great surprise, Adam felt nervous. He had spent time alone with so many girls and women and had never felt nervous or had to struggle for the right things to say. Through all the years that they had known each other, he had never allowed his thoughts or feelings about Fay any space or time to gain a life of their own. Now he was hoping that his uncertainty was not obvious. He needed to make an instant decision to follow the heat of his desire or clamp it down under control. What to do? He couldn't think about it any longer. He felt forced to act and let his subconscious make the decision.

He suggested that they sit on a bench facing out toward the ocean, and without waiting for a reply, he led her gently by the hand. But as they drew near the bench, he stopped at the board-walk guardrail. His fingers trembled as he reached for Fay's other arm to turn her towards him. His eyes locked onto hers with the same fire as on the dance floor.

She felt even more vulnerable now. She could feel her own heat rising. Ellie and Bernie were motionless as they watched with amazement and waited to see what was going to happen.

Adam continued to peer into her eyes for a long silent moment, perhaps searching for some clue there. His jaw clenched tightly. He wanted to tell her that he wanted to let go, to give into his desire. But fear froze him, fear that he would be making the biggest mistake of his life, that he would be destroying something he didn't really understand.

He suddenly stood up and took her to the car. As they drove she tried to talk to him, but he was closed and cold as an icebox. He looked at her and said, 'I'm not a good person, and I have problems. I'm incapable of love. This was just a weakness, so you better go'.

'Did you hear that?' Ellie, who felt her own heart break at that very moment, looked at her sister in despair.

'I told you, all men are heartbreakers and not to be trusted.' Bernie furiously glanced at Adam who was robotically driving his SUV.

Fay was left speechless. She ordered him to stop the car, but he refused until he finally arrived at Wilshire Boulevard and stopped at the Thompson Hotel. She didn't even look at him. She simply left the car and spent the whole night crying. Ellie and Bernie felt extremely helpless. They watched another mistress cry because of a man. 'If she were a shoe she wouldn't be as emotional, for one she wouldn't have any tears to cry' admitted Bernie.

'And she could look in the soles before falling for them too' ardently said Ellie.

'See that is the issue I have with the human race, they are more fragile than us even though they seem so gigantic and tough, behind all that beefy and muscular body there a really weak heart that is broken faster than a Baccarat crystal glasses.' Bernie said fervently hoping none of the other objects in the room overheard her criticism of the human society.

The next morning Fay booked her return flight, and the three of them flew back to New York, where things felt somehow better with no more Adam. He was among the non-discussable subjects.

Confessions of a Bohemian Moccasin

Before you criticize someone, you should walk a mile in their shoes. That way when you criticize them, you are a mile away from them and you have their shoes. –Jack Handey (American comic writer, comedian and actor)

While a lazy man's best friends are his slippers, good, old, worn-out Moccasins are perfect for Bohemians. No, we are not the occasional weirdo Moccasins. A genuine Turkish factory-made, comfy Moccasin, that is who I am. My bottom is a single piece of leather stitched around a last. My vamp is attached by whipstitching to the bottom of me so it encloses the foot. It sounds horrible, but I actually feel comfortable with the stitching. By the way, my name is Keko, and my brother is Hako.

They often say that I am airy. That is not because I have holes on the sides of my inner soles, not at all; it describes more my free-minded character. I admit that at times I have an unpredictable nature, like the ever-changing air currents on the ocean drive.

My brother and I have realised throughout the years that we will never be happy with a monotonous lifestyle. We love trying out new things and meeting new shoes. We basically embrace constant changes.

See, my brother and I are what they call 'Bohemian Moccs.' Our free-minded spirit is often very different from other male shoes.

We say, 'Don't judge other shoes.' And we almost never do. We try to remember that all shoes have a soul and mind. So there is reason behind the way other shoes act, even if the reasoning seems dumb to us. Instead of being insulted or offended by others' lifestyles, I've become intrigued by what makes each of us different. We try to live peacefully with other shoes and respect them all.

We are Bohemians. Our objective is to take pleasure out of this world without causing any harm. We try to live an artistic lifestyle and place freedom of self-expression above all other desires, including wealth, social conformity, and the so-called shoe status.

See, I have travelled a lot, thanks to my energetic old man. In fact, he's only in his early thirties, but we like to call him 'old man.' Don't ask why. He is a famous photographer named Eren Acar. You might have heard of him. And of course, as is true for all Bohemian artists, my master, my brother, and I are criticized and looked down on because of our free lifestyle.

In defence of Bohemia, writers, artists, poets, musicians, and philosophers could commonly be found leading Bohemian lifestyles as far back as the nineteenth century in Paris, France.

Drugs, alcohol, and a freer attitude towards sexual expression were considered part of the subculture too. Not that we feel it is a good thing, but let's face it, give freedom to people and their shoes and let them decide for themselves what is right and what is wrong.

Bohemia is somewhat romantic, I think. There's no strings attached to our actions. What else would an artist like me dream of?

Today, any slipper who leads a non-traditional lifestyle is often called a Bohemian. And I am not talking about the countless new shoes in the fashion market that cost more than gold and are shockingly stamped as Boho style! Just because a few eccentric details were added on and the leather purposely washed off doesn't necessarily make the shoes into freedom-loving Bohemians, full of unconventional, unique ideas. On the contrary, these new fashion shoes are like manufactured robots. They know nothing about this lifestyle they were artificially made to fit.

These Bohemian shoe wannabes have radically changed the concept of true Bohemia. Today's Bohemians will be the offspring of the wealthy and can thus afford to play at being Bohemian by purchasing Boho-style shoes and clothing in high-end department stores and paying exorbitant rent in popular parts of town.

Bohemianism today is just a big lifestyle pose undertaken by those who can afford it. It has become a fashion statement by celebrities and artificial artists.

That is not our case at all. We came from a shoe factory in Edirne, a city in the central part of Turkey. When we were manufactured, our siblings told us stories and legends about the great Tulip era. Since childhood we have dreamed of getting at least a little taste of what it was like to live back then.

I still fondly recall talking with vintage Turkish slippers dating from the 1920s. They were made of a red wool fabric, and they had gold metallic thread soutache embroidery work done in a decorative Art Deco geometric design.

The slippers belonged to the big boss of the fabric factory who loved vintage slippers, and these were his favorite. These ethnic Turkish-style slippers were hand-stitched with squared toes, and they were fully lined inside with a white silk grosgrain fabric. I reckon they had only a couple of tiny moth holes that were almost impossible to see with the human eye. Well, these glorious slippers taught us history and etiquette.

They told us about the Tulip Period, which when the sultan and administrators immersed themselves in pleasure and enjoyment, forgetting about the outside world. We heard a lot of stories about the extravagancy of the imperial court, the Western-inspired parties, and the whole elite pleasure culture seen and felt everywhere. Lasting from 1718 to 1730, the Tulip Era (in Turkish, *Lale Devri*) was a transitory period in the Ottoman Empire marked by cultural innovation. During this period many reforms were made in art, literature, architecture, technology, the military, and science.

Wise old shoes used to call the period the Ottoman Renaissance. In fact, the period gets its name from court society's passion, or shall I say craze, for tulips. Tulip-growing became so popular that hundreds of new varieties were cultivated, and in the spring these beautiful flowers transformed the city into a riot of colour.

Tulip bulbs were imported at great expense and planted by the thousands. And their blooms were celebrated in candlelit tulip illuminations in gardens throughout Istanbul.

That free-styled, pleasure-oriented period couldn't have lasted forever, though. Order was imposed by the people, and the Pasha was killed, and government funds were spent more wisely for people's needs rather than beautiful tulips. Nevertheless, the era is still represented by songs, paintings, and architecture.

Well, now you probably think that I am a history teacher. Not at all. I just love imagining how people and their shoes lived back in those years. Shoes were much more appreciated, since they were all handmade and there were fewer of them.

In fact, my brother and I had a long-term relationship with a pair of white leather slippers. They were born in early nineteenth century. I still remember their two white silk tassels that were embroidered with silver metallic thread in the Turkish style. They were made in Turkey for the European market in conjunction with Napoleon's Egyptian campaigns from 1798 to 1806. The soles of the slippers were imprinted with three circles. The toes were very pointed and slightly curled upward. Even though they were...well...I hate to call them old—they were very mature and well preserved—they were full of exciting stories. Most of all, they seemed more alive than young, newly manufactured, empty-headed dolly shoes.

They also had a gracefulness and class that I have never seen in another pair of shoes. But our relationship was great until they were sent away to a museum, where they are still admired by thousands of people. Aria, my beloved, and Zara, her sister, were in a very good condition until Aria got a tiny split at the side seam. She was never the same after that; we would fight all the time, and she became very jealous towards any other female shoe. She kept saying that I would be unfaithful to her, and it truly hurt me that she would ever think so because she was the love of my life. It was becoming unbearable, and when she heard about her exile into the museum, well, it was time to part.

I then had a few other affairs, but it was really just to get her out of my shoe system. None could ever be compared to Aria. Her tone, her ways of expressing herself using old Ottoman Turkish expressions, it was like I lived my romance in the Tulip Era.

My old man Eren has begun countless travels due to his job, and we have stayed in many hotels. But in the New York Mercer Hotel, my brother and I found ourselves in the room with really hot-looking pale-white, soft, fresh slippers.

Not only were they extremely sexy, but they happened to be Turkish. Except they immigrated to the US right after they were born. These Turkish slippers were made with double twisted thread, so they were extremely absorbent, durable, and soft. The thick sole provided the best support for arches and made walking in them extremely comfortable. At least, that's what Eren claimed while thinking out loud, as he often does.

Even though they were practically married to the gigantic hunk bathrobe, they found a way to escape him since he was always left in the bathroom. While he was behind the closed bathroom door, they cosily wrapped around my brother and me. It was great to cuddle with them, but that too didn't last long as we had to leave early in the morning.

They were so pure in a sense; they never left the hotel room, and their life expectancy was incredibly short. However, they lived their life luxuriously and comfortably, without any injuries or brutal walking experiences like the cold, stoned streets we have encountered.

Our old man Eren, a true Bohemian photographer, chose the perfect spot to live in the whole of Los Angeles.

Welcome to Venice Beach, where the beautiful people of Southern California come to feel Boho and where unemployment is a studied art. Everywhere we look, we see stunt performers, roller-blades, mystic religion practices, incense burning, Reggae street musicians, and people dressed in colourful hippie clothes.

The Boardwalk is a narrow strip of shops, cafes, and clumsy tourist attractions wedged in between wooden beach cottages and broad Pacific sands. It is full of people and their shoes screaming hope and self-expression as ambitious yet undiscovered artists. They play out their fantasies to an audience of tourists, day-trippers, casual strollers, and, most of all, themselves.

Californian eccentricity and individualism does not welcome high-heeled stilettos. Most shoes here are easy-going slippers, thongs, moccasins, sandals, and flats. All are a little worn-out and covered in sand.

Like a movie, Venice Beach is removed from the rest of the world. Likewise, struggling actors, writers, cocktail waitresses, estate agents, and roller bladders are all representative figures in this movie-like scene. They embody modern reincarnations of the poets and underground rock musicians and hustlers who back in the sixties gave Venice Beach its reputation.

Vintage shoes can be seen everywhere, and that is exactly what Hako and I love about this place. We get to meet mature shoes: those that have lived hard lives and walked on all sorts of streets and rocks. Those shoes can teach us rather than gaze at us like we are some kind of shoe gurus. They all have a story to tell, and that is what I love the most in my shoe life.

Some shoes were here way back at the beginning of the whole Venice Beach concept. The story of the beach began when tobacco millionaire Abbot Kinney dreamed of creating a genetic experiment in which the tallest, blondest, most muscular Americans would meet, absorb the high culture, and procreate.

Bob, my fellow shoe friend who has lived here and there for almost one hundred years, claims he was reincarnated into his new shoe body about five years ago but has perfect memory of his past life on the beach. He said that Kinney's experiment failed mainly because the new Venetians were far more interested in funfairs and sideshows. Thus, in 1912, the state board of health declared Abbot Kinney's sixteen miles of canals to be a public hazard and filled most of them in, shattering his dreams of creating a sophisticated beach suburb.

This century, however, Venice has become a strange melting pot of clashing cultures and shoes of all styles and different backgrounds. One can easily find everything from Havaianas to with a vintage Dior Haute Couture, from Timberlands to Spice Girls '90s style platforms. Bohemians, struggling actors, drug-dealers, modern oil vendors, and fun spooky comedy shows make living in this place so unique.

Chapter 7
London Shoe Escapade

The slight breeze from the window awakened them. The weather forecast did say it was the coldest day of the year. Nevertheless, the twins embraced every surprise of life. They were finally living again with an amazing young woman who took such impeccable care of them.

Today she chose to wear them with a gorgeous, petite, dark-blue cashmere coat, super-slim dark-blue jeans, and a classic black Chanel bag with a gold chain that added something extra to her outfit. It would have been wiser for her to wear a warm pair of boots or at least a pair of flat shoes. It was supposed to snow, and the twins were more of a spring/autumn evening pair.

Fay analysed herself in the mirror and smiled at the twins as if they were her children who so wanted their mother to take them with her.

'People will think I'm foolish wearing you two, but what can I do? I feel good in these beautiful shoes!' she mumbled as she grabbed her keys and rushed downstairs. She handed the heavy keys with its massive wooden holder to Gilbert, the receptionist who glowed every time she entered or was left the hotel. His smile almost out-shined the main chandelier in the middle of the tiny lobby.

Capital Hotel, in the heart of London's Knightsbridge, was very well-situated on Basil Street, adjacent to Sloane Street, and just a few steps from Harrods and the many shops and restaurants in the area. The boutique hotel appealed to the mistress, as she felt very familiar with the staff, which had remained largely the same for the past decade. The friendly entourage and personal service were enough to make her always stay there when visiting London, even though the rooms were extremely miniature, especially compared to the American standards of spacious living.

As Fay quickly moved her little feet, the old Harrods porter thought there was something odd about the young, exotic-looking lady. She had such an amazing presence that she almost beat out the mannequins in Harrods's windows. Why did she refuse to wear another pair of shoes in this weather? he wondered.

As he observed her coming towards him, he was amazed at the neat-looking shine from the snowflake-like high heels.

While Ellie and Bernie were taking their mistress around, they had some obstacles. The weather was not in their favour today. At one point Bernie almost slipped while Ellie tried hard to maintain balance. They thought about how human beings take their shoes for granted. The twins knew that humans think shoes are simply a garment for feet—something to keep feet warm and ease walking while maintaining a sense of fashion. Humans never thought about how some shoes had a soul and feelings and genuinely cared about their owners and wanted to ease walking and make their mistresses feel more confident and sure of themselves.

Fay felt that when she wore Ellie and Bernie, her posture became more statuesque and her legs seemed longer and her mood was constantly great. They made her feel gorgeous like a model, or powerful like an empress.

Most people used their shoes and then threw them away. In lucky cases shoes were given to vintage stores, as happened to Ellie and Bernie. The twins never understood those girls who wore their favourite shoes to the nightclubs and got wasted so their shoes got stepped on and drinks spilled on them. For the shoes it was a slap on the face, disrespect. How dare a woman get drunk and lose control when she was wearing her newborn baby shoes? They must be shown off in bright light and not have drinks and cigarettes spilled on them.

Luckily, Ellie and Bernie's second mistress had a lot of respect for them. That was why they tried so hard to make her happy. After all, what could be a better friend to a girl than her favourite shoes?

Ellie and Bernie were not simple shoes with a soul. They had truly positive intentions. Interestingly enough, they had been born different in many ways into the shoe society.

When Bozzi was working on their final formation, he never imagined that they could actually be alive. Tremendously artistic shoemaker genius Balthazar was so inspired while working on the twins that he gave them many of his own characteristics, two of which were optimism and positivism. They felt different from other shoes, and they preferred to look at matters from the bold, straightforward view they had inherited from their father's artistic nature. This enabled them to be much better partners to their mistress. They understood her better than any other shoes could. They were her best friends.

It would eternally remain a mystery how Maestro Balthazar created shoes that were living objects. Was it some kind of spell he performed, or was it simply a spur-of-the-moment sensational miracle that the universe had performed through Balthazar's highly gifted hands?

'London seems like it hasn't changed since we last came here for the movie premier with Crystal,' stated Bernie.

'Did you see those glass buildings? Apparently they have the most expensive penthouse. Its over 150 million pounds!' exclaimed Ellie.

'It looks absolutely awful, four huge pieces of glass next to such a beautiful building as the Mandarin Hotel Knightsbridge I saw a picture in the magazine the other day,' replied Bernie.

'I heard a few people talking about these Hyde Park buildings. Apparently most apartments are not sold. However, one penthouse was purchased. Can you imagine?' Ellie giggled.

'Yes, I can. People are getting richer. I can see by the huge variety of shoes in the shoe departments. There is obviously a huge demand for stylish shoes. And I see a lot of Russians, Turks, and many other nationalities that were not as present before,' Bernie said.

'Turkey's economy is growing very fast. In fact, their prime minister was on the cover of *Time* magazine. I saw Fay flipping over it the other day,' Ellie proudly said. Ellie loved to tell Bernie something she did not know.

The two sisters giggled at their semi-political conversation and continued marching down the beautiful streets of Knightsbridge.

There was a huge line in front of the main entrance of Harrods. Fay wondered what was happening as she heard the women in the line quarrelling about who had cut in front of whom.

'I've been waiting more than an hour to get in. I left work early. And, believe me, I will not take someone cutting in like this!' one woman growled.

'Oh, sorry, ma'am. I have a project to write. It's the most expensively guarded shoe there. I really have to get in as soon as possible. It's for my work. I have to write about it,' a young girl explained.

'That is not my problem, dear!'

The girl pushed herself through the crowd and right inside the store.

'Did you hear that, Ellie?' Bernie asked.

'Bernie, what if it's one of our kind? Another Bozzi?' Ellie exclaimed in joy.

'I doubt it,' Bernie said. 'Plus, even if it is, I doubt Fay would spend thousands of pounds on a pair of shoes as all this fuss is probably about a very overpriced pair of shoes.' Bernie shook her shoe head.

'I just wish we could meet some relatives and not be the only ones anymore,' Ellie said in despair.

A tall lady was speaking into a camera. The twins carried Fay towards her to hear what she was saying.

'It is an age of motion and touch sensors and every other kind of high-tech gadget for security of precious goods. Harrods in London recently took a unique step to protect a pair of very expensive shoes, an elite pair of $120,000 sandals. The store rented a poisonous cobra to stand guard over a pair of Rene Caovilla sandals festooned with rubies, sapphires, and diamonds during the launch of the shoe collection,' she said.

'Ellie, Bernie, is that you?' came a voice from the ladies shoes department.

Lola and Lila, the red pumps, recognized Ellie and Bernie by their elegance.

'My God, it has been ages!' exclaimed Bernie.

'We are here with our mistress. We moved to England as she is working for a British channel now,' said Lola.

'Ellie, Bernie, how have you been? How is life?' enquired Lila.

'Oh, we're happy. We have a new wonderful mistress. She's young and full of travels. Of course, we miss our dear Crystal, but life is treating us pretty well, I must admit,' Bernie said.

'It is incredible to bump into you, my dear Lila and Lola!' said Ellie happily. The shoes smiled at each other and discussed the shoe with the snake.

'How justifiable was the idea of using a poisonous cobra as a guard for luxurious sandals?' demanded Ellie. The look of the snake's eyes scared her.

'I can tell you this much: thank God we are not in that vitrine!' Lola exclaimed.

The four twins hugged, giggled, and said their good-byes as their mistresses began to move away.

The twins strolled the streets with their mistress, had a marvellous lunch at the Wolseley, and were heading to the Lanesborough hotel for afternoon tea. Suddenly their mistress almost fell while meeting her friend, not because she was nervous, not at all. Bernie pulled to the right while Ellie pulled to the left, and poor Fay tripped on the white marble stairs outside the Lanesborough Hotel. Fortunately, the twins quickly mobilized and kept her from falling, even though it made her look for a second like a modern-art caricature at the Tate Museum.

Superstitious Ellie was convinced that Fay's stumble was caused by the negative energy of the hotel, which was previously a psychiatric hospital. Fay was fine, though slightly embarrassed, while her friend was rather sweet and acted as though he hadn't seen her almost trip. While Fay was enjoying her tea and scones, the twins observed the people around her.

'Do you think she's in love again?' asked Bernie.

'No, not at all,' answered Ellie. This boy was just a friend. Ellie could feel Fay's feet were relaxed and not trembling at all from nerves.

It was the beginning of February, and snow covered the streets of London, making it look like a Swiss ski resort. Ellie and Bernie were the indoor types. Lying on their soft ivory cashmere material shoe cover, they observed Fay playing with her freshly blown-dry golden locks. She seemed rather thoughtful, and she grabbed the TV remote to switch on her favourite channel, Fashion TV, and lay back cosily in the bed. Not a minute passed before her facial expression changed. Her eyes widened, her skin turned red, her mouth slightly opened, and she turned up the volume.

Bernie couldn't see the TV clearly from her right side. Ellie was peeking at the television and at Fay, and she was all excited by the new adventure that was going to happen.

Bernie leaned towards her sister, who was almost falling off, and demanded, 'What is it?'

Ellie slowly made a soft gesture with her heel that meant to wait.

Once the catwalk began, Fay switched off the TV and threw the remote on the floor. She was infuriated and grasped her much-loved velvet chocolate box filled with caramel Godiva chocolate truffles. She devoured several pieces, one by one, until she felt the need to nap and forget she had ever seen those images from the TV.

Ellie finally turned to Bernie and explained, 'They showed Adam. He was on the Galliano fashion show in Paris with some blonde model—a famous one too, I think. She was someone's face...can't think clearly of whose...but they were rather close, and he was smiling and sipping on his champagne!' Ellie said.

'I always knew that guy was not good for her. He's trashy and not good enough for her. She should just get over him. If he hurts her now, I don't want to think of what could await her in the future,' Bernie said harshly.

As Ellie watched her sister, she couldn't help but pity Fay. 'She loves him, Bernie, and he cares about her. He just doesn't know how to show his feelings, and he is trying to hide them!' Ellie insisted.

'Right, Ellie, he's hiding his feelings at Paris fashion week while he's hand in hand with a top model and his glass of champagne. Very hidden to me!' Bernie watched Fay drop a few tears on her creamy pillow, then said, 'It's better if she suffers a little now and is done with it than continuing to hope! He's nothing she or you, Ellie, should be interested in. She needs someone more like Marlon Wesley, but younger of course and not married. A true gentleman at heart—anyone like him would be great for her!'

'I thought you said he was a heartbreaker,' persisted Ellie.

'Indeed, he broke Crystal's heart, but I can't blame him. He saved his family life, and he never acted like this little fellow Adam, who has no manners whatsoever,' barked Bernie.

The twins quarrelled for hours, both stubborn and extreme at times. Ellie, the deep romantic, and Bernie, the realist, lay on either side of Fay, their beautiful mistress with big, sad eyes.

She had left New York to be far away from him, and here she was feeling like she had been slapped by the television. She kept on thinking how if she had watched another channel or perhaps not even turned on the television in those few minutes that they broadcasted Adam she would not have seen him and been hurt. Then she went on wondering if he did it on purpose. Did he know she would see him? Did he simply not care for her at all? Was he happy now?

* * *

The twins toddled on the worn red carpet in Harrods, making their way to the Egyptian escalators that would take them up to the urban retreat hair salon where their mistress would get the usual pampering. All the fashionistas would eye the shoes, as they were perfectly familiar with the twins' exceptional, high-quality, excellent appearance.

After all, they used to be on the cover of magazines and rated as the shoe of the year. What could be a better self-esteem boost?

But Ellie and Bernie were more concerned about placing themselves in the intellectual hierarchy. They felt the need to prove that not only were they gifted with natural, beautiful looks, but they also had smarts.

They very much enjoyed philosophical conversations between each other and at rare occasions with other fellow intellectual siblings from the shoe society. They did indeed make fairly interesting points and have a very different approach on matters. Their approach was from the shoe perspective, which often clarified certain issues human beings couldn't see.

Bernie often remarked how those who had poorly maintained shoes were more likely to be untrusting people who could not manage and organize their lives and in many cases had very few if any prospects. Bernie was easily irritated by those who took care of their belongings poorly, especially shoes, who carried people around all day and smoothed out the way.

Ellie was less critical. She preferred to look at matters from a more human point of view, and she thought perhaps that the poor fellows who had no time to pamper their shoes had more important issues to solve in their lives. She didn't feel as egocentric as Bernie, who had too much respect for her origins. If Bernie were to be a human, she would probably be an extreme nationalist. Ellie would be a free-spirited artist who would try to maintain peace and enjoy life filled with its beauties.

As they moved hurriedly, they thought about a certain concept many shoes had been concerned about for ages: shoe compatibility. The twins knew that human beings might not be able to envisage their life without the help of their fellow shoes. Always present to comfort their needy feet, shoes embraced humans and made them feel safe and comfortable through their journeys. The twins found that each foot was different, and people needed perfectly fitted shoes that could walk the distance at the right speed, on any surface with style. Shoes needed to match peoples' weight and stride.

As much as there was compatibility between humans, Ellie and Bernie knew there was also compatibility between shoes and their owners. Humans' feet must feel good with shoes, or the relationship could turn ugly. Shoes could get heavily injured and ruined forever, becoming handicapped, which was the worst that could happen to a shoe, as they would lose their value and could walk no longer. Ellie and Bernie thought about how ruined shoes became useless, left to watch the world go by while they were motionless, touched continuously only by dust that never failed to descend upon them.

Suddenly, the twins noticed a chalk python Marlowe sandal with partially enclosed instep. It was a shoe designed by Sophie Gittins. Her name was Marla, and she was glowing more than any other shoe on the decorative shoe tables.

'Hey!' She winked at the twins.

'You are gorgeous,' spoke out Ellie.

'Indeed, you are the most glowing shoe around here,' said Bernie, smiling in approval.

'Oh, it's my heart that makes me glows. I feel absolutely in love from the tip of my heel to my whole sole!' she exclaimed in a British accent that sounded fabulously melodic.

'Who is the lucky one?' Ellie and Bernie asked at the same time.

'He's over there, the right shoe of Dior shoes salesman. He's the love of my life!' Marla waved at her beloved one, who was drawing her heart signs by the Dior shoe section bench.

Both Ellie and Bernie were very curious about this shoe love story.

'How long have you been in love?' asked Bernie.

'Oh, it's been over a month, and I'm loving every second of it,' Marla replied tossing the dust that lay on her open front sole.

She took a deep breath and continued, 'It's not easy to be a shoe and observe how other shoes such as those Dior fuchsia pumps are trying to get onto my man!' she said furiously as she watched the Dior pump sensually rub on to her beloved Jasper.

Jasper was a regular black shoe with no specific handsomeness or quality. At least from the outside he seemed very average. Yet both of the twins observed that he was the biggest playboy in the shoe department. Shoes like Berluttis or Tom Fords spent time planning how to start a simple conversation with Marla or other beautiful shoes so they could ask for a date. But Jasper just came on to Marla with no fear of rejection. He told her he loved her heel; he cooed to her that her python skin was the most beautiful skin he had ever seen. A few hours later, she was deeply in love.

Jasper didn't allow any other male shoe to approach her. Even when the sale began he made sure she was going to stay untouched and placed on the highest shelf. He was a protective lover, but he nevertheless continued to flirt with other young candidates. He threw compliments right and left, leaving all the most beautiful shoes crazy in love. Jasper's brother was a quieter shoe, though. He was said to have been heartbroken after last year's sale, when his beloved one was snatched and he never got to see her again.

'She seemed very happy,' Ellie said as they twins toddled down to the escalators.

'Yes, she did,' answered Bernie thoughtfully.

'I also want to fall in love and live a happily-ever-after love story.' Ellie verbalized her real dream.

'If you are meant to live one, you will, sweetie pie,' replied Bernie as she pushed her sister to hurry along.

'I want to have a relationship,' said Ellie while staggering her heel.

'Do you even know what a relationship means?' asked Bernie.

'Think about it, it is a connection between two beings in a moving ship that will eventually sink if there are constant battles. *Relation* and *ship*. Just like the constant relation we have with feet. One must be able to bend and twist the shoes. When a foot flexes as one rolls through a step from heel to toe, if the shoe is too stiff, the sour foot will fight it with each step. It will then be a constant battle, and that sort of relationship never ends well,' Bernie said.

'Now that is an interesting way of looking at it, but I don't mean such a relationship. I meant more like Marla and Jasper,' Ellie whispered, not wanting the whole of Harrods to hear her confession.

'Jasper didn't seem very honest, and Marla seemed blind,' bluntly said Bernie, and the conversation was closed.

They continued sauntering and firmly embraced their mistress's feet that were so sensual, delicate, and soft. They felt happy to have such beautiful little feet, and they made sure not push too hard on them and spoil their fresh French manicure.

Confessions of an Aspen Ski Boot

I was born and manufactured in the US. My name is Mary. My brother Jerry and I were very happy with our lives at the ski store until a middle-aged woman purchased us because we looked cute. Her English had a strong accent. It was her first time in Aspen, and she refused to rent boots, so she bought us. And we were still so young that we didn't know there were other countries besides the US. We hadn't skied even once, and we had never felt the real breeze of the Colorado mountain air.

Our mistress's name was Yvonne von Malzimerstein. She was half-French and half-German. She had been married to a German real estate magnate, Von Malzimerstein. After she buried him, she continued flying around jet-set towns and enjoying her nothing-to-worry-about life.

Skiing was amazing with her. She never tired us. After a few slopes, she always sat down to a long lunch session at the restaurants in the ski lodges. Some of her friends were from interesting backgrounds. There were artists, actors, philanthropists, and politicians. All had stories to tell, and we picked up all the information that was bursting from the table.

She only used us for one year, but we went on a world tour thanks to her. We headed to Gstaad for the World Animal Trust gala. Though she would always wear fur, for that one night, she would wear a simple cashmere coat. She headed to St. Moritz for the New Year with her German family. She flew to Verbier for the concerts and Megeve for relaxation and spa weekends. She loathed Courchevel, so we never got the chance to visit it. One day Yvonne screaming on the phone awakened us. She was shouting so loudly that the teak floors trembled from her voice. 'Impossible!' she cried. 'I have trusts in Switzerland! Call Zurich now! I cannot be bankrupted! I am not giving up my chalets in Gstaad. They can do whatever they like! I refuse!'

The call was from her banker. She had made false investments based on the recommendation of one of her politician friends. She was an inexperienced investor, and now she had debts so high that her only option was to sell all her property. And she would still have to find more funding for the rest of the debt.

The financial crisis hit, then Bernie Madoff was exposed, and it was the end of our mistress's easy days. There would be no more skiing for Yvonne; she was too busy searching for funds and selling her antiques. We were left dusting up until she left and never returned. The house was sold and we were sent to charity. Somehow my brother and I got lost from each other. Because of our heavy structure, they must have packed us separately. At my arrival I was all alone. Thank God a young Asian boy decided I was still useful and made me his favourite toy. I was a big ship in the local water dump. I was happy for that; nothing scared me more than being broken up in pieces.

Yvonne showed us an interesting human life; however, she also showed us how fragile humans are. They have become so materialistic that one financial crisis can sweep them out of their lives, destabilize their entire situation, and make them disappear. I lived in a French orphan house, and my days were slow. I observed the kids play and missed my home. A mountain shoe should be skiing in the snow. I really hoped that one day someone would take me back to the snowy Aspen where I belonged.

One morning I was still half asleep when my dear brother reappeared next to me. In a matter of a few hours, we were packed. The trip took forever. When we opened our eyes, we found ourselves in Aspen. An American family from Colorado had adopted the young Asian boy. He had been searching for the other ski boot to make me a pair, and by luck he found my brother on a weekend market sale of odd objects, just a week before he received the news of adoption. Our life has transformed like a dream. We ski and feel the snow, and every day we thank God for such a beautiful life. I don't miss Europe or Yvonne;, I have learned that nothing is better than home. Our home is Aspen and its snow.

Chapter 8
New York: The Return

The twins returned to the city of magic energy, the city that never sleeps. New York made them feel at home. They glimmered from the faint sunshine peeking through the yellow cab, which felt like a carriage as it jumped up on every bump. It was a yellow carriage with invisible horses, or at least it seemed that way from the floor of the cab.

Fay sprayed herself with Bond Union Square, her signature, the aroma of freshly cut flowers with a touch of the ultra-urban city.

It was a comfortable journey. Ellie and Bernie rested inside of the Louis Vuitton hand luggage and were later moved into the maxi dark-purple Balenciaga, as Fay liked to have them close to her in case there was a fire and she had to run with only her handbag.

The twins felt privileged by this gesture. They were placed right by her passport, patent red valet, BlackBerry, and travelling jewellery. They were the only shoes in the handbag. It certainly was a great place to be, as her bag also smelled of the two-hundred-dollar Bond perfume.

The taxi carried them through the long avenues till it finally reached 22nd and 3rd Avenues, where Fay had a penthouse any girl would dream of. It was her parents', but she was the only one who used it. As the twins were carefully carried into the house, they couldn't help but remember the day Fay's mother had purchased them at the vintage store.

Time flew. As Fay was getting ready for the night, she put on a fabulous leopard-print Bordeaux dress. Her beauty mesmerized the twins as they waited with excitement. Was it their lucky day to embrace her little soft feet? As she slowly picked up the crocodile clutch that her grandmother gave her last Christmas, which matched the twins, they watched with anticipation as she picked them with a big smile on her face, exclaiming, "It's your day today!"

With her brown golden locks and her ever-perfect smoky eyes, her plump lips shiny as freshly cut plums, she would be the star of the night. A bright white smile flashed from her bronzed skin, and she wore a big fluffy fur that made her look like an A-list actress: she was glowing.

As she stepped out, her tiny legs shivered from the cold. The twins were proud and stable. They marched like they were Oscar nominees right across the street to Rose Bar. Fay's friends at the entrance warmly greeted her. As she stepped in, like animals before an earthquake, the twins felt her legs shiver dramatically from more than just the cold. That never happened to her. She was a strong woman who could stand up to almost anything. What could it be, they wondered?

As she slowly leaned into Eva, her best friend in New York, the twins had time to get a glimpse of Adam looking better than ever, as he had lost a few pounds. His skin looked evenly toned, and his sharp eyes managed to see nothing and everything. Even the twins caught their breath when he quickly analysed them as part of Fay's outfit.

It was Jean Paul, an old friend from high school, who jumped on Fay to salute her. As an actress, she had learned how to manage emotional displays, and she stretched the biggest smile one could. Jean Paul was so surprised to see her, while Adam remained behind him looking at every move she made. As Jean Paul and Fay said their good-byes, Adam appeared rather friendly for once. His face actually made an effort to make a slight movement, which eventually made it look like half a smile. She kept her same big smile, though, while she just breathed for a second or two.

'Hey, Fay!' Adam cried to her.

'Hey, nice to see you,' she said without looking at him.

He tried greeting her with a kiss. She wasn't sure if it was part of his walking to the table or an actual attempt to say hello, so she chose the safe way of not moving one inch towards him.

The whole "Hello" process was surprisingly quick, and after a few seconds it felt like a dream, she was at his table with a bunch of celebrities.. Fay was in her own world, while the twins put all their energy into trying to convince her ego to walk towards him. She was too strong and blocked their attempt. The Victoria Secret angels that were by his side didn't make her feel confident, she remained still and spoke to the mutual friends that were beside her.

'I'm only going along with your attempts now because I cannot bear to hear you say that we should have done more,' said Bernie, who wasn't pro-Adam.

'Just please, for once, do what I ask,' Ellie pleaded.

Fay was like a piece of ice in the freezer. She remembered that horrible night in LA and figured he must have been too drunk to even remember. She thought he probably acted that way all the time with thousands of girls.

Was it love, she wondered? Is love a never-ending game? Fay was watching her shoes as if crying to them for help.

It was quite obvious there was certain chemistry between Fay and Adam. They were like big children who peeked at each other, but neither would make the first move. She was afraid, and he was confused.

Bernie got upset when Ellie forced her to cooperate with her to move Fay towards Adam.

'Leave them alone!' Bernie said. 'Don't you remember how much he made her cry that time in LA? Or should I remind you about the state of that room in Thompson?' Bernie looked sharply at Ellie.

'But they are human beings. Everyone makes mistakes. Don't be so harsh on him. He's just a lost boy, and he can't control his emotions,' Ellie told her sister.

'That sounds like a woman to me, and Fay deserves better than a freak that loses him at the most romantic spot and time ever. It's like he spoilt my happy-ending movie by acting like a true psycho!' Bernie insisted persuasively.

Nothing had happened that night but the twins had a long quarrel that had ended when Fay decided to march right out and back home.

* * *

Interminable days of silence passed one after the other. Fay had been leading a somewhat passive routine. Ellie and Bernie were placed in the huge wardrobe along with the other pieces of art.

Ellie enjoyed the gentle caresses of the new collection, a bright red silk gala dress that was hanging innocently right on top of her on its massive lime-brown hanger. Bernie, who was only inches away, had a mini Swarovski-garmented cocktail dress that was custom-made especially for Fay by an haute couture atelier in Paris. Bernie was deep in her thoughts, thinking how great it was she was not born as a dress.

True, this dress was the most beautiful dress in the whole world and had no flaws. It was absolutely perfect in all dimensions and made of the best material to embellish and glamorize anyone who fit into it. But even though she was so gorgeous, she had a fairly short life, Bernie thought. She had been worn only once, for Fay's twenty-first birthday, and that was all. It was a one-of-a-kind of dress, with more photographs taken of it that day than during an actual Oscar red carpet ceremony.

It still glimmered just like on that first day when it had arrived. Only now it was just a piece of cloth fully incrusted with crystals that shined when the light hit them. It hung still and motionless, when other clothing danced to the wind that occasionally came through the door.

Like a white marble statue it stood there amongst the more vivacious living pieces. Whereas the black American Apparel leggings always had incredible stories to tell, as they saw more of the world than even some people, as they were Fay's favourite for everyday.

Indeed, the leggings had a soul too, but they had lost their memory of how they had gotten it. Their life was happening at a very fast pace, so they at times had blackouts in their memories. Early Alzheimer's perhaps? Or too much of a social life? Bernie wondered.

Fay would match them with tank tops, her grandmother's vintage belts, dresses with soft cashmere V-necks, and a few accessories she would find before leaving the house.

Bernie enjoyed some time off to do some thinking, arranging her thoughts, and fighting depression. While Ellie was always in a party mood and a real extrovert, Bernie was always the mature, strict one. She felt every bit responsible for Ellie, and for Fay, for that matter.

Financial Crisis: Cruella

Financial crises hit the economies of the world, taking mostly from the rich. Television, radio: the news of it was everywhere. Some prognoses claimed that certain countries would be completely broke.

For high-end fashion designers and brands, this was a total disaster; far fewer people would agree to spend thousands on clothes and shoes in this market. Lots of Hermes's famed Birkin bags were left unpicked in the stores, as the economy had been much better three years earlier when they had been ordered. Many shoppers' husbands had been promising investment bankers at Lehman Brothers and J.P. Morgan.

As Fashion Week started in New York, the fashion industry was wondering just how much more stress the retail markets, and even the resilient luxury sector, could take.

'You must buy one dress a month and stick to it. Now is the time to save!' Fay's mother would tell her over the phone.

Fay had gotten two already. The one for summer was super chic, but she could literally wear it more than thirty different ways: strapless, butterfly sleeves, tie-neck, as a skirt, and so on.

Her second was a new-season, hot-pink Herve Leger, which she planned to wear with the twins, of course.

Ellie and Bernie had realized that something had changed in the air. People seemed more depressed and grumpy. Fewer people were out in the streets, and the stores were more like museums during the weekdays. People would admire, but never touch, as though things were made of diamonds.

'I cannot blame people for not shopping as much for clothes and shoes at Bergdorf, Saks, or Barneys. Their pieces are more expensive than a month's rent,' declared Bernie.

'What about all the Cruellas that still shop?' asked Ellie.

She was traumatized by the same type of a woman that they have observed in many cities. They can be spotted in very expensive and luxury stores.

A big-shot lady in fur, Cruella, as the twins would refer to her, would swamp over all the shiny shoes, bags, and most expensive clothing as though she were going to eat them. To their horror, a Cruella type appeared right at their feet one day. Even her shoes were made of fur.

She moved quickly, pushing everyone out of the way. Nothing could stop her.

Dressed in a '50s-style full skirt and a cropped, gull-length chinchilla coat from Jitrois, well known for its heritage and expert knowledge of luxurious fur and leather, she kept her eyes hidden behind gigantic black sunglasses. Her figure seemed lost in her massive greyish fur. Careless of her surroundings, callous about animals, she lived for herself, disdaining environmental issues. Such things were not her problem.

Her days were filled with exclusive parties and champagne glasses filled with Dom Perignon or perhaps Cristal Roederer. Her friends? They were just like her. Their wardrobes were bulging with fur and leather and crocodile Firkins bags; thousands if not millions of dollars were stocked in animal corpses in their private mansions in Chelsea and Mayfair.

As she walked past the fur protestors in front of Harrods, they screamed at her, exhorting her to pity animals, trying to explain how cruelly her coat came to be. She gave them a haughty look, stiffened her back, and aggressively pushed open the doors to march her way in. The crowd was shocked by her behaviour and flashed her hateful looks. She moved on like a ship at full speed, her hair a sheer platinum blonde to complement her ever-present deep red lipstick.

'Cruella de Vil!' a childish voice cried out. The character from *The Hundred and One Dalmatians* is not just a pitiless woman from a cartoon; she's a template for thousands of men and women, whether they know it or not. Animals have been killed for millennia for people like the renowned Disney character. The child's eyes were filled with fear; his red cheeks were getting brighter as he hugged closer to a woman who seemed to be his mother.

Following her stride into the jewellery department, Cruella felt the familiar desire, almost a need, for her favourite department in Barneys. Situated on the second floor, the fur coats varied in size and price. She seemed disinterested in the sale pieces. Her medium-long nails stretched to the white, fuzzy-fox petticoat, her eyes delighted by her new finding. It could feed her everlasting desire for real fur.

What exact thoughts were running through her mind remained a mystery. Could she hear or see all the desperate people outside, holding posters and reaching out to her and those like her? Did she even have a clue how those animals were brutally killed? Perhaps she did, but she continued her shopping, hunting for more and more until the end.

As Cruella disappeared from their sight, Ellie and Bernie were left wondering what the future of their shoe society would be. Would their life expectancy increase from this financial crisis, as people would stick to the same pair of shoes? They had already faced a few exploited siblings. These shoes had cracked skin from the cold, washed off heels, and dirty soles. One even had chewing gum crystallized in the sole as it had been stuck there for a year.

However, they were happy. They had been walking and running and seeing the world. The ultimate dream of a shoe is to be worn, and to always be together with their siblings, as they accent one another.

Financial crises would enhance the possibility of shoes living a much more active life, of shoes being passed on to children and worn by new mistresses, and of shoes being restored and cleaned at the shoe repairer to give them that newness and youth they lost with age.

As Ellie and Bernie moved swiftly, they watched the newly placed Louboutins in Barneys, untouched, virgin-like, sensual pairs of shoes. They were just on mannequins. Some shoes gained a soul only after having been bought. The excitement and love of the buyer enhanced their process of soul creation. As there were no buyers these days, the shoes remained as lonely and cold as newly made statuettes.

The twins were like shining stars, enjoying the gentle feet of Fay and slow promenades around town.

Crisis! Crisis! Crisis! People talked about it, shoes gasped at it. They had once felt so wanted, so hard to get. People would place themselves on wait lists, and those were very successful people. Moderate, educated fashionistas would start aggressive fights to win the shoes from one another. They were the centres of global attention, portrayed in Hollywood movies, fashion photographs and magazines, the Internet, and shopping temples. When the end of the season would begin, there would be lines waiting outside to get them for still exaggerated, but at least slightly discounted prices. Like confident striking princesses, they would flirt back, but not be touched until the right fit would appear.

Going from being the most wanted to now impossible-to-get and not on any priority lists was a disaster. Many fellow shoes fell into a deep depression where they could not envisage a brighter future than the great past they once had and perhaps hadn't appreciated enough at the time.

Now they could only rely on an extremely rich clientele, those who would treat themselves to a spot of high-end retail therapy.

They could only depend on these high-net-worth people who would hopefully sustain the luxury goods market through the current crisis. However, there were too few of these people, and they could not possibly adopt all the shoes at once, not even half of them.

Shoes went from being overwhelmingly famed, wanted, and dreamed of, to now feeling impractical, too delicate, and too expensive. Shoes wondered if they would soon be sent to some discount store where they would not even be recognized.

'Do you think it can hurt us?' asked Ellie. The twins walked on a copy of *The New York Times* and scanned articles on the crisis. Bernie twisted the paper with her heel so quickly that it seemed only natural.

She took a deep breath and said, 'A crisis doesn't hurt purchased goods like us. It's not a monster, sweetie!'

'Then how come it left all those shoes in all those stores as orphans?' Ellie asked with tears in her eyes. 'No one can afford them any longer. What's happening to the world? Can't they just produce more money and give it to everyone?' cried Ellie.

'I wish it were so easy,' Bernie said. 'Money is the part of humanity I never understood. It's obviously the worst invention, as it causes only problems and it's so hard to get hold of. Moreover, it makes others judge those who have lots of it and spend it on shoes, for example!' Bernie breathed heavily.

Ellie and Bernie watched a young girl pick up a pair of boots, turn it around to gasp at the price tag, and drop it on the table. Even markdowns were still much too pricey for people in these days.

As Fay headed out to Uptown Serafina Pizzeria on Madison for a quick lunch with girlfriends, Ellie and Bernie watched the interesting shoes walking in and out. This was indeed a concentration of amazingly exquisite, elegant shoes. Some marched while others stared blankly. The waiters' black shoes looked friendly and happy. As the menus for Fay and her friends were laid down, the twins could see the rather high prices.

While the girls chatted about the usual love problems, the four pairs under the table discussed important global issues.

Ellie described the financial crisis as a destructive monster that wanted to eat all the money. 'The next thing you know, it will eat the fashion houses, forcing them to stop producing!' Ellie exclaimed.

Jiji and Ju, the other two shoes that were under the table, futuristic booties with floating insole on carbon fibre heels, laughed at the remark. 'We are survivors,' said Ju. 'Even though we get to be our masters' slaves, we will help them to get through it!'

The shoe friends giggled at the human misery. It felt good to be shoes and not to have to worry about such things as finances.

Bernies Confession on a Shoe Sample Sale

Even during a recession, no one can resist at deal, especially for Bozzis. Yes, the legendary shoe designer, our bellowed father, who attained fame with Hollywood actresses wearing them on the red carpet, was now having his work displayed on sale stands. This meant prices were way below what you'd find at retail. Leather heels started at $100, for instance. They were not the old, exclusively handmade Bozzis.

After the death of Balthazar Bozzi, the company was purchased by a chain of fashion companies who continued the Bozzi name without the same quality. The designs were still outstanding, but the comfort level was not there. Its new logo was, "For beauty we will suffer," now an inside joke in the shoe gossip world.

And considering the original retail price of at least $575, $100 was a total deal. So, of course, the lines were insane! Women started lining up at 6:00 a.m. Wednesday for the private sale, but mobs of shoe-obsessed Bozzi fans continued to linger all morning, even after the doors opened to the public at 11:00 a.m.

The scene? It was what one would expect: total mayhem, with everyone pouring over tables upon tables of high-heeled sandals, pumps, boots, and even some flats. Yes, Bozzi made flats. Shoes were divided up on tables marked by size number, but soon the matching pairs were single with their mates scattered all over the place: on the floor, in the corner, on another table.

A tall brunette was trying to decide whether to spring for a pair of leopard-print embellished heels for $225 after spotting two pairs for herself and for her mom. 'My friend told me about this, and I'm a shoe fanatic,' she told Fay, who was amazed by the sheer number of Bozzis, all looking fabulous.

Did that lady know that both Ellie and I were carefully examining her soulless shoes? Good craftsmanship, but something was clearly missing. Fay was a shopaholic and would purchase much more than she actually wore. Luckily for us! I mean, if she wore all the shoes she bought for the past two years, we wouldn't be worn as often. Our lives would stop, and we would be bored out of our minds!

You must understand that being a shoe is a whole different kind of life. It might be the same world from the outside, but we have to stay neat, able to walk, and fabulous!

Bozzis always bring vitality and sexy glamour. The store was filled with really strappy sandals, with lots of decoration and attitude, and clean-cut, '80s-inspired clothes. There were crystal embellishments, studs, animal prints such as zebra, and accent colours of red and blue to give the shoes that real power. While glamour was the key to the skyscraper high heels, Bozzis were also cropped Cuban-heel boots as well as the essential ballet pumps.

Were these women aware of the US economy being on the verge of collapse? Of the problems with the banks?

If politicians in Washington did not make progress on raising America's $14.3 trillion borrowing limit in the next few weeks, it would put the US rating on review for a possible downgrade. The Treasury Department warned that if the country's debt ceiling were not raised by August 2, the US would exhaust its capacity to pay its bills.

However, judging by the hungry look on their faces, it really didn't seem like these women cared about default so much. In fact, I think they looked at things from a different angle.

I think these ladies cared more about the number of shoes they would be able to purchase if the economy collapsed and shop owners put out more sales to pay their rent. In fact, I think that these women would be very joyful if, for example, Saks Fifth went bankrupt. Then all their shoes could go on a massive sale, including new collections.

But then again, there is another major factor. If America had a default situation, the US dollar would fall in value, and these women's credit lines would also be lowered, unless they were foreigners. If they were American, it would only damage them along with the shop owners and every other American.

Europe is not doing any better, as the shiny lizard high heeled boot told me the other day. She was originally Greek and confirmed that Greece was really doing badly. She explained the while Greece is in debt, Italy is also going down the drain, along with Spain and France.

In a way, we are all connected and affected by the world economies going chaotic. The shoe industry is not going to do any better. The other day I stepped on a newspaper and was saddened by the amount of negative news: Libya in war, a Norwegian terrorist killing over eighty students in a summer camp in Norway, Syrians rebelling against the government, Iraq having one crisis after another, and now all the financial crises, and the ever-present hunger in the African region where people die of starvation every second. Sometimes I start to wander if we shoes were to rule planet Earth, perhaps we would have a better take on things and better understandings of how to manage it. It feels like humans create institutions and universities, NATOs and UNs and UNHCR, yet problems still occur.

It's very interesting to watch all these crazy women filling their shopping bags with their zillionth pair of shoes and having no idea about the world finances while I as a shoe watch them and don't understand how the world reached such instability in the financial sector. Is it the fault of the shopaholics, perhaps?

Dinners and Social Events with Shoes

Social life was essential for the twins as much as for their mistress, who enjoyed a few glasses of champagne and small talk with cute strangers.

This time the party took place on thirty-seventh floor of Trump Tower in a six-bedroom apartment. Fay's close friend organized a birthday for her brother with very different kinds of people and their shoes, from the most sophisticated young fashion divas to investment bankers, and from artists to doctors.

The shoes varied from simple, elegant, extravagant, and practical to orange top Havaianas—which were supposed to be the staple footwear for summer, but now were apparently the new winter item too.

These shoes perfectly reflected their laid-back Aussie-lifestyle owner, PC, a chocolate heir who was striving to be a Bohemian artist. Unfortunately, he hadn't figured what his talent was. He couldn't decide between being a painter, photographer, or sculptor (a recent interest).

The human's face could be seen through his choice of shoes, once said a pair of vintage shoes that had once been worn by Elizabeth II to her wedding ceremony. Gentle and smooth, they now travelled around the world and at one occasion had encountered Ellie and Bernie. Surprisingly they were not snobbish at all, contrary they were very down to earth and had lots of funny stories about the British royal family and the Buckingham Palace. Back to the dinner party Ellie and Bernie perceived the socially active Havaianas who were mingling from one spot to another.

The Havaianas catered perfectly to PC's personality. He matched them with a vintage shirt and a pair of purposely torn jeans.

By the window one could perceive a pair of butter-soft, slouchy leather boots that stood out with bright red soles: a true fashion statement on a true fashion girl, Rebecca Diz, daughter of the Fashion Guru and former model Randall Orsay-Diz. Mari-Anne chose to stick to her light brown python Louboutins that always embellished the wearer's legs to make them look twice as long and thin.

There were also a few tall men looking very similar with their dress slacks with glossy lace-ups. Others were in sleek, dark suits, simple button-down shirts, and camel brown, handmade Lobb shoes.

There were many latest trends on display, as well as well-balanced pairs that were a mixture of funk and style at the same time.

They mingled around in their very different shoes. Some were new, others were old; all had lots to share.

One pair of chunky black loafers belonged to the former Lehman Brothers' banker who lost his job and now was actively working on his daily blog, "How Not to Commit Suicide, by Andy Brown."

The pair consisted of Jo and Bob. Bob had been deaf since his hysteria at the news that he and Jo were going to be worn by human feet. He was very emotional and couldn't handle the fear and stress of something that moved inside of his newly created shoe body.

They were a great pair for men as they were super-comfortable to walk in. The leather slip-ons seemed very enthusiastic, even though they had had a pretty tough time lately. The leather had that lovely matte texture, and the rubber outsoles would keep feet enormously comfortable.

Unlike the Jamie Bernstein shoes that could be compared to the stiletto-clad ladies in the clubs, Jo and Bob looked perfect with pressed linen trousers and the off-white shirt with gold Patek Philippe cufflinks left to him from his Swiss banker grandfather that Andy chose to wear for the occasion. They were malleable yet still suave.

As Jo approached Ellie and Bernie, he took the initiative to introduce himself as a self-made shoe who used to be worn only on Sundays to the pub with the pals. Since Andy's career-ender, he had stepped down to another, more relaxed schedule, and Andy had turned to his good, old, comfy loafers who would least distress his tired feet.

'Looking good, guys!' said Bernie, who felt the need to be inviting and nice to newcomers in the society.

'Oh, thanks. Thank you, Bernie. I have heard of you two sisters a lot. I'm so pleased to finally meet the jewels of the high-end shoe society!' he said in a shaking voice. He wasn't used to that kind of smooth language. It sounded fake to him, like he was not meant to speak that way. But it still made him feel good to share a few minutes with them, as if he were a high-standard shoe as well.

Bernie and Ellie smiled and said in their truly feminine, courteous manner, 'So sweet of you! Thank you so much for such beautiful words!'

They were the true daughters of Balthazar, as he had been the politest man in the world.

'So, Jo,' Bernie began, 'what can you tell us about this atrocious epidemic that has taken control of the world's economies and even hit our fellow newborn shoes around the world? Did you hear Andy talk of it at all?'

Jo wasn't used to all this attention, especially from such gorgeous, delicately curved sexy heels. He took a deep breath and began his long speech about the world economies and the banks and credit and what the term "credit crunch" meant and how it affected the rest of the world and the prognosis of Andy who seemed to be very pessimistic on the matter.

He explained, 'The most important thing is to keep in mind that while previous crises were regional, this one is global. It is happening all over the world, and it is unlike any previous financial crisis. There is no one solution to fix it. It has led the world's leading economies to lose billions and billions of dollars.'

Bob shook Jo to congratulate him on his speech, though he hadn't heard a word once he saw those beautiful shoes listening carefully to what he had to say.

As Ellie and Bernie chatted with their friend, they suddenly noticed a modern painting of a red stiletto shoe. It was simple, with a black background and no other elements, just the shoe.

The twins grew up knowing they were very important, but they never knew what the core meaning of their importance was.

While dresses can be outgrown, pants can be cut, shorts can suddenly not fit, bikinis can go out of fashion, socks can be lost after washing, underwear can be thrown away, and fur coats can be holed by insects, shoes remain the same over the years.

Even when they go out of fashion, one can still fit into them, no matter the time of the year. The age of the person and their weight changes do not matter to the eternal fit.

Shoes are the stability everyone is in search of. They stabilize the posture and place the feet well, giving them just enough space to mingle between each other, but not so much space that they feel lost.

The twins slowly drifted away from the heavy talk of the male shoes to look at the gorgeous Manhattan view. Luckily, the windows stretched down to the ground, so they could comfortably see out.

There she was: Madame de Fleur and her twin, Mademoiselle de Grange. They looked identical, yet one was the madam while the other her shy, quiet version. Apparently, Madame de Fleur refused to carry the same title as her twin, so she diminished her twin and changed her surname. She behaved as the older sister who had been educated at de Grange. Little did Monsieur Louboutin know that these elegant velvet stilettos were not as modern as they looked to the naked eye. In their souls, they were old French aristocracy, two sisters who immigrated to New York along with their families in the 1950s.

They were very much into shoes. And after Europe, the new market of the US truly made them wish they were as diverse and fun as their shoes. They grew to be snobby and antisocial, but as one day they were metamorphosed into shoes, their lives changed. They became much more confidant and happy. Finally, they could attend dinner parties without worrying about extra pounds gained or their skin having blemishes.

In shoe society they were famous for their human past and their happy integration into the shoe world. Their mistress, Mrs Ackerman, was of German-Jewish descent. Very well connected, she wore them on many socially fun and important occasions. As Mrs Ackermann was a very well-respected lady, and so were her favourite black evening shoes. Many didn't believe their human past, calling them liars, fantasy makers, and dreamers. Madame de Fleur was said to be a fictional name, and the same with de Grange. Their shoe accent was declared fake and their stories fiction.

Ellie and Bernie liked to listen to their stories from time to time. They were different and amusing, and their analyses on situations were different from those of the Nike sneakers or young Louboutins, who were too egocentric and only talked about X actress, X major event, and the best-nominated shoes in Hollywood.

Madame de Fleur talked about Louis XIV, and the stories she heard from her grandmother about the legendary parties at the Versailles summer palace, and the French revolution where people took over, and even about modern France.

Ellie and Bernie loved traveling, even though they felt intimidated every time they were placed into the X-ray machine. They didn't enjoy some stranger seeing their skeleton and their everything, often grabbing them and throwing onto the sad-looking plastic tray. But they loved the concept of waking up in a whole different atmosphere with different roads, and even different asphalt that felt different and smelled different. The shoes they met on their travels were quite different from those of their home.

'We were in Paris recently,' said Madame de Fleur. 'I must say the shoe situation there is not as good as it used to be. Printemps and La Gallerie Lafayette are not as rich in variety as they used to be. I wonder if Carla Bruni is any good to this country.' She couldn't help but stress her name with such an untrusted audience.

Mademoiselle de Grange explained that her sister had some jealousy towards beautiful and successful women, and Cara happened to be one of them.

'She's not even French! She's Italian!' exclaimed de Fleur.

Bernie was already bored with the conversation. She stepped a few feet away and watched crumbles of the chocolate cake fall on the dark oak floors. She wandered how it felt to eat food, to chew it and to swallow it, what affect it had. She had observed for quite a long time how people ate and got all excited by a tasty dish, while sniffing disdainfully at bad food. She daydreamed about this very interesting concept of eating.

Part Two

Chapter 9

Two girls: Isabelle and Daisy

They are easily perceived on the street, their statuesque walking, their colourful and luxurious clothing, their freshly cut and brushed hair, their perfectly lined eyes, their powder-bronzed skin, and finally their most wanted handbags, cars, watches, and jewellery. One's eyes get lost in the count of the things one sees when checking them out.

They live the easy life, financially much better off than most of the world, having seen it all, done it all, in the jet-set circles, of course. They are helpless without their family or, as it often is, those trust funds that give the comfort of life and make it all seem fantastic and easy.

The world seems like a big city for them even when they travel, which is much more frequently than for the rest of the world. Every weekend or so, they bump into each other: the same clubs, restaurants, shops, private parties, and after-parties for the underground wannabes.

As they walk and talk and meet and have relationships that end as new ones begin, life seems perfect. One notices that it becomes one big, or, better, small circle that knows almost too much about one another and has done almost too much with each other and each other's girlfriends, boyfriends, yet again parents, and, God knows, grandparents.

It all stays covered up, but secrets don't stay secrets for long. Everyone is conscious of the truth, but good manners from schools like Le Rossey, Aiglon, Beau Soleil, Monte Rose, and College du Leman have taught them to be rather diplomatic. One should be sure to know it all, but also to keep it to oneself or just a few of one's friends.

Isabelle Labrier-Albrecht and Daisy di Castelonni

Does anyone ever wonder whether it's possible to get bored from having simply everything? Beauty, money, family status, all those gadgets, the latest sport cars, no limits on credit cards.

She was from a very well-off family who tried to give her everything from affection to education, with extracurricular activities like chess and ballet. She spoke six languages, studied in the best Swiss private schools, and knew the children of society's top people. Her connections were incredible, but she never used them because she simply had no idea what she wanted to do.

Life was very easy and smooth for her. The biggest problems were those of love. Money, health, or anything along those lines was never an issue. She was young and beautiful, in her early twenties, and living in her vacuum. The world suddenly seemed like one small city where everyone knew each other and went to the same places at the same times of the year: St. Moritz, Gstaad, in winter, St. Tropez Ibiza, Marbella, and Sardinia in summer. In September, New York and London, perhaps Paris from time to time on the weekend direct first-class Eurostar from London.

From one town to another, it almost felt like she was in one big city as the same faces all connected somehow, often from exes in common. No wonder "It's a Small World" worked so well as a song.

Her friends were in the same situation, all lost and simply running away from the sad reality, some to drugs, others to hardcore partying or intense relationships that completely devastated them and left them not only heartbroken, but also completely destroyed and in need of therapy.

Daisy and Isabelle shared one true passion that was holy to them: their dedication and love for their shoes. They had shelves and shelves filled with shoes in all colours and shapes.

Isabelle's dressing room was focused on hip styles. The overall branding component evolved out of that initial identity: a whimsical word that incorporated circular elements from which patterns were easily created. Images of shoes' silhouette were applied to the walls and tabletops and incorporated into shoe displays. It wasn't a clothing room; it was a shoe palace where the temperatures never exceed twenty degrees Celsius.

'Sometimes I wish I were born as a Christian Louboutin pump,' Isabelle said. 'Honestly, I love my shoes more than myself.' She laughed.

Indeed, Isabelle never checked her dear shoes when she travelled. She always packed them carefully into her hand luggage that ended up being heavier than the main luggage. However, she managed to sneak it in the plane. And there would always be a kind, strong man who would help stow the three-toned mini Louis Vuitton roll-on filled with shoes.

Once an old man bickered at her that he felt his vertebral colon shift and that he was almost sure that if his lower discs were worn off it was because of such irresponsible little girls who made men carry their heaviest bags. She was petrified by his words. Couldn't he understand that it was of paramount importance to her to have her favourite shoes on board, safely placed above her head?

She didn't let the old man spoil her mood. That same very day, she went straight into Browns on South Molton Street, London, and purchased a new classic and very elegant look, topped off with lovely ankle-strap, zebra-print sandals. After all, she had to get the frustrating image of the mean old man out of her nervous system.

Isabelle and Daisy were very much alike in that sense. Both had recently graduated. Both attended boarding schools in Switzerland when they were teenagers, and now they were both starting their first jobs. Isabelle was lucky to get a job through her friend at Quintessentially Event Organizer Company, while Daisy was starting her internship at Sotheby's.

New York, especially for newcomers, could get very chaotic and frantic. At times the girls felt a deep need for a getaway.

They hung on to the simple philosophy that, when it was time to step away from the distractions of everyday life and get back in touch with their spiritual core, they didn't have to go far to go deep.

In the age of BlackBerrys and emails, iPods and Xboxes, they found themselves disconnected and adrift, in need of renewal and healing in a world that was becoming more and more challenging, arduous, and time-consuming.

But how could one step off the grid of modern life and reconnect with the spiritual? The answer for millions of people was to go on a retreat. Retreats were a means to look within in stillness and silence, to locate what may be missing in life, and to appreciate what has always been there. They require that participants set aside only the deadlines and obligations that besiege daily life and find solace and sustenance in comforting quiet and simple routines.

Isabelle and Daisy chose their own way of pure distraction.

The place had to be the equivalent of what they understood as being heaven, where one was filled with only happy, positive feelings, which created endorphins and made their skin shine and glow.

That holiest place on earth, where they truly felt peace within themselves, was nothing less than a shoe department of one of the luxury department stores. And the best part was that there was a piece of that heaven in every major city. In New York, they adored Barneys, Saks, and Bergdorf; in London, Harvey Nichols, Selfridges, and Harrods; in Paris, Le Printemps and La Gallerie Lafayette. They also enjoyed the angels' nests, their name for the little hidden shoe boutiques around the world that often offered new brands not yet discovered by heaven.

As they slipped on one pair after the other, the world just seemed like a better place. This was the spiritual get-away, the one they cherished and lived.

They were still single, going on new dates almost daily, and in their free time they emptied the stores, especially the shoe departments.

For them entering a store offered an unexplainable feeling. And they accented each other. They had that spark in their eyes at the sight of a new pair that could totally satisfy their craving.

* * *

Typically, they would not actually eat during their lunch breaks. 'Why eat if you can economize on food and hit the shops where you can buy so many gorgeous things instead?' Isabelle said to herself. As a matter of fact, there was a stock clearance that day in that super-cool vintage store in Gramercy on 22nd and 3rd.

It had the most fabulously preserved antique collection of rare and collectible vintage clothing: from a deep blue Mulberry street dress to an LA highway grey stumping jacket or a faux-retro sailor swimsuit.

Hence the two friends Isabelle and Daisy would walk for hours with unfathomable energy. They grabbed all sorts of objects: dresses and bangles and shoes

'Oh! And those stunning sunglasses! They are so '60s!' Their excitement was increasing as they checked the price tags and found everything at 70 per cent off.

'It's my last time this week,' Daisy exclaimed to her best friend who was too busy grabbing almost everything in the greediest way.

'I don't need anything anymore.' Daisy tried to calm herself as she left the store. But then she looked at the new collection arriving at the shop across the road and hesitated. 'Well, maybe not for a few weeks. I could do some studies instead. It's time to play.'

Her face glowed with pure happiness and satisfaction. Shopping was so much more appealing than any meal. What she bought she could wear, touch—it was hers forever!

Well, perhaps until the end of the month when she would feel the urge to replace it all.

How many times have millions of girls felt this feeling? And then, when the excitement has faded away, when you've worn the dress a few times, you move on and gradually forget about it.

A never-ending love story, repeating itself over and over, no matter the location, whether Paris, London, Moscow, or New York: the human modern society has become addicted to fashion.

The two girls were very much aware of their shopping addiction and worshipping devotion for shoes. They just did not feel any wrongdoing regarding it, as it didn't hurt anyone but their families' pockets. They just loved shoes and didn't think it should affect anyone but them and their dear shoes.

As they grabbed one piece of clothing after another, they both paused at the sight of the most original, exquisitely stunning pair of shoes.

Daisy's facial expression was already sad, as she had made a quick mental calculation of what seemed to be the size of the pair placed on the highest part of the hefty wooden shelves. It was a size 6.5.

At times she hated being tall, especially when there was a sale and all the prettiest shoes left were 6.5s and 7s, never a 9.

Isabelle called the shop assistant, a baby-faced man in his late thirties, who hurried up to the girls.

'How can I help you ladies?' He looked at their Balenciaga and Chanel purses, both in skinny J-Brands and very expensive-looking peep-toes, and figured they were to be called 'ladies' rather than 'girls.' He thought maybe they were older than they looked but had gone through some serious surgery. Who knew these days what women would do in order to look young? To stay on the safe side, he preferred to be overly polite with his clients rather than familiar.

Isabelle said ardently, 'Can I see those shoes right there on the top? And what is their price?'

'They are reserved, ladies, but I can surely show them to you.'

He climbed up a stepladder, gently took down both shoes, and put them on the counter.

'They have are very unique a brand. You might know Bozzi, except these were handmade in the late 90s,' he said.

The girls gazed with their mouths almost dropping on the floor. It was like an archaeological find. They had found that rare diamond.

'Indeed, they were handmade by a legendary Italian shoe-maker, Balthazar Bozzi. One of his US clients, a very high-end businessman, ordered a pair of shoes to be a last good-bye present to his mistress. Bozzi was extremely touched by this gesture. He even wrote about it in his memoir.' Daisy and Isabelle stared at the shoes.

'Are these the very ones?' Isabelle demanded.

'No. It is a similar year pair, but not the legendary ones,' he said.

'I know about him!' Daisy said.

'There was a whole section about the famous actress and the man who made shoes for her, the "high-society, celebrity shoemaker," if I recall correctly!' said Isabelle, who was very informed of the shoe history.

Before the young man had time to continue, Daisy got out her BlackBerry, got online, and frantically typed something. Just a minute later, she read out: "Balthazar Bozzi, the emperor of the female shoe! He made each pair with his deep passion and love. His shoes, creations, were like his family...."

As she read, she glanced at Isabelle, who was bewitched by the shoes. As she got closer to the young man, whose name, "Bob," appeared on his name tag, she pulled up a flirty face.

'So, Bob, how much would I need to pay for these marvels to be mine?'

'I am very sorry, ma'am, but they are reserved for someone else. In fact, she will be here soon,' he said as he checked his watch.

'I'll pay you twice the price!' she exclaimed. She could hear her heart beat strongly. It would pump out at any minute. Those shoes had to be hers, she decided.

'Three times more! Come on, buddy!' Daisy joined in.

Bob felt attacked. The two girls had joined forces, and now he felt what it was like for his buddies who had gone to Iraq. He was trembling, as the pretty girls now seemed like little Draculas. Their eyes, they said it all. He wanted to run away, but there was no way out.

'I have promised a girl to keep them for her,' he mumbled.

'What if she died? Honestly, it's New York,' Isabelle said. "She might have been hit by a bus in Brooklyn or something. Come on, you'll make money. We are here. She is clearly not, so let's not waste each other's time."

'Fine. five hundred,' he said at last.

'Three hundred,' Daisy countered.

'Four fifty.'

'Here, I have four hundred in cash,' Daisy said, reaching into her purse. 'It's all yours. Just hand those babies to me now!' she said impatiently.

He shyly took the cash, counted it, and slipped it into his pocket. No one saw, and he had done it before from time to time, when he felt that it was thanks to him an object was sold at such high price. Therefore, why shouldn't he, Bob Lewis, keep it to himself? He had worked with his inner self previously as well, in order to escape that anguish and culpability.

He forced a smile, switched his concentration to the sunny weather outside, and tried to meditate on the schoolyard sneakers that lay horizontally on the floor.

Isabelle and Daisy jumped out of the store, laughing their hearts out.

"Daisy! You're such a bargain-hunter! I love it how you haggled the price down!" Isabelle said gleefully.

Daisy giggled hysterically. 'Did you see his face? He was, like, totally scared of me! It's all the Istanbul grand bazaar experience of this summer!' Daisy said.

'Come on. Let's get a cab. We need to celebrate these beauties!' she cried.

Third Avenue was a very busy road. Cabs were coming from all sides, and finally one managed to see the two tiny silhouettes with, interestingly enough, one shopping bag. The girls had spent so much energy on getting hold of the Bozzi pair that the rest of the clothing was left forgotten in the changing rooms, never even having been tried on.

Taxi Ride & Metamorphosis

Speeding yellow cabs can make one feel like she's on some roller coaster or a horse carriage in the centre of Manhattan. Jumping, sliding from one side to another, Isabelle and Daisy were knocked together and down, right to the bottom. A sudden blackout…

Moments later, they both woke up with a faint, dull ache they had never experienced before.

'I have such a bad hangover,' Isabelle whispered as she rose from her uneasy dreams and felt a surprisingly light sensation that was not like her previous hangovers. She couldn't feel her body, just an awful headache.

'Rape drug. I think we were drugged. I don't recall anything,' Daisy managed to say. She felt like she had been beaten up.

'Arghhhhhhhh!' A scream came from Daisy.

'Arghhhhh!' And then she could not stop screaming. It was the most horrible thing she had ever seen in her whole life. Her MAC make-up cover was wide open, and she saw herself in its mirror. She saw a shoe. And when she tried to move and search for her body, all she saw was the shoe twitch back and forth. Both of the girls felt heavy spasms. They trembled from the shock.

They both yelled *'Help!'* but it sounded like a soft screeching of wood in windy weather. The whole world seemed suddenly very different. Both girls tried to remain still and wait it out, to see what would happen, to wake from this scary dream.

'We are shoes!' Isabelle yelped. 'We are not us! I don't know! Tell me it's not reality! Tell me it's a dream, please. Tell me it's a dream. I'm scared! I am really scared!' Isabelle cried heavy tears, which ran through her now new shoe cheeks. Indeed, the girls had become their newly purchased pair of shoes.

Isabelle was shocked by what she saw and now began to feel that her heel and sole and nose tip and whole body were now all parts of a shoe—a Bozzi shoe—the one she just purchased! Except now she was the actual shoe. It seemed like a mean farce, a scary tale they taught you when you were a child. 'If you don't behave, the monster will eat you.' Except they never said, 'If you don't behave, you will be your favourite shoe.'

She instantly remembered the story of Athena and Medusa, where the beautiful but greedy Medusa became a sea monster. But this was not a movie or a tale. This—she was feeling this from every part of her face and body. Could it be a dream? Isabelle wondered.

Let's stay calm, she thought. *It will pass.*

Daisy shouted, 'Isabelle, are you still there or am I hallucinating? Maybe we ate something with mushrooms and now we are living this bad trip. Could that be it?' Daisy cried, her eyes full of paralyzing fear.

Isabelle shouted back, 'I am here, and I hear you, and that scares me because it just doesn't feel like a dream. It feels very real.'

'For God's sake, we are huge, giant shoes!' cried out Daisy.

'I can't believe it. This is a joke…a farce…it's a nightmare!' yelled Isabelle.

However, they then realized that they only looked gigantic because they perceived each other from a shoe's perspective, and not a human's.

Both were lying on their hard, wooden-with-a-beige-sole backs, and when they tried lifting their heads a little, they could see the taxi doors. The MAC makeup was their only source of reality. But then they also saw each other, and it was the same as the image shown in the mirror.

The Indian cab driver opened his door.

'This is nonsense,' Isabelle insisted.

However, Daisy forced herself towards Isabelle and rolled onto her heel. She shut her eyes to keep from seeing herself as a shoe.

They began praying, tried to meditate, and say 'Ohhmmmm,' but every millisecond in this shoe body seemed like an eternity. Patience was key, yet so hard to feel. Too many emotions came all at once with no time to decipher reality from dream and fears from truth.

Suddenly, *boom!* A loud footstep was heard. *BOOM!* An even louder step. Then came continuous, harsh footsteps heading in the direction of the back of the car. Daisy and Isabelle tensed up simultaneously, and both looked at the gigantic, hairy hands that were moving in their direction. An awkward moment held until the rough, jagged face of the cab driver appeared as he picked the girls up. His eyes were black with sleep deprivation, and there was an obvious intoxication about his movements.

He looked at the shoes with disgust, and then slowly walked to the vintage store. Anger filled his dark eyes; his fists were clenched. They felt awful. His stiff fingers threw them on the counter where Bob Lewis was meditating on the sneakers on the upper shelf.

Chapter 10

Confession: Daisy the girl shoe

It was probably the thousandth time we had stepped into a vintage store, but this time we were brought by a taxi driver who angrily handed us over to the shop seller, who handed the driver a wad of money.

As the shock of the moment faded, I found it a peculiar feeling to be carried—quite light and easy. Our bodies felt quite numb. Sensitivity was missing compared to before, yet it felt good. Nothing was hurting, but everything felt far away.

With my consciousness, I realized the gravity of the situation. Whether it was a dream or some crazy joke, I would normally scream and cry and make a big show, but I had a bizarre, creepy feeling. I was actually calm and fine with the present situation. I didn't quite realize how it happened, why I couldn't hear my heart pumping out, why my beautiful long hair was gone, and why I was motionless on the table feeling so petite.

I could hear them. There were too many voices. The young shop seller seemed gigantic, and other voices, different ones, sounded different, lighter, and I could distinguish them from the human voice. Were they spirits, or was it the sound of the old radio? Something was bizarrely wrong.

Vintage Store

'Welcome home, twins!' said the light-grey family reunion dress from its high hanger.

The new shoe twins watched her with total amazement; something was bizarrely wrong. They couldn't quite understand how they were where they were, and they questioned their own sanity.

Isabelle begun whispering into Daisy's shoe ear, 'I cannot believe it! We are shoes! Do you understand that we are shoes?' Isabelle cried out.

'What do you mean? Take a breath, Isabelle. You are so stressed.' Daisy laughed. 'Just calm down. I'm feeling different, too, but not to that extent, I mean. Did you hear yourself? Are you high? Or is this just a bad dream? She will wake up,' Daisy said reassuringly.

It just all seemed too funny. She thought it was probably a nap, and she would wake up any minute to laugh about it. No need to live a nightmare. 'I'm positive it is just a dream, no matter how real it seems. I will wake up.' She told herself so a few dozen times before Isabelle screamed.

'It's not!' Isabelle said. 'Can't you see we became those freaking shoes you bought? Can't you see your face? Body? Everything is a damn shoe!'

And suddenly it hit Daisy. Perhaps they were not dreaming or under any drug. They were shoes. They could overhear other pieces of clothing speaking, whispering, 'Poor things, they must be so confused.'

'Confused about what?' Isabelle asked.

'It is actually a very interesting sensation, a great dream to re-member, so let's get the most out of it,' Daisy said, still thinking it might be a dream. She looked around in hopes of waking up soon.

'A dream? Did she just say a dream?' the voices whispered, giggling.

'Oh, sweethearts. It is not a dream. It's reality, but it's not bad. You will learn to live and appreciate your life as shoes. Don't be panicked about it,' the reunion dress said.

They felt themselves touched, lifted, and once again they fell onto each other. They clumsily felt each other's leather just like the shoes they had bought before they hailed a cab and then…they didn't remember anything.

'It's not a dream!' Isabelle screamed. 'It's freaking reality! I don't know how, but I just feel it. I can't even think what it is!'

The situation was becoming unbearable. There was too much panic and clothes talking and pitying the shoes. Daisy didn't quite understand any of it yet. She started to feel her silhouette, which did feel like a shoe, but it also felt so natural that she supposed it had to be a dream.

'A cute little dream, like that dream I had when I was five that I was a princess dinosaur. I felt just the same, except everyone around me was happy, and we played and enjoyed it. I guess it was my age. When I was five, a dream could only be sweet and happy. Now I am older, and all the bad things I've seen throughout the years have gotten stuck in my unconscious, so they are coming up in my sleep and disturbing the beautiful positive reality,' Daisy said.

Isabelle looked at her friend, and with tears in her shoe eyes, she mumbled, 'I was seeing a shrink to get rid of my deep fears, but now they are poisoning me. I could have resolved it and been much happier now.'

Daisy shook her heel. 'Hmm, I'm sure the shrink would have told me to go up against my fears and talk to them,' she managed to say. 'So we are shoes!' Daisy said.

'And hot ones, too,' the red mini-dress exclaimed flirtatiously.

'Get lost!' Isabelle screamed as she dissolved into grunting sobs.

'Calm down, Isabelle,' Daisy said.

'Calm down? I am a shoe, and some cheap red dress is trying to make me feel good. It's hell! Now I know what hell is. This is it! When are we going to burn?'

'You are being dramatic,' Daisy said. 'Come on, it's not that bad. It's all in your head. I promise you, if you just close your eyes and think about it.' Daisy tried to reassure her friend.

'I don't have eyes, and neither do you! Do you hear me? We don't have eyes that need mascara. We have shoe eyes that see but have no eyelashes! We are shoes! Identical shoes!' cried Isabelle in despair. She was always a drama queen. However, this time she completely lost her temper and she was heartbroken.

'So, let's explore our situation,' Daisy said. 'Then let's be shoes. It's temporary, anyways. You see, in the blink of an eye, we will wake up. You feel that it's forever, so just relax and don't get all stressed about it,' said Daisy reassuringly.

'You are even more lost than I am! Keep your positive thinking for other times. Now it's time to be realistic. I don't know how long it will last, and I do feel that I am a shoe, not a human anymore. I might sound crazy, but I am not! For God's sake, look at that mirror. Can't you see yourself? Try to move. You can't! You are as numb as I am. We are together in this, and say whatever you want, it's not pleasant. It's a horror movie!' Isabelle yelped.

'It is tragically funny,' Daisy conceded. 'I mean, think about it. We always wanted to have the best shoes in the world, and here we are feeling like we are shoes. It's quite ironic, don't you think?' asked Daisy.

'Except we don't just *feel* like shoes, we *are* shoes! That's what you are missing, and we've been shoes for half an hour. It's not a dream. I feel everything. Dreams are different. They can't feel this realistic.'

'It is quite realistic, I agree. But that clock is just in your imagination. Try to imagine we are in a candy shop with lots of candies, and we will be there, you see,' said Daisy in a soothing voice. She was very therapeutically when it came to crises.

'If that clock is in my imagination, how come you can see it as well?' demanded Isabelle.

'Well, I guess *you* are in *my* imagination, and your worries and frustrations are my inner fears that manifest themselves through you,' replied Daisy sarcastically.

'All right, Dr Freud, enough of your theories,' Isabelle snapped. 'Instead of claiming it's a dream, we should figure out how to get out of it!' Isabelle demanded.

'See, that is where I say we should just stay still and enjoy the time,' Daisy told her. 'You are just looking for an adventure, a war, a problem to be solved, obstacles to be overcome; it is not the path I choose. I will be very calm and happy and grateful for my present situation as a shoe,' Daisy said. She wanted to look positively at the situation because it had begun to feel quite fun to her.

'I can't even move properly, Daisy. We can't walk or dance or wear clothes,' Isabelle cried.

'Just trust me. It will all be OK. Now relax and try to stay positive,' Daisy reassured her.

Whatever the purpose of this situation, it was quite mentally charged for both Isabelle and Daisy. Just the thought of being an object was very new to them.

'Why would this ever happen? Why am I a shoe, and not a dress?' thought Daisy.

'People say you often dream of a fear of something you have imagined, but I have never imagined becoming a shoe myself, not even in my wildest dreams. I have bought a lot of shoes throughout my life, so perhaps that influenced my subconscious. I have probably given shoes too much importance, and with time my brain has decided that I would love to feel what it is like to be a shoe,' said Daisy, voicing her thoughts out loud.

Isabelle was not talking anymore. She had lost all her energy in her grief at being a shoe.

'Any better?' asked the reunion dress.

'Well, a little thoughtful. I have all these deep thoughts running through my mind,' answered Daisy.

'Maybe I could be of some help to you,' insisted the dress.

'Oh, well, tell us what happened, maybe?' Daisy managed to ask.

'That would be difficult,' said the dress. 'All I know is that two beautiful ladies came by this morning and bought a soulless pair of shoes. They seemed tough in negotiating, very tough. Next thing I know, the shoes were back, and they were, well, you two,' she said.

'Wait a second,' Daisy said. 'You said "soulless" shoes. I feel a sole in my shoe body.' Daisy giggled. It was very amusing to be a shoe, she thought.

'I said "soulless", not "sole-less." Soulless, without a soul, you see, an empty object like that wool beige coat.' The dress pointed.

'Wow, you are getting into an even deeper talk than I am. So, you are saying clothing have souls now?' asked Daisy.

'Indeed, look at yourself. The fact that we are having a conversation means we have a soul. In other words, we are alive!' said the reunion dress, smiling.

'Interesting,' said Daisy.

'You don't believe me, do you? You think it's all just a bad dream?' asked the dress.

'No, not at all. On the contrary, I think it's a good dream. My unconscious is manifesting itself, and I am really trying to explore the inside of my deepest thoughts,' said Daisy.

'You are being way too philosophical, sweetheart. You will have plenty of time to be having these thoughts, and at some point you will be so tired of thinking. As you get stuck with un-answered questions and the thoughts become deeper and deeper until they are almost unbearable, you will be angry, but you will not be able to express it. No one will be there to reassure you that there will be a happy ending. It will be your choice to live as you wish and believe in whatever you please to believe in,' the reunion dress said.

The dress took a deep breath. 'I had a family. I miss them dear-ly.' The reunion dress became melancholy, and at the thought of her family, her lower part was now dangling sideways.

'What happened? Tell me and I will help you!' Daisy insisted.

'Oh, poor child, if you only knew my age,' replied the dress.

'How old are you?' asked Daisy.

'As a human I would probably be dead by now, as it's been over forty years since I became a dress and I was already fifty-three. So unless I lived as a human to be over ninety, I would be dead now,' said the dress.

'How did you end up here? How did you become a dress?' asked Daisy.

'Oh, child. I have no knowledge of how I became what I became. All I know is that I loved dresses. I even starved myself at times to fit into a certain dress. I would love my dresses more than my own children. Dresses were sacred to me, and one day I found myself being worn by some woman. It was the most awk-ward feeling.' She took a deep breath. 'I later realized that the woman who was now living in my house, sleeping in my bed, and making love to my husband was his new wife, and she wore me clumsily. She didn't care to take me to dry cleaning. She just threw me in the washing machine along with the dirty socks and underwear. I was devastated. Watching being replaced in this way was simply disastrous.' Her sleeves moved gently as she looked around to make sure Bob the salesman wasn't anywhere in the proximity.

'The final straw was when my youngest daughter started crying whenever she saw me lying on the bed. She said, 'Throw it away! That dress, I hate it! Mommy loved it more than me! I hate it!' she looked down.

'Can you imagine how I felt? My little daughter felt that I loved a dress more than her, and the worst part of all was that she was probably right. I had not realized at the time the importance and time I gave to my dresses. I placed them higher than even myself.' The dress looked down at Daisy, who was like a little child, mesmerized by the incredible story.

'That is so sad. I'm so sorry, and what happened next?' Daisy asked gently.

'Next I was sold to a local vintage store along with all of my other designer dresses, and then I was shipped from one store to another. No one has ever bought me, but the shop owners feel I am a very unique piece, so they all hang onto me. That's my story,' she said quite graciously, assuming responsibility for all her faults and accepting the reality of things.

'You seem dazed,' the dress noted.

'I'm…well…actually, I am quite touched by your story. It must have felt horrible to be there and watch your life being taken by another woman, and worst of all being worn by her,' Daisy said with concern.

'Yes, but that was my past. And you know what we all say here?'

'What?' asked Daisy.

'The past is dead. If you keep hanging onto your past, you will just go crazy. Live the present, as you can't do anything to change your past but learn your lessons,' said the dress.

'Now let's talk about you and your friend. Or shall I say your twin, since you are identical now?' The dress grinned.

'I don't know more than you how I ended up here,' Daisy said, confused.

'I do,' Isabelle said as she awakened. 'That taxi driver must have drugged us with some experimental drug that affects the brain cells and makes you feel like a shoe,' she said anxiously.

'I used to think that way as well,' said the dress. 'All of us have had millions of theories that it was a dream, a drug, an experiment, a mental disease, a bad trip, or simply not real. But it has been forty years that I have been living as a dress. And that armchair,' the dress pointed with her long sleeves to the armchair that was graciously placed on the left side of the store. 'Mr Hugh has been an armchair for the past thirty years. And those little pink ballerinas have been there and lived that way for five months. All these objects have had the same metamorphosis. And, trust me, all of them refused this reality at first. My advice as the eldest is just to accept the reality and try to see the positive. I mean, at least you did not become a garbage can or underwear. You are an exclusively gorgeous pair of shoes. One of your siblings once belonged to a famous actress in Hollywood. You now have history, and a glamorous one at that.' The dress smiled.

The girls looked around for the first time as though it were reality. They still had doubts.

Fine. Let's try feeling as though it is real. I have nothing to lose, thought Daisy.

As they gazed at their surroundings, they now saw things slightly differently. They tried to keep in mind that the objects they saw were all alive or had a soul, as the reunion dress had explained.

'Wait a second. What is your name?' Isabelle asked the reunion dress. Daisy blushed because, even after their long conversation, she hadn't thought that a dress could have a name.

'Margaret.' She paused. 'It is Margaret.'

Isabelle leaned into Daisy gently. 'We are together in this. Let's stick close,' she said.

'We are,' Daisy muttered.

As they looked around, they could now perceive the others. The objects were all perfectly aligned: the Chelsea Pier loafers, Olympian Brogues, Bourbon Street ankle boots, postmodern peep-toes in python, bright yellow chorus line flats, bibliophile heels, cage heels, and countless others. Vintage dresses hung on the right side of what now looked like a gigantic store: a cherry-covered bridge dress, a crimson pleated dress, a burgundy berry-basket dress, a pale tulip dress, and a red miss Scarlet dress. At the top hung the most respected dress of all, the hoary-striped family reunion dress, who was carefully watching the newcomers.

The left side of the store offered a few coats: an auburn leather motor scooter jacket, an ashen shirley holmes trench, and a delicate, light-brown cashmere crème caramel coat.

They now all seemed alive and to be curiously watching the girls.

'I am Daisy, and here's Isabelle,' Daisy said to them as she banged her heel on the ground.

The Chelsea loafers said in one voice, "We're Jack and James."

The bourbon street ankle boots spoke up, 'We're David and Gina! You probably wonder...well, we were husband and wife. But he always loved his boots, so I took too much care of them. I gave myself to their maintenance, and next thing we know, we are those boots. But we are happy, together forever.' They smiled.

The postmodern peep-toes said, 'Rebecca and Cynthia. We used to be as beautiful as you two when you stepped in the store! You know, maybe it's nice you disappeared at the peak of your beauty. At least everyone will remember you as beauties and not old wrinkled grandmas.'

The bibliophile heels joined in. 'We're Kelly and Betty. We were designers. These sandals are our very own creation. They were such a success; even now our names are printed on them. These were the very first pair sold.'

The cherry-covered bridge dress said, 'I'm Chelsea. Welcome, girls! I am just a simple down-the-block girl.'

She had no time to continue before Margaret interrupted, 'Chelsea! Just because they are newcomers doesn't mean you can lie!'

'I'm sorry. Fine. I'm Chelsea, and I was stealing clothes and being a rather mean girl who did a lot of harm to people. I always lie; it's my passion. But I have learned to be honest about it, which makes me a better person, right?' she said.

Isabelle and Daisy were now overwhelmed by the situation, and all these names and stories left them totally confused and, for once, speechless.

* * *

Shoe chats at the vintage store

Along with the other pieces of vintage clothing and accessories, the new twins were placed next to the rest of the old and abandoned shoes. A Trussardi suit with holes in the right pocket, as though still upset at the economy for having fired his owner, now hung passively on a two-dollar hanger.

'I was wrapped in a newspaper the other day before I ended up here. There was an article there about Crocs,' said a hefty tweed blazer that seemed like a fossil. He took a deep breath and asked the twins, 'So, how is it going for shoes these days? I read that some are being rejected,' insisted the tweed blazer.

'Rejected? Ridiculous. How could you even consider shoes out of all clothing minorities to be rejected? Shoes are the must-haves, the most-wanted and cherished parts of women's and men's closets,' said Isabelle.

'Well,' he said, 'Crocs are one ugly pair of shoes, and a recent article about the dangers of wearing Crocs on escalators caught my attention. The Washington Metro has even gone so far as to post signs warning riders about wearing Crocs (and Croc knock-offs) on its escalators. Apparently, the soft, grippy shoes can grip the sides of the escalators and get twisted and pulled under. Or they get caught if the person wearing them does not step over the teeth at the end of the escalator ride.' He flipped his tweed pockets to make sure everyone heard him.

'Makes one wonder, though...in all these cases, is the shoe really to blame? Or is it the owner? Or is it just bad luck?' asked the Trussardi suit.

Daisy and Isabelle lay back to listen to the other items talk. They were now in a semi-calm mood, and a comfortable shelf was the perfect place to rest their tired shoe bodies. Stress really tires human beings, but it also affects shoes.

Days passed with no one touching them. Then one day a young woman entered and glazed at shoe section.

While Fay was gently moving her pretty little feet towards the shoe shelves, Ellie and Bernie noted the ever-present dress that had been hanging there since they had left the store with Fay' smother.

'Any new gossip, sweetheart?' Ellie asked the dress. Bernie tried not to show her own deep curiosity.

'New? We've got some very interesting news that might be of major interest to you, my little intellectuals,' Margaret, the reunion dress, said with a smile.

'Tell us right away,' they chorused.

'It's been a week now since we had the most peculiar incident. One day, two young, slightly arrogant girls walked into the store. One bought a pair of Bozzis, the second pair we've had in the store since you two were bought. In less than a quarter of an hour, they reappeared in the store, except this time the shoes were the girls. I mean, the girls became the shoes.' Margaret's lower part began to flow. She seemed animated just by the thought.

'We have had such cases before, like the minister's armchair and you,' she continued. 'But we never actually saw it happening like that. And they were so young, barely in their twenties,' she whispered.

'They must feel horrible. I mean, it is a change from a human body to a shoe one,' said Ellie.

'Oh, yes, poor things refused to accept reality, thinking it was just a dream. Now they still hope to become human again, but what can you do? Faith dies last, as they say,' said Margaret, the dress.

Before they had time to finish chatting with the dress, Fay grabbed the new Bozzis and exclaimed to the seller, 'I want these! I can't believe you haven't called me! I am a true fan of Bozzis, you know,' she giggled.

'Ma'am, they just arrived barely a week ago.' Bob the salesman replied.

'A week ago!' she exclaimed. 'They are destined to be mine!' She smiled. 'Oh, my little babies, I will take a good care of you. Don't you worry,' she whispered softly to Isabelle and Daisy, who somehow looked frightened. After all that had happened to them, they were now fragile creatures with no arrogance left.

Before they all knew it, they were beautifully wrapped, and sitting on the seat in Fay's car on their way to her Gramercy apartment. They were royally placed in the shoe closet right next to Ellie and Bernie.

'What is happening, Daisy? I can't even think any longer. It's just too creepy!' Isabelle fell into tears while Daisy couldn't keep herself together any longer. They both cried in misery, even though no real tears would slide down their shoe cheeks.

Bernie tried to comfort them. "Come on, girls, no time to cry. It's not that bad to be a shoe. Plus, you two have the privilege to be Bozzi shoes!' she commanded.

'We are not supposed to be shoes!' Isabelle wailed. 'It's a total error in nature. I don't know what it is, but it's so wrong! We are human beings. We have a social life, families. We have an existence. This is not where we are supposed to be!' yelled Isabelle.

'You are here now, though, so let us try to help you at least for the time being. I assure you, we will help you to be the most respectful shoes while you are in this state,' reassured Bernie.

'Life is too short to cry. And as Bozzi shoes, we have to learn to be calm and ladylike. After all, we are what they call in the shoe society the aristocratic shoes, handmade from the most exclusive materials. And every one of us is unique, unlike many other factory-made shoes that are all over the stores,' Ellie added.

After a few seconds, Daisy looked at Bernie and Ellie, 'Will it hurt when I am worn by a foot?' she asked innocently.

'Sweetheart, not at all,' Bernie assured her. 'It might feel awkward at first and tickle very lightly. You will feel full, and you will even look nicer and feel much more confident, especially with Fay's feet. You see, she has what they call Egyptian feet. They are the ones used by ancient Roman sculptures for the gods. Fay's feet are very smooth and curved, so the only parts that will actually touch will be the back and the front. The middle has open air space,' Bernie said.

The new twins were getting used to their new life, and Ellie and Bernie enjoyed being older sisters. They began to develop protective feelings towards the new twins who seemed very lost and unhappy with their shoe reality.

Chapter 11

Why Us? Why Now? Why Humans-to-Objects?

It is often said that the human society has become one where materialism rules, where money equals power, and where expensive luxury objects play a too-important role.

A rumour goes around town that a famous jet-setter, Louisa, while got engaged to Brandon, her six-year boyfriend, but all she really cared about was the size of her flawless Harry Winston engagement ring. She talked about it as though it were the most important object in the world. In fact, she looked at it and smiled constantly, and she spent more hours contemplating it than she did her actual engagement. In fact, she had little in common with her fiancé except for their love of material goods; he loved his sports cars, and she had a never-ending appetite for diamonds. Unfortunately, one day Louisa and Brandon disappeared. Both were said to have become their favourite objects. She became the Harry Winston ring, and he became the red Scuderia Ferrari. An urban legend or truth, most shopaholics have heard this tragic story.

Hence, Ellie and Bernie had come to realize that human beings were merely objects themselves. Just like shoes, they had a price tag and could be bought, perhaps not with a credit card at the mall but they were placing their material dream object so high up that it was their price. For that object they basically gave away their life, without realising of course. With time their life became around that object, its maintaining and caring for, and next thing we know, the human being has lost its human touch and became that very object. Ironic, indeed, but in a way makes sense at least to shoes it does.

Isabelle and Daisy were now learning how to live as shoes. They were still confused and often refused the reality that they were marching under Fay's feet. They stomped back and forth across the wooden dark oak floors until she slipped out of them and placed them beside the twins.

This was the typical afternoon teatime, except, of course, no tea was served for shoes. They were juxtaposed: Ellie, Bernie, Isabelle, and Daisy.

Anna, Fay's close friend, didn't miss an opportunity to wear Fay's newly purchased Bozzis.

'How was your day, girls?' Bernie asked.

'It's so nice to hear you say "girls"!' exclaimed Daisy.

'Yes, indeed, I almost forgot what it felt like to be talked of as a girl and not "cute shoes,"' Isabelle snarled.

'Ellie and I have analysed your case, and we have some thoughts we would like to share,' Bernie said.

'Sure, we've got all the time in the world!' replied Daisy.

'Go on,' said Isabelle coldly.

'Now, don't be arrogant. We are just trying to help, since we feel your misery being shoes. We want you to understand why this might have happened to you two,' Bernie continued.

'I am deeply sorry that Isabelle is not happy with this situation and is venting her anger and frustration on everything around her,' Daisy said.

'No, I'm not. I just don't see what there is to analyse. It is just a mistake that someone will soon realize and fix.' Isabelle closed her eyes and zoned out, not wanting to hear any of the twins' thoughts on the issue.

Daisy kept her eyes wide open, hoping to understand everything better.

'Sorry about her,' she said.

'No worries. Pessimism towards life will not make her become human again,' Bernie outlined in a strict voice.

'Now, Daisy,' said Ellie, 'tell us a little about yourself. What did your life consist of, your friends, your dreams, your life aims, everything?'

'Well, my name is Daisy Sella di Cassolini. I come from an aristocratic Italian family. My mother was a true American beauty of the '70s from Colorado. I studied in the most prestigious Swiss boarding school and never had a financial limit, except for one time when I demanded a plane for my eighteenth birthday, and my father refused, saying I already used the family jet more than him and my mom, so why would I need a second one?' Daisy laughed at her past that sounded more glam than anything else.

Ellie and Bernie listened carefully and were more interested in her character than in her former materialistic achievements.

'To cut a long story short, I have had everything, from beauty to money and friends from all over the globe. Now, as for a life's aim, I guess I never really thought about having one. I was pretty busy with all the social events and parties. Shopping also played an enormous part in my life, as well as Isabelle's. We would literary buy out whole shoe collections when we went shopping. It was a sort of a therapy.' Daisy paused thoughtfully. 'I had never even thought about how it would feel to actually be a shoe,' she said.

'How does it feel?' Ellie couldn't help but ask.

'It is different, but I am slowly learning to kind of like it. I mean, we could have become underwear, as Margaret explained to us. It could have been much worse. At least we have company, and our mistress is gentle while wearing us, so it is by far not as bad as I thought it would be,' Daisy said.

'I see a mature Bozzi in you. I loved your analysis of your past life. You had practically everything one could dream of, except love and passion, which are vital in every life,' Ellie said.

'Look at us. We were born together as twins. We have been shoes all our lives, and we try to approach every experience we've had with love, passion, and gratitude. We appreciate our history and ourselves. We hold the name of Bozzi, and we used to belong to a famous Hollywood actress, Crystal Baron. She died years ago, but we are still here and very happy to be us,' Bernie said.

The twins smiled at each other.

'So, what do you think I should do?' asked Daisy.

The twins thought for a minute, then Ellie looked at Daisy and finally said, 'You see, Daisy, the situation is pretty simple. You don't really have a choice but to learn appreciate life as a shoe or mourn it and live in constant grief.' Ellie pointed at Isabelle, who was deeply inside herself, closing her eyes to reality, preferring not to be present.

'Just like when you have changed countries and moved to new places, you always have to make yourself familiar and comfortable with your surroundings in order to play a functional role in society. In this case, your new surroundings are the shoe society,' Ellie said proudly.

'And you are lucky, you know that. After all, you didn't end up as any old shoe. You are a Bozzi, one of the most wanted shoe brands,' said Bernie.

'How do you expect me to live happily when my best friend and now other half is not cooperating?' Daisy watched Isabelle in despair.

'She will learn to live. Don't worry. Stubbornness has a time limit,' Bernie reassured her.

'So, why do you think this happened to us?' Daisy asked.

'It is hard to say, but we have seen cases of jewellery, sport cars, yachts, even planes and dresses and cigarette boxes having human souls. All in the past had idealized and gave too much importance to the object they eventually became,' Bernie said.

'Let me tell you about the Davidoff red oak and gold cigar box that we met the other day at a party uptown. His name was Everest Smith. Originally British, he had been a real estate tycoon who had owned most of Manhattan's top-rated buildings. His hobby was collecting cigar boxes. He had thousands of all kinds and types, but he had a special attachment to his very first one, a present from his father. He took greater care of that wooden box than of his own children,' Ellie said.

'The room where it was kept had to be a certain temperature, and the woman who came to clean had to use the special organic cleaning products on it. If there had been a fire he would most probably have died saving the box rather than running out to save his life. Without realizing it, all his love was going into that object,' Bernie added.

'Not surprisingly, one day he woke up to realize that he was now the cigar box, and since he had been gone, his daughter had placed his favourite box, now him, on the window of her uptown

Park Avenue apartment. And every time she would show it to a guest, she would say, "And here it is, Daddy's jewel. He loved it more than he loved me." She would giggle as people would touch and feel the famous box,' Ellie said.

'And what happened to him, to Everest Smith?" Daisy asked.

'Well, he is still there at the very same spot at the window. We saw him there when we went to a party at his daughter's apartment. He was complaining that the sun is bleaching the top. However, his daughter is less caring of the box. She just looks at it as a simple wooden piece that her dad cared too much about,' Daisy replied.

'I understand, but it must feel horrible for him,' Daisy said thoughtfully.

'No, not really. He told us that he finally found his inner peace. He sees his daughter and grandchildren much more often now, and he has a magnificent view of Manhattan. And, thanks to his daughter's social skills and amazing dinner parties, he sees all his old friends. He notices how old and worn-out they look in their grey suits all complaining by the window about the financial crisis and the stress it has caused them. All in all, he is happy being a Davidoff cigar box,' Bernie said.

'Incredible, I would have never thought that it could be possible,' said Daisy.

'Neither did anyone else,' Bernie said. 'It's a life full of surprises, and new ones are to come. Just be open to them.'

'I have met another case that might interest you girls,' came a voice from the upper shelves. The shoes looked up at an old Louis Vuitton sac-voyage that used to belong to Fay's mother.

'When I went to Washington, Fay dropped me at her uncle's office, where I had an interesting encounter with a Mac Computer. The Mac asked me if I was human in the past too, and I said no, I was born as a sac-voyage (meaning a travellers hand bag in French) and proud and happy to be one. The Mac then told me his life story. Apparently, he used to be an engineer and loved Mac computers. He could spend days on the computer doing his engineering calculations. One day, he woke up being one, and he said it was the happiest day of his life, since he had everything he could ever dream of in him now,' said the old, cranky voice of the sac-voyage.

Bernie, Ellie, Daisy, and Isabelle listened carefully to her voice.

'He showed off his numerous features and colours and modes and programs in Mac as well as his relationship with the Internet. He said he had a love-hate relationship with the Internet that drives him crazy and gives him this particular thrill about life that he had never felt while being a human engineer.' The sac-voyage stopped and laughed, 'What is the ultimate happiness, but being in love?'

'May I correct you?' Bernie asked.

'You don't agree with the concept of love?' asked the sac-voyage.

'I do agree that love plays a role of paramount importance in our lives. However, it doesn't mean we need to be romantically in love with someone. I would prefer to say that we should be in love with our own selves,' answered Bernie.

'She means love our lives and ourselves without the exterior material objects to it, but find true happiness in our present lives,' added Ellie.

'True, I never thought of it like that. As you know, we just travel and observe. My inner self is peaceful and satisfied, as long as I fly private or first-class, of course,' the sac-voyage laughed.

Ellie, Bernie, and Daisy laughed with her. Daisy's laughter made her leather shine and her cheeks blush. Her whole shoe look was now fresh and gorgeously cut, while Isabelle still refused even to open her eyes.

For a second Daisy realized that it had been the first time she had laughed as a shoe. She felt better, happier, and not alone anymore. There were others, and perhaps she could be happy like the Mac and the cigar box. Who knew? She might become a shoe celebrity and have shoe love affairs, and maybe she could simply forget she had ever been a human being.

They were a team, a small team but a friendly one. Bernie and Ellie were the older ones who would guide the new ones, and Fay was simply the best shoe owner that could possibly exist. Daisy remembered how messily she used to wear her shoes, and that after two times her shoes were no longer good enough to be worn so she gave them all to her cleaning lady, who by now probably had a massive collection of high-end, brand-name shoes of her own.

Daisy wondered if any of her shoes had souls, or if they were even human souls. She thought how different shoes would seem to her now if she were human again. However, that thought brought sad feelings, so she switched her thoughts back to her sweet shoe reality, where everything she had imagined was pink and beautiful.

Her only concern was Isabelle, who literally boycotted any kind of communication from anyone. The only time she would talk was when Fay would wear them, and then it was only to criticize and nag about how much she hated being a shoe.

Finally, after days of self-imposed isolation, Isabelle awoke to her most despicable shoe reality.

No matter how much Daisy tried to persuade her of the positive aspects of their lives as shoes, Isabelle refused even to hear about it and preferred to change topics and talk about anything else.

'I must say, her taste is not awfully bad,' Isabelle declared.

'You mean Fay's?' Daisy asked.

'I didn't remember her name, but yes, Fay's. It's not as good as mine, or yours, for that matter, but it's still good. I like her dresses, except it seems that she just buys and never actually wears them,' Isabelle said, observing the grey suede mini dress that still had its tags on.

'That's how we used to be, don't you think?' Daisy asked.

'Quit with the "used to be," please, and secondly, I always wore my stuff at least once...or maybe not, but I planned to,' Isabelle snapped.

'You know, I thought about it. We were too much, you and me,' Daisy said.

'What do you mean too much? Too good to be true?' Isabelle said sarcastically.

'No, I mean too much into unnecessary things like shopping. It was like our life purpose to buy out the whole collection of everything, and especially shoes. I mean, just think about last Christmas's sales in the Saks shoe department!' exclaimed Daisy.

'Oh, my God, it's too soon,' Isabelle groaned. 'I can still feel the energy, the blood flowing in my cheeks. It was better than anything. That was the happiest day of my life! Those fuchsia pumps, remember? For nothing!' Isabelle grinned.

'Yes, I remember, but look at us then. That was the ultimate goal of life. It's just wrong, don't you think?' Daisy asked.

'Wrong? No way! What's wrong about spending your own money on nice things? Anything is good if it makes you happy! Plus, shoes, what harm could they possibly cause?' persisted Isabelle.

'Maybe we cared just slightly too much for shoes. Maybe we were supposed to care about more important matters than shoes and clothing and those parties. Where did they lead us?' questioned Daisy.

'Those parties? Did you lose your brain on the way to becoming a Bozzi shoe? We met at one of those parties, and we were the stars of those parties along with the rest of the world's most influential and famous people, jet-setters, and artists. So many contacts any PR person would dream of having,' angrily barked Isabelle.

'Except we were not in PR and never thought of using any of those contacts. All we cared about was the party and the happy mood. We strived to be the hottest and most popular. It was aimless, totally empty!' cried out Daisy.

'I loved my life, so think whatever you want. Stay here as a shoe if you like. I refuse to think that way. You go a enjoy being a shoe!' yelled Isabelle as she turned away.

'I'm just trying to understand, why us? And honestly, Isabelle, I know very well just as much as you I was not appreciating my life at that moment; I was not satisfied with anything. You even cried for a week when your dad blocked your American Express card I mean, a whole week of your life gone, for what?' demanded Daisy.

'I had my reasons at the time. And anyways, what's up with you being so philosophical? For God's sake, you're starting to sound like that yoga teacher I once had. All he said was, "Detach yourself from your material world and feel free." No, not my cup of tea. I feel good having my friends, my money, my family, and my damn shoes!' Isabelle yelped. She was so infuriated that her pump was detaching from the sole from all the stress.

Bernie and Ellie listened carefully to the argument between the two younger ones and couldn't help but feel sorry for Isabelle. Indeed, they were saddened by the new shoes' depressing attitude. They simply couldn't accept their new reality as Balthazar Bozzi pumps.

'Did you know that the plain pump started out as a heel-less shoe worn indoors?' asked Bernie.

'No,' Isabelle said.

'So, they were basically slippers?' Daisy asked.

'Not really, but later on, around the nineteenth century in the UK, the flat pump was considered somewhat sophisticated, and was worn by both women and men,' Bernie said.

'And in Paris in the mid-nineteenth century, Count d'Orsay introduced the new version of pump that was low-cut on the sides to expose the curve, and it had a heel. Pumps suddenly had a totally new, sensual, toe-cleavage exposure!' added Ellie.

'This is interesting, but why are you giving us a shoe history class?' Isabelle asked impatiently.

'I am actually enjoying it!' Daisy said. 'What about Hollywood? What role did your ancestors play in Hollywood history?'

'For God's sake, Daisy, you sound like you're back in college! You are a freaking shoe under a table in an LA hotspot where normally you would be sipping rosé, and all you care about is the freaking shoe history!'

'Easy there!' Bernie commanded.

'Never mind, she's just upset with…you know,' Daisy said, trying to soothe the conflict that was bursting out like that volcano on Mauritius Island that memorable spring break when all the girls went back in 2006.

'Hollywood loved two types of women's shoes,' explained Ellie. 'The high-heeled pump, which always looked glamorous despite its inappropriateness to the many action scenes the heroines were depicted in while wearing them, and the thin strappy sandal as worn by Hayworth, Garbo, and Davis, which represented a willing partner to seduction.'

'All that is to say, now that you girls are shoes, you should be as proud of our history as we are! Your mixed feelings are understandable. Change is often hard to accept. However, one should let go with time. Just try to enjoy your life as a glamorous pump!' said Bernie.

* * *

Shoe Lessons

Bernie, as the older sage, began, 'We are handmade. Many shoes in today's world are machine-made, however we are all manmade. Machines are made by man too, so ignoring our relations with the human world would be absolutely wrong and unfair.'

Isabelle snapped immediately, 'Thanks for that piece of information. I am a human, and I know better than anyone here that shoes are manmade!'

Daisy whispered to Isabelle's shoe ear to calm her while Bernie continued with the lecture.

'Being an excessive shoe lover is not always great. Unfortunately, people tend to forget that shoes have a long life and don't need to be fed. All they need is careful wearing.'

'And a little pampering,' giggled ever-happy Ellie.

'Fashion character Carrie Bradshaw from *Sex and the City* is best known for her love of shoes. Shoes are not to be separated from the lives of women. A publication of the *United States Shop Smart Consumer Reports* surveyed more than a thousand women in the US. On average, each woman has seventeen pairs of shoes and has spent about four thousand dollars for them all. Among all the shoes they have, only three pairs are used regularly.' Ellie read out loud from the old magazine lying in the bottom of the closet room of Fay's apartment.

'Dear shoes you must remember that we are living in New York and everybody walks here, that's how we go just about everywhere our trains, cabs, or…limos won't go. Where, for instance, in Los Angeles or Virginia you might think a trip to the corner store should be made in a car, in New York that's a walk, pal—maybe because it would be too hard to find another parking space, but more likely because not many have a car so more walking for us meaning be cautious of the way you walk not to dehydrate your soles and not to have scars that take long to go away' said Bernie facing Isabelle and Daisy. In the meantime Ellie was analyzing her soles that seemed very much neat.

'It is quite exciting, I never thought from a shoe perspective when I was a girl - a walk just seemed like a natural thing to do and not a strategy based one' Daisy said smilingly.

'On the sidewalks, it is all about knowing how to place your heels and to move quickly and accurately. Always watch where you're going. Ferret out a path, and take it. Be predictable, you're not running interference for the Jets: No serpentining, no running, and no getting too close to your fellow walkers shoes. Jostling another walker is harassing the other shoe and might be perceived as pushy and arrogant; it isn't done by any properly educated shoe, and certainly not on purpose, and if it happens, must immediately follow with an honest apology. Likewise, a true, full-on 'wreck' may require an exchange of insurance information.' Daisy said on her last breath worried she missed out on some important information.

'May I? asked Ellie excitedly.

'Of course, I am having a black out dear sister, can't think of anything else to teach these girls' said Bernie hopelessly.

'Nothing we haven't heard before' distressed Isabelle and tapped her hill as to turn away when Daisy stopped her and gave her a very big shoe look.

'Please continue, I'm really enjoying this shoe lecture on walking, I mean if it is not shoes, then who else will know better about walking?' lightly giggled Daisy.

'You are right my dear' Ellie replied.

'Tell them about the subways.' said Bernie.

'Oh I will, but first crossing the roads! A few basic rules to remember my dears: *Look both ways*—even if you're crossing a one-way street. You've had your own share of wild cab experiences, so you should know that anything goes for drivers—and an errant cabbie could flatten the unawares jaywalker. Move quickly. There's no reason to dally in the middle of the street. No skateboarding trick that begs to be performed, no moonwalking maneuver that must be seen to be believed. Get out of the street, and fast.' Said Ellie

The three shoes were mesmerised by Ellie's fun story telling style of the walking lecture.

'On Escalator Lanes as on the great superhighways that stretch across this land, so too on the escalator: If you're not really moving, stick to the right. The walker shoes who stops dead in her tracks on the left, riding the escalator at her leisure, inconveniences and annoys her fellow walkers. Stand on the right, walk on the left, and make everybody happy.' Said Ellie taking a breath and continuing.

'Now on subway stairs mass makes the rules. A rush-hour train's worth of stair-hogging passengers has more to do with who's going where than whatever resolve you think you have. Squeezing yourself down the narrow side of an oncoming wave of shoe walkers is pointless, dangerous, and exactly like driving the wrong way down a city street that's switched direction, without warning. So: Be sensible, wait at the top the stairs. Yes, even if it's raining.' She laughed as she could see the terrified eyes of Isabelle, who had never taken the subway even as a girl

The four shoes were slowly building a friendship. Daisy was putting a lot of effort towards realizing her previous mistakes. She was working on her inner self and trying to live her new reality as a shoe positively. At the same time, Isabelle refused to cooperate and was upsetting all of them, especially herself.

Shoe Promenade

'These comfortable insole liners are made of ultra-soft fibres that help to reduce the friction between the foot and shoe and absorb moisture to prevent feet from slipping in the shoes. And they're so easy to use. Peel off the plastic film on the stilettos to ensure a smooth surface. Trim liners according to your shoes, remove the protective layers, and place them firmly on the shoes. These Softins come in leopard, zebra, polka dots, pastel floral, and green dots. You're really spoiled for choice. They can be easily removed without leaving residue,' read Fay out loud. She then faced the twins and said, 'I wouldn't be needing any of those; my little ones are the most comfortable shoes in the whole wide world.

Weekends with Fay's best friend Anna in town meant all-day shopping and catching up because Anna never bothered to pack her suitcase. She would literally decide to go from Switzerland to New York and jump on the plane the same day with her wallet and passport and ever-present black Birkin. She preferred to buy everything in New York or borrow a few things from Fay, as their sizes were exactly the same.

Ellie and Bernie were on Anna while Daisy and Isabelle were on Fay, and they danced through the streets on their way to Saks Fifth Avenue.

Serious-looking office men in their grey and black suits were curiously watching the two happy-lady figures, who were giggling at everything around them and lightly jumping as they sang a little passage of every song that came to their minds.

At a red light, a former banker specifically looked at their ever-moving little shoes and thought, *How much fun it must be for girls to wear those little leather pumps.* He greatly appreciated the classic, smooth, and feminine lines of the heel and the top sole. He had even decided to get a pair just like that for his wife, but was disappointed when the girls ran straight up to Saks before he had time to approach and ask them where they had found such marvels.

The shoe department at Saks Fifth Avenue in Manhattan was getting so big, it was even gaining its own government-approved zip code. As of mid-August, the fabulous shoes that were on the fourth floor were moving up to the eighth. Choos, Manolos, Louboutins, and more got a grandiose 17,500-square-foot home, 9,000 of it for storage, fittingly called 10022-SHOE.

Chic shoppers were able to take an express elevator into the salon, which had a residential feel, and shoppers were encouraged to interact with one another. Hand-blown glass walls and chandeliers provided the light.

A baby screamed while her older sister stumbled around the store wearing a pair of $200 shoes that had been handmade in Spain. The shoes her mother was wearing fit as if they had been made for her, but the colour she wanted wasn't available in her size.

Ellie, Bernie, Isabelle, and Daisy marched confidently next to the mother and daughter, who were quarrelling about shoes. But, in contrast, the shoes they were wearing seemed very happy. One was singing, and the other was dancing.

'If only they could hear us,' said Bernie.

'Then Isabelle would be out in the trash,' said Daisy, laughing. 'With all the stuff you said about Fay…' She giggled.

'I wish someone could hear me and make me myself again,' said Isabelle, grinning.

They mingled around and spotted a few hotties, who were all sparkling and new.

'They are so beautiful,' said Ellie.

'Of course they are,' said Isabelle. Except after one day out and about, their multi-leather stiletto with elastic crisscross ankle will look all worn-out and have heel scars,' she uttered.

Daisy spotted a peep-toe wedge with open design and sipped quarter, but then she realized she was in no need of shoes anymore.

They marched a few floors, watched all the other shoes, and felt relieved that their beauty was lasting, compared to other shoes that at first sight might look impeccable but after having walked miles wouldn't be as practical and new-looking.

* * *

Another day with the Shoes

'Shoes, shoes, shoes! Needless to say, all can see how important we are and why the fashion world fusses about us and women obsess about us,' Bernie said proudly to Daisy and Isabelle.

'There are, however, a few lessons you two should learn since you are shoes right now. We have a certain self-maintenance in order to stay beautiful and young. We can offer just a few tips that will help you in your daily lives.'

Ellie turned towards the old pair of Ferragamos on the upper shelf. They were full of dust and looked like they dated from the past century. One could still see a lighter shade of orangey red under all the dust. The wide and flat shoes had faded over the years, probably due to sunlight. In fact, Isabelle and Daisy didn't understand why such a worn-out pair would still be in this magnificent closet-room.

'They used to be beautiful,' Ellie said. 'I saw a picture of Fay's mother wearing them. They were totally different from how they look now.'

An old grouchy voice came out of the shoe, 'It's age. You will see. The whole enthusiasm of life fades away. Before you know it, you'll be a dust carriage just like us, forgotten and not loved.' The shoe's sad grumpiness was apparent. Indeed, no matter how much the rest of the group tried to make them talk and appreciate what was left in their life, they utterly refused, choosing to sleep a sort of a clinical death. They let themselves go, having gained a few layers of dust, making them appear even more grey and old.

Bernie and Ellie comforted them, trying to make them feel better, but the Ferragamos refused to listen and closed themselves once again.

'They rarely wake up,' Ellie said.

Daisy and Isabelle were gazing at the Ferragamos, thinking to themselves that never had they had so much sympathy and pity for an old pair of shoes.

'You see, when people buy expensive shoes, they're usually paying for the brand name, as well as for quality craftsmanship. But after immersing themselves in the most luxurious designer shoes in the world, don't you think they should pamper us?'

Ellie and Bernie now gently pointed to the elegantly placed pair of Chanel ballerina flats that had been bought in London some years back for about seven hundred pounds. These sophisticated ladies were still resting elegantly in Fay's shoe wardrobe.

'So what are the rules to keep us shoes in condition as good as new?' Daisy asked.

Golden Rules for Shoe Owners

Throughout the years, the Bozzi twins came up with a list of golden rules for future shoe owners.

'A new pair of shoes should never be worn for many consecutive hours. Once your feet are completely accustomed to the shoes, you can begin to wear them all day,' stated Bernie.

Ellie continued stating the "Golden" rules:

- Never wear the same pair of shoes two days in a row. Let them rest for at least a day before wearing them again.
- Use a shoehorn when putting on your shoes.
- Before removing a lace-up shoe, loosen the laces completely so the shoe slips off more easily.
- Once shoes are taken off, insert the made-to-measure shoe-trees or the "moulded" paper that comes with it.
- Shoetrees should also be used when shoes are wet from rain. In this case, the shoes should not be rested on the soles but on their sides and left to dry for an entire day.
- Each time you wear a pair of shoes, they should be cleaned and polished, even when they still look shiny.
- If a pair of shoes isn't worn for some time, coat them with a thin layer of polish and put them in the cloth bag provided in the box.

At the end of the day, it's important that one doesn't buy a shoe just because of the name. Buy a shoe based on how it fits and how comfortable it is. When wearing a shoe, the brand tag isn't going to do your feet any good.

Confession of Daisy, the Slim Heel

Oh, what, Keanu Reeves? Is that you? Didn't recognize you because you are so cool and casual with that messy, dark, long hair of yours! Instead of *The Matrix*, *Bill and Ted's Excellent Adventure* immediately popped into my head, and I almost wanted to ask you to do just one line in that California-surfer dialogue. But I refrained, obviously, since I am a shoe!

Yes, I am a shoe-fabulous, high-heeled, Italian, handmade, black pump. And I'm of best quality. At least, that's what they said at the vintage store where I was savagely dropped by the taxi driver. If only he knew that I was that very same girl who sat in his taxi on 3rd Avenue in Manhattan with her best friend. And God knows what happened before I knew I was a shoe!

Nevertheless, whatever. I am a shoe now, and my best friend is a shoe, and we have a few fellow shoes to help us out and orient us, shall I say, into the shoe society. That's what they call it. It has its own rules, you might be surprised to learn. I would have never thought so before, but guess what? Life is just full of surprises, so beware whom you might wake up as tomorrow morning!

I even had some silly thought that the taxi driver cast some livid spell on us because maybe my friend was arrogant when she hailed him. After some thought, though, it didn't really make sense, since I can still recall his distaste when he didn't get paid. He probably assumed that we ran out at the light and forgot our new shoes in the backseat.

No! No! I know exactly what you are thinking, and, trust me, I was thinking the same at the first moment. And, yes, I have watched, *The Hangover*, and no, I hadn't taken any drugs that day. I simply went shopping, and this is reality no matter how much I wish it weren't. It is not a dream, unfortunately. But, hey! What can we do? Sometimes life continues, and at least I am trying to stay positive, like *The Secret* says to do.

Actually, that law of attraction kind of makes sense in my circumstances. I thought so much about shoes that it's no wonder I became one. Except I wasn't aware that, by fantasizing about new shoes for the new season, I would literally become one myself.

I assumed that it would mean I would get more shoes. I never could possibly imagine. I still get shivers at the thought.

You know what I say, though, it's not as bad as it seems. I have a nice petite nose, and my bum looks so athletic and sexy thanks to my smoothly polished heel. My skin is of baby crocodile, which in shoe terms means ageless! Indeed, I will be preserved young all my life, and even if a piece of me breaks, there are always shoe specialists to whom I can be urgently sent. Besides, even when I was a human, you know, I had a few small operations, or shall I call them improvements, made upon me.

Solitude and loneliness were often making me sad when I was a girl. I missed my friends and family, but guess what? Not anymore. I am constantly with my best friend, Isabelle, and thousands of other shoes who all look up to us since we are what they call "The Shoe Aristocracy." When we are out of the dressing room, we are mingling out and about. We have a very social life since our mistress loves parties and cocktails. In fact, if we were still human, we would make a great friend circle. She does the things I would do, and she spends her days just as I would. So boredom is out of my vocabulary list.

In love it is a little hard. There aren't too many good shoes out there, male shoes especially. They are either too serious or stuck up, or way too casual, like Converses. Not the type I would introduce to my family, if you know what I mean. I wish designers would feel at least for a day what it is like to be a shoe and understand that we need to love and to be loved too, by other shoes, not just women. Women love us as though we are their babies, which means a great deal. However, romantic love wouldn't harm us at all. It would add some spice to our shoe life.

Of course, I miss the human stuff too. But all in all, being a shoe is not that miserable. Look at me! I am in LA in the Chateau Marmont Hotel. Where else could I possibly want to be?

On all sides, celebrities are walking down the halls in their beautiful, eccentric shoes, wearing leather designer clothing and gorgeous handbags, all looking like they just came out of the TV. There are moans, laughter, cries, and tears coming from all sides as though the hotel itself is alive, breathing some sort of madness into the lungs of its residents. The walls are the flesh of a mythical beast that feeds off peoples' desires. Indeed, there is something about this hotel that makes insanity make sense.

Despite all my enjoyment, however, being a shoe is ruining my relationship with my best friend. She simply refuses to enjoy life as a shoe. Stubbornness sometimes destroys people, but what can you do? If they refuse to recognize it, there's not much to be done.

Maybe my friendship is on the rocks, but this place is giving birth to crazier feelings and thoughts! I feel like I am part of a movie. It's not so much the hotel as it is an entity that coexists within.

But it is all good. Being in the midst of celebs, screenwriters, producers, and directors—it is just so LA!

Enchanting is the word that comes to mind. I feel the old-world charm wrapping around me and taking me into a state of euphoria. I don't know if it is purely my enthusiasm at being here or if it is the whole shoe metamorphosis that has made me so hyper and happy, but I must admit I am loving the present moment to the full extent.

Trust me, if all shoes were as happy as I am presently, the world would definitely be a better place, because, hey, just take a minute to think about who carries you around all day and night when you are out. Indeed, shoes, shoes, and shoes again! They protect you against the cold, and at the same time they accessorize your outfit and comfort your feet. What do they get in return? Nothing. They are replaced by a new pair as soon as they age or go out of style with no pity or care; they end up in the garbage. Sad reality, the law of the jungle is true for shoes too—the weak lose while the strong survive, with exceptions, of course. Mother Fashion teaches the world that shoes and other old clothing tend to come back into the fashion world, so keep them with care for their return.

I must admit, it is hard to be a shoe when one sees, like now, the desserts on a nearby table that just look too good. The fruit tart with custard is huge and so fantastic, the crust so light and flaky, and the vanilla custard so creamy and overflowing with fresh berries. Mmmmm. And that chocolate cake! Mmmmm!

Enough! For shoe's sake, I cannot look that way any longer. I can only comfort myself at the thought that if I were back to being human and ate all those delicious things I would probably be a beast by now and fall into a deep depression, and then I'd lock myself in some nutrition spa in the Swiss mountains, far from human sight. For that matter, I should be grateful once again that as a shoe I shall never gain an extra pound and can live ever happy, as I always dreamed of.

Being a shoe means a lot of time for observation, hence a lot of fun details to gossip about later with the girls. For example, what can be worse than an old lady who is dressed as though she just came out of the Playboy Mansion, except she lost count of the years that went by her, or decades, to be precise? As my mistress crossed her legs I got a new view of the back patio, and there she was, an old, rich-looking lady, judging by her full diamond Daytona and a big, fat, heart-shaped sapphire ring that resembled that one in the *Titanic* that the old woman threw in the ocean.

By the way, how crazy was that? Why would she throw it? Just think about it: millions of dollars gone for the sake of some romantically driven emotions. Anyways, going back to our old lady who obviously thought she was in her early twenties. She had her old, wrinkly boob out, giving us side cleavage that almost made our heels throw up!

Now it is time to take a tour while our mistress makes her way to the ladies' room. We—as in I, since my best friend has decided to zone out again—follow her, checking out the rest of the people and shoes. Back from the ladies', we take the steps up through the charming, tiled entryway up to the lobby and out towards the garden dining area.

Back in the shaded sunlight, we sit in the elegant but simple digs and take in the beautiful arches, windows, fountains, and lanterns that comprise the hotel architecture and detail. I don't know if I would appreciate this place as much if I were human. Everything as a shoe has a much grander appearance. For example, I note the one-too-many cigarettes lying on the ground, all lit by the hotel's matches with a naked flapper on the matchbook cover. I don't think I ever would have noticed the image of the matchbox before. Perhaps this is insignificant, but it is still interesting to note such things, or to simply appreciate how wonderful lazy LA afternoons are while relaxing and engaging in casual conversation.

While the waiter was taking our mistress' order, the waiter's shoes, Bill and John, told us about the tales of shamelessness that started and ended here. The likes of Gram Parsons, Jim Morrison, Elizabeth Taylor, and Hunter Thompson. just to name a few, were notable legends that caused a glamorous brawl within the walls of this infamous hotel.

As the shoes of the young producers at the neighbouring table said, 'Chateau Marmont is the ultimate Hollywood charm, which essentially means it's sort of shabby-classy.'

I most of all enjoy the gate into the gardens; it's like *Alice in Wonderland*. A narrow stone path leads you up the hill, and you glimpse the pool through the trees. Periodically, paths lead off to the various cottages. As you wander, you pass little wrought-iron seats scattered along the way for weary travellers and, whimsically, come to a Ping-Pong table. It has a lot of charm and a certain mystery to it, and grounds are comfortable to walk on, of course.

Confession of Isabelle, the Arrogant Pump

"Three quarters of the miseries and misunderstandings in the world would finish if people were to put on the shoes of their adversaries and understood their points of view." –Mahatma Gandhi

I am completely Daddy's Little Girl. He'd do anything for me. My nannies still probably do my laundry and clean my room even though I've been away. My dad even went to the ends of the earth to get my dog back.

Then he gave it away.

Just because I wouldn't talk to him.

He couldn't take it.

My parents created a monster. Or perhaps it was simply that I haven't really seen them that much. They thought that sending me off to a Swiss boarding school would make me happy. And I did meet my best friends there, but, as sad as it sounds, I never had that happy family reunion dinner for Thanksgiving. My mom, well, she never cooks, and my Dad was always away. Even when we were on vacations, he never stopped using his cell and talking about important issues that sounded like Japanese to me.

For that matter, I got used to manipulating them into getting anything I wanted and making them feel guilty for having abandoned me in the Swiss Alps. And it really worked.

I came to New York, got unlimited funding, and fun was everywhere, until once again I got bored of that too.

What I most regret about when I was human would probably be that I held grudges with loved ones if I didn't get my way.

I know this makes me sound incredibly bad, but I'm not. So I get what I want when I want. And if I don't—watch out. It's that easy. I like being spoiled. It's fun.

Then my whole world turned upside down. I fled Europe. Everything seemed wrong there, or perhaps it was just not enough. The party circle got smaller and smaller, and to be honest I did not enjoy them any longer, either. I loved shoes and shopping, but, God, I never thought I would be one myself.

That is just the worst. It hurts me even to say it. I do not understand why such a disaster happened. I mean, I was not perfect, but I haven't killed anyone! I would prefer to be in prison. At least I would be me, and not a piece of wood and leather. I remember my past, but it seems like it was a very long time ago. I have lost count of the days of this new life. I still hope somewhere deep inside that it is a bad dream and that I am lying in some coma and will wake up soon.

I try to accept the situation, try to be happy, but I can't. I hate it, and I cannot accept it. It is beyond my power and my will. I think hatred is the only genuine feeling I have left, the only place where I feel strength, since all my other tools, like my voice and physical power, are long gone. I can only be alone with my misery and wait for a miracle that I have lost hope in too.

Everything annoys me. Especially sounds. I find myself overwhelmed and stressed over every little thing. I can't find any motivation. I am tired all the time. I have almost daily headaches. I know I should be a happy. I am at least alive, even though I am a shoe. But the very word *shoe* makes me sick.

Why am I so angry and sad? I don't think I am depressed. I don't want to hurt myself. I do have low moments. But they aren't too extreme. I can totally see how I sound like a textbook description of depression, and when I was in college our psychology teacher always told us that depression is a parasite. It steals your life from you, but I am a shoe. What else should I feel, excitement? I'm not even a red suede mule with colourful jewelled ornaments; I'm not a silk satin T-strap shoe with a gold leather trim and woven upper. I am a simple, dark-brown shoe pump. Yes a Bozzi, but so what. If I have to be a shoe, at least I could be the glamorous and sparkly, not a brown pump!

I feel that my only escape from this atrocious shoe reality is to zone out. The more I sleep, the less I think. Often I have difficulty falling asleep. These thoughts don't let go and make me feel so miserable that I could literally dream of being savagely thrown away, and then again, I am a shoe. The worst that would happen is my soles would break and some beggar who would find me on the streets would use me for their feet.

At least I have my best friend in this chaos with me, and our mistress seems like a cool girl, but I just can't hide it. I hate her for being the girl I should have been. At times I feel that she is living my life and sees my type of people, flirts with the guys I would, and dresses just the way I would. Worst of all, I have to watch it every time she wears us. I have to accept the fact that I am a shoe who is carrying Fay's foot around. No matter how well conditioned, creamed, and pedicured her feet are, I am Isabelle Von Albrecht. I should never be at anyone's feet. If she only knew whose soul her Bozzi pumps were. If only she knew.

As to the other two Bozzis, they act like they own this world. They keep on giving us lectures. Shockingly, Daisy seems to enjoy their company, unlike mine, but that is just because I have difficulty being myself in these shoe circumstances.

Ellie and Bernie were born as shoes. How could they ever understand us? We've seen the real life, the life they will never get the taste of. Actually, I guess I should remove the word *never* from my vocabulary. It's ironic how just a few months ago I would never have imagined my current situation.

So the twins, they are classy indeed, but so annoying. They love criticizing, especially me. I am so negative, and so ungrateful, and so spoilt, blab la blah. What else do they expect, honestly? Do they think I should be jumping with excitement, or what?

Ellie is more or less easy to handle. She is just a hopeless romantic and lives in this pink little world of herself that Daisy admires so much. As if Daisy weren't human. She has actually pulled herself up to fit in the shoe society. I think I lost her, and whether this is an alien experiment or God who decided to entertain himself for a vacation, I will not allow the shoes to get into my soul. I might be physically a shoe, but deep inside I will always be me, Isabelle Von Albrecht.

As for Bernie—and did you hear her full name, Bernice? What a grandma name. She is actually the strictest shoe I've met around here. She's like the military chief in the army, the one who sets order and never loses her head. I just hate her. She should understand her place. She is a shoe, not Queen Elizabeth.

I just get a big headache when all of them start talking to me. They think I should fall into their happy mood. Why can they not just leave me in peace? And the vintage store was the worst. No one considered our shock. All they were into was telling us that basically we were punished; it was karma. I wish I had my mind straighter at that point to shut them all up. For all their holiness, they were happy deep inside for our misery. I am sure about it. All that sweet-talking was just part of the game.

Chapter 12
The Miracle Trip to LA

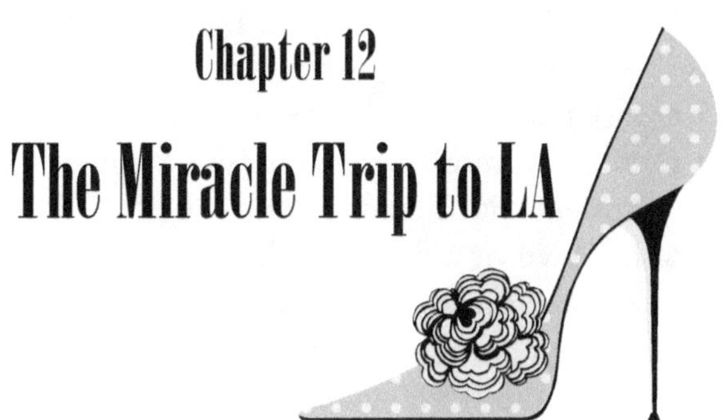

Some were stuffed with dirty underwear and stuck in suitcases with no space, not even a millimetre, to move and aggressively thrown into the commercial flight luggage check-in along with all other over-packed, extra-large bags. Other more fortunate ones flew on private jets with all the space and comfort needed, always in their custom-made box, silk on the inside and a sort of transparent window on the right side of the box. The way to Los Angeles was wonderful. Fay's mother's friend agreed to take her along on her private Gulfstream G4 plane. She was travelling alone with her niece and nephew, who were going to summer camp just outside LA. So she happily invited Fay to fly back to California with them.

Fay always thought that seeing the shoes in the box was of paramount importance. Otherwise, how else could one figure out which shoe was where? Thus she used the custom-made boxes with windows.

The old lady Fay was traveling with, Countess de Montfleurie, was also a shoe lover. Not only did she make her maid pack each pair of her shoes carefully, she demanded they be taken out and aligned in the open space, as she was persuaded that shoes might absorb negative energy while being left alone in the dark. She did not want them to transform any harsh energy onto her feet.

The countess considered her shoes her children; she never had a child of her own or a pet. Her clothes were all she had, and they were always there for her—to comfort her on the tough days and make her look glamorous on happy days.

The staff of the airplane was by now used to such unusual requirements. They had grown accustomed to certain old ladies and men that have all the money in the world but lack family and people to love.

To cater to their young clients, such as the niece and nephew, the company had developed a special menu, including peanut-butter-and-jelly sandwiches, chicken fingers, and ice-cream sundaes.

Ellie could not help but watch the black trousers of the boy in his early teens. His slacks were slightly too long, and his shoes were too big.

'My goodness, are you guys fine there? You must feel so flabby with those small feet!' Ellie asked the shoes.

'Eleanora, we heard about you and you sister, the princesses Eleanora and Bernice! You two are the luckiest to have been purchased by such a shoe lover!' exclaimed the right shoe under the long pants that covered half of his face.

'We are on the same plane aren't we? So I suppose you should consider yourself lucky as well,' Ellie said proudly.

'Perhaps we are on the same plane, but, trust me, walking around with kids in the mud and dirt is not comparable to your luxury tea parties on the silk Persian carpet,' one of the boy's shoes said with slight envy.

'Well, you are a man, so I suppose, just like some human men have to attend the army by law, the same goes for you, my friends. It will teach you how to be a better, more disciplined, and trained shoe!' Bernie said. 'It's such a turn-off for a man to run away from his manly responsibilities. How will you ever be able to take care of your girlfriend, or wife, for that matter, if you have never stepped into the mud, run on rocky mountains, and slipped on wet bananas?' Bernie demanded, as if she was truly worried for such unmanly male shoes.

'Experience, my friend, is the right path, so enough of the nagging.' Ellie smiled in her very motherly way.

The two shoes were now silent. They hadn't expected such classy, quiet little lady shoes to come back at them with such strong arguments.

'I guess you are right,' the left shoe murmured.

'Did you meet our Korean slippers?' asked the left male shoe.

'They are permanent residents of this plane, and whenever ladies' feet hurt they choose to cuddle in the slippers. Moreover, they know about absolutely everything that's happening around the world. They travel all over the globe and meet thousands of people. And they hear all the latest gossip the stewardesses pick up on while going out and about at this plane's most peculiar destinations.' He pointed at the two slippers relaxing by the exit door.

'Hi, everyone,' said one of the slippers. 'I'm Bong-Chol, and this is my sister, Ja-Hoon. Welcome onboard!' They both sniggered.

'Nice to meet you, Bong-Chol and Ja-Hoon. I'm Bernie,' said Bernie

'I'm Ellie. Pleased to meet you,' said Ellie.

'Oh, let's put aside all the politeness. We are all brothers and sisters. Hallelujah to the shoe society, and I wonder what the human race would do without us,' proudly said Bong-Chol.

'Indeed!' They all laughed in satisfaction.

'So how are things back in Korea?' Bernie asked.

'As far as we are concerned, it is simply perfect!' Bong-Chol said.

'Oh, tell them, tell them. They won't believe it!' pushed Ja-Hoon.

'The city government of Seoul started to paint four thousand nine-hundred and twenty-nine public and private parking places pink throughout the city, with thousands more slated to go under the brush next year. The pink parking spots, reserved for women drivers so they don't have to walk so far to work or the mall, are part of the South Korean capital's Women Friendly Seoul Project. It's an effort for the notoriously macho Asian city of more than ten million to transform itself into a safer, more heel-friendly space for women.' Ja-Hoon stated.

'Isn't it extremely thoughtful of the Korean government? I mean, now our fellow shoes will have a longer life expectancy. They will walk less and look younger, for that matter. A shoe paradise, I would call it,' Bong-Chol said.

'Wow.' Ellie and Bernie considered moving to Korea for a minute, but then realized that out of all the existing shoes they were probably living the most luxurious life, where they flew private jets, had special sympathy and love of their mistress, and special occasional pampering and treatments. A pink parking spot wouldn't change their lives much anyways.

'What's the crying I hear?' demanded Ja-Hoon.

'Oh, never mind. It's coming from that pink bag.' Bernie pointed to the back of the plane.

'You see, Isabelle is still upset about being a shoe, and her best friend Daisy, who happens to be the second of the pair with her, is probably at the verge of breaking her own heel to survive her friend's constant nagging,' Bernie said. She was still annoyed about Isabelle's immature attitude towards her life as a shoe.

'You see, they were initially real human girls who cared so much about shoes and gave them such a big role in their lives that one day they became shoes. And they don't have a clue how that might have happened,' Ellie clarified.

The Korean sisters looked at each other with not a single blink of surprise.

'We've had many cases such as that in our plane, mostly spoilt people bored with their life who one day became the material object they had placed higher than their heads,' Bong-Chol said.

'What do you mean, 'higher than their heads'?' asked Ellie and Bernie at once.

'She means they become the objects to which they have given lots of importance. Another way to say it is that they have placed the objects so high and have given such importance to them that they see the object as even higher than themselves,' Ja-Hoon clarified.

'For example, in developing countries people are even becoming alimentation, as in bread and water. Some become stones as they give such importance to houses and apartments that they are prepared to give their lives to them,' Bong-Chol explained.

'In developed countries, on the other hand, people tend to become money or gold, and Birkin handbags, shoes like your fellows in the pink bag, cars, and even credit cards!' Ja-Hoon added in amazement.

'That is very intriguing! I mean, why would anyone want to be a credit card?' Ellie wondered.

'They don't realize it. They don't actually tell themselves, "I want to be a credit card." It's just that they care so much about their credit cards that they are ready to starve and not sleep and sacrifice so much in order to keep that Black American Express. They feel that the card is associated with them and that without the card they are nothing, so they unconsciously make the card more important than their human selves. They become nothing more than a slave that with time incorporates into the object."

'And is there a way back?' asked Ellie.

'Unfortunately for them, we have never heard of a way back into the human body, and we know about current affairs. Every day people are said to be lost, and their relatives think they were kidnapped or even killed, when in reality they are often still in their homes as their favourite objects.'

Ja-Hoon and Bong-Chol were now exhausted; all this talking made them sleepy, so they fell asleep on their shelves along with the other shoes and slippers.

Ellie and Bernie were left to think while Daisy slept and Isabelle feared now for her future.

The flight was so comfortable that the shoes didn't want to leave the premises of the jet. They said their warm good-byes to Ja-Hoon and Bong-Chol. Before they knew it they were out in LAX airport, where a driver in a black Cadillac was waiting for the countess and another driver was waiting for Fay.

* * *

LA: Out and About

The day went at a very fast speed. The twins were this time left to rest at the Sunset Hotel deluxe room, while Daisy and Isabelle had their first real night out as shoes.

The walls of the club pounded with the boisterous dance music. The crowd wove in and out between the bars and the dance floor. They were a team. Even Isabelle was obliged to obey the direction in which Fay's feet were moving.

For the first time, she truly felt like a shoe, and every piece of dust and dirt that from time to time stuck her face was the worst feeling she could have ever felt. Her head was going around with the amount of feet and shoes she encountered, and most surprisingly all those people seemed like total giants with extremely long legs.

'It's utterly disgusting, all those girls who think that it's sexy not to wear underwear!' Isabelle exclaimed.

'Isn't it kind of cool that we get to go clubbing even as shoes? I mean, this is totally the sort of place you and I would hang out in. Check out all those guys. They are so hot!' Daisy laughed.

'Why don't you check out their shoes instead? Since you feel so good being a shoe, you might consider liking male shoes as well,' Isabelle sneered.

'I am just trying to live the present moment and make us a team. I can't believe you have so much anger inside,' snapped Daisy.

Before they had time to finish their argument, they were lifted up and hung in the air for a few moments.

'What is happening? Did Jesus come to save us?' Isabelle exclaimed.

Daisy peeked through the feet and the legs to see a male silhouette holding Fay up high.

'Who's this guy?' the shoes wondered.

'Adam! I didn't know you'd be here!' Fay said, laughing out of nervousness. It had been a while since she had seen him, and it was a pleasant surprise to bump into him.

'I'm just here for a few days to see my family, then it's back to New York,' he said shyly.

'She's so obvious. I mean, hello-o, don't show the guy that you're so into him,' Isabelle said, full of sarcasm.

'Wait a second. Wasn't that Adam the Bull?' Daisy asked.

'You mean, as in Adam my ex?' Isabelle said.

'Yeah, I mean Adam the Bull, the guy you were obsessing about. And then you dumped him for Julio. Or was it Ted?' asked Daisy.

Hip-hop songs were jolly, and all the shoes around were having a blast while Daisy and Isabelle suddenly realized they knew this mysterious, gigantic man.

'Julio. Ted was three months after that,' Isabelle said. 'So basically, the girl who owns me is into Adam? If she only knew what a loser he is, she would change her mind,' said Isabelle, smirking.

'He never seemed like a loser to me. Just because he doesn't talk too much doesn't mean he's empty. It's actually pretty mysterious and sexy,' Daisy said.

'No way, you like him? You had a crush on him all these years?' demanded Isabelle. The tip of her toe approached Daisy in a mischievous way.

'Not at all. I just like to observe people and have my own opinion on each one of them. Is that a crime?' Daisy asked innocently.

'No, of course not. But liking your best friend's ex is not a cool sisterhood thing to do. That's all I'm saying,' said Isabelle.

'You know exactly whom I liked and when and whom I went out with, so please take it easy with your accusations,' declared Daisy.

'Did you see that? Who the hell does she think she is!' shouted Isabelle suddenly.

A grey suede platform with metallic snakeskin signed Nickolas Kirkwood had just meanly stepped on Isabelle's shoe tip.

'I'm Ella. And who are you, poor, old thing?' said the shoe sarcastically as she turned her heels and was about to march. But then her mistress took her and her sister off and threw them across the room, shouting, 'Sure, I'll take off my shoes! I haaaaa! I wanna party like a maniac!' The woman was barely able to stand on her feet. The Bozzis caught just a glimpse of Ella's face as she smashed on the wall, and that was a scene to remember forever.

'You see, justice exists!' said Daisy excitedly.

'Did you see her face? I cannot believe shoes can be such...' She paused to listen to Adam and Fay, who seemed to have gotten closer as their feet have approached.

'Whatever. Let's concentrate on what's going on here. It's quite fun here for once!' Isabelle exclaimed.

'I'm sorry for that time,' Adam mumbled above them.

'I already forgot. Don't worry,' Fay said with a piercing look that said it all—she hadn't forgotten a tiny little detail.

'Anyways, I have to go to this party in Hollywood hills. I'll see you some other time,' said Fay coldly and rushed to the door.

Out of breath, Daisy and Isabelle tried to understand what had just happened, but it was way too complex for them at this point.

In the car Fay seemed sad. But she lit a cigarette and took what seemed like the longest puff of enormous pleasure that brought back a smile to her beautiful face. The two shoes felt even more confused.

'Did you see that? She smoked it like it was some happiness elixir,' Isabelle noted.

'Indeed, I just realized how much I miss being human. We could drink and eat and smoke and talk and be heard. Look at us. We don't even have hunger. I can't even remember how it felt to eat the Four Seasons mini burgers! They were my favourite, and now I cannot even picture it in my mind! Isn't that crazy?' Daisy exclaimed.

'Welcome to shoe land!' Isabelle said, smirking.

'But, in fact, I bet it would have disturbed me when I was a human if I knew that my shoes fantasized about having a burger!' Daisy laughed.

'If I could clap right now, I would, you know. It's amazing how you can entertain yourself all alone with your own declarations and change your views and make them funny for yourself! It's tragic. Our situation is totally tragic!' Isabelle cried.

'That's exactly why, my dear, we should at least try to cheer ourselves up. Why be mature at this point? No one cares if shoes are mature in a nightclub, so let's go live to the maximum. Just don't think about it,' Daisy urged her.

As Fay walked into her room, Isabelle and Daisy were happy to see Ellie and Bernie, who were patiently waiting for their return.

'How was it, girls? We'd expected you to stay out longer. Did you hurt her feet?' asked Ellie.

'Not at all,' they said.

'This Adam guy appeared, who is actually my ex. But interestingly enough, he's kind of into Fay, although she seemed pissed at him,' Isabelle said.

Bernie was very proud to hear the news. 'I never liked him. I'm glad she didn't lose control this time!'

'Lose control to Adam the Bull?' Daisy asked.

'Why do you call him "Adam the Bull"?' asked Ellie.

'Because he is extremely stubborn and shy! He seems arrogant, but in reality, deep inside is a really shy baby bull,' Daisy said.

'Whatever happened, he probably freaked out,' Isabelle said. 'It's typical for Adam, and tonight he really seemed to regret his behaviour.'

'Regret,' said Bernie with a smirk.

'He'd better mature if he wants our princess,' Ellie added.

The shoes sat closely at the shoe bench and watched the beautiful view of Los Angeles. They had become close in the past months, and they enjoyed common shoe gossips. Isabelle told Bernie and Ellie about Ella, and they all laughed at the accident of the mean suede platform.

It was almost morning, and the shoes were enjoying their chat as they fell asleep without even realizing it.

* * *

The Shoe Makeover

Los Angeles was known as the place for beautiful people and their beautiful shoes.

The shoes were all aligned in front of the television watching a show about Hollywood stars and their cosmetic surgeries. All the stars seemed to be gorgeous after the miraculous doctor had worked on their imperfections.

'Did you see that?' exclaimed Ellie. 'The before and after barely look like the same person.' She giggled.

LA was one of the best places to go for cosmetic surgery. The city was full of so many options, but Los Angeles had a very high cost of living, so most people living in Los Angeles had money. Most people with money felt they could afford certain benefits, including cosmetic surgery. Cosmetic surgery could include breast augmentation, face-lifts, or body shaping, and people wanted to spend their money on the best surgeon they can find to do the job.

Thus, Los Angeles, with its many fine people, would have only the best surgeons to work on their bodies to make them worthy of the camera. Los Angeles cosmetic surgery offered the best equipment, the best qualifications, and most of the procedures for the masses to make money and to help others stay beautiful. Indeed, everything could be improved, not only faces and bodies, but also shoes!

'Lady shoes of our status must attend to fashion. To allow oneself to become outmoded, behind the times, is to become irrelevant. When people cease to be intrigued by a shoe's appearance, they sense a tacit permission to ignore her walk, words, and ideas,' said Bernie.

'Moreover, while ladies can talk and everyone can hear them, we are only heard by our own kind. For humankind, we are beautiful objects, and only our appearance and popularity rank within the fashion industry count,' Ellie added.

'It is hard to be a female shoe. Men's shoes may last decades, and no one dares to say a negative word about them. But we must look our best and be in shape in all times. We must also be in fashion—a very slippery business, very easy to fall out of,' Bernie added.

'So what do you propose?' demanded Isabelle.

'I heard Fay mention she is taking us to the shoe spa,' replied Bernie.

'A little lift on my skin and some hydrating cream wouldn't do anything but good to Ellie and me.' She checked her leather.

'I want to go as well!' Daisy said excitedly.

'I hope she'll bring you as well,' said Ellie.

They heard a sudden sound of walking bare feet. The two pairs were up, and before they knew it, the four Bozzis were placed in a Barneys bag and on their way to the shoe spa. Squashed Isabelle was laughing nervously. 'Stop tickling me for the shoe world's sake! Stop iiiiit!' she screamed.

The shoes laughed at Isabelle, who was for once genuinely laughing. Ellie, Bernie, and Daisy hugged her, but she pushed them away. 'Get away from me. I don't need your shoe hugs!' And she closed down her eyes and zoned out.

Ellie, Bernie, and Daisy were used to Isabelle's bad temper and left her in peace. They were too excited for the spa to quarrel with her.

They arrived at 10 West 55th Street (between 5th Ave & Avenue of the Americas). The cobbler/shoe spa was wonderful.

A few hours later, the Bozzis looked immaculate. Spanking new, as the saleswoman called them. Their muscles were relaxed, their leather was smoothed, and their soles were newly painted. They felt wonderful.

'Love it. Feel like a queen,' said Ellie.

'You are. You are Bozzi and one of a kind,' Bernie reminded her.

Daisy enjoyed her first experience in a shoe spa, though it was different from human salons. This one smelled bad with a lot of plastic and paint. There were no pleasing aromas like the spa in Bali she went to a few years ago. Suddenly she missed her parents. She felt anxiety, but she had learned to work on herself and change her thoughts.

Isabelle hated other people touching her, even when she was a human. She despised the shoe polisher, but she kept calm as no one was there to help her out. She still refused to accept her shoe reality, and she found it comforting that Daisy was there to listen to her nags.

Fay seemed particularly happy at the dinner invitation she had received from Adam. She wanted everything to look flawless, including her shoes, of course.

Fay was glowing after the shoe spa and her own time at Frederic Fekkai salon. Ten new outfits later she was heading to Cecconi's wearing her favourites, Ellie and Bernie, with a pair of leather pants, a black silk top, and a pair of gold bangles on her ears.

'Can you believe it?' whispered Daisy.

'Yes! He called her thirty-seven times. I saw it on the phone screen myself!' Ellie happily announced.

'He said he wants one more chance and that it means "the world to him" that she comes,' Ellie said.

'I don't trust this boy,' said Bernie.

'He's a loser,' said Isabelle, who had begun to feel possessive of her ex.

'I'm very excited for her,' Daisy said happily.

Before they had time to finish their conversation, Ellie and Bernie's bodies started to tickle. Fay's feet were sliding in; she was nervous and they could feel it.

They stomped down the lobby, and there he was in his Berluttis, just like the first time.

Bernie curiously watched them, and Ellie checked Adam's expression, which she thought was like a little boy who had just gotten his cake.

Adam took Fay's hand and kissed it. The gesture was straight out of a fairy tale, especially coming from Adam, who had been so uptight and cold in the past. It was almost hard to believe.

In the meantime, his shoes, Biggie and Biggie-Mo, were mesmerized by the beauty of the Bozzi sisters.

'So you can talk now,' said Ellie flirtatiously.

'Indeed, we can. We always could. We're just not that social during huge events,' replied Biggie-Mo.

His fine, dark-brown colour and handmade Italian shoe body was close to perfection. Ellie and Biggie-Mo had an attraction towards each other since that first day they met. But being obedient shoes, they placed their mistress and master first before their own flirtation.

Bernie also chatted with Biggie, who seemed like a decent shoe to have a proper conversation with. She enjoyed the company of fine-looking male shoes. All these women and their gossips were tiring smart Bernie, who wanted newness in her shoe life.

The shoes approached each other just as they realized that Adam was officially asking Fay out. 'I love you, Fay. I always have. I was just scared of my own feelings. But you never hated me for it. Please forgive me for the way I was,' he said.

She looked into his eyes and kissed him.

Biggie-Mo and Biggie were dancing with Bernie as they realized Ellie was high up in the air. Indeed, Fay had watched too many movies and wanted to imitate the old-fashioned first kiss with the lifted foot.

The evening went by beautifully, and Adam invited Fay to a reception held at his grandfather's house the next day. Fay didn't expect Adam to introduce her to his family so fast, yet she was pleased to see him acting like a true, mature gentleman.

Chapter 13
A Dream Coming True

The Countess, who was a rather cold lady, decided to show amity to the young Fay, whose company she had enjoyed on the plane. She called Fay up to invite her to one of her old friend's dinner parties up in Bel Air, but she found out that Fay was already going with her new boyfriend. The Countess was happily surprised that Fay was invited to such 'a hard to get in' Hollywood's most desirable receptions.

For the occasion, Fay put on her wonderful Bozzis, Ellie and Bernie. She also brought Isabelle and Daisy, just in case she felt the need to change shoes which was almost never. However she didn't want to drive all the way back to her hotel to change shoes.

It was a joyful day for Fay. Barry White's "Just Another Way to Say I Love You" played in the background, and the vivacious colours chosen by the family-event organizer delighted the eyes of the numerous guests. Fabulous cherry blossoms with purple daisies perfectly matched the satin table cover, the pastel cherry blossoms, and the pale-coloured ivory oval shaped plates.

The classic Mediterranean villa was originally designed by Paul Williams in 1931 and completely rebuilt in 2005. Located behind iron gates in the most prime section of Bel Air, it was hidden from public view behind massive greenery.

Incredible craftsmanship, quality, and authentic details adorned this pristine property. Beautiful public rooms opened to an incredible courtyard with a fountain and an outdoor fireplace. Two motor courts provided off-street parking for more than forty cars. There were also an amazing 35 mm theatre, a library, and a game room for billiards.

Spectacular grounds, formal gardens, manicured lawns, amazing pool, tennis court, and guesthouse: it seemed too big for an old man living on his own.

'*It must have been super fun to growing up here*', Ellie thought.
'This place is sprawling!' exclaimed Bernie.

As the twins marched in, they loved the warm and light atmosphere of the reception. Isabelle and Daisy were left at the cloakroom. Still jet-lagged from the trip, they were both deeply asleep.

The women were plentiful and different: tall, short, blonde, brunette, American, Latino, Asian, European, African, Russian, and Arab.

Princess Noor of Saudi Arabia walked about in some very high, and very hot, black Louboutin pumps. Their soles were shining, they haven't been touched by the rough outside streets. All they knew were the car interior and the inside of the enormous Bel-Air mansions

By the Bellini Bar that was specially brought in from Ciprianni a typical blonde LA private school girl danced about in sexy, skimpy, ankle-strap sandals.

Adam's mother, a very elegant lady with striking brown eyes went open-toe velvet, while Marlon's personal assistant looked graceful in stunning, silvery sandals.

Some elegant-looking young woman showed off the wild red-patent platforms that matched her wild, feather-layered dress.

A girl next to her, perhaps her daughter, looked sophisticated in cute, open-toed pumps.

A tall, blonde Victoria's Secret model was in classic retro and as shiny as one could possibly be.

Next to her was a Hispanic lady in stunning two-tone pumps with gold cap-toes.

A Russian wife of an oligarch was looking sexy and elegant in bright emerald, pointy-toed pumps with cut-outs.

A lively yellow, over-the-shoulder dress with a lovely pair of peep-toed pumps walked by, though her head was held too high up, hence the twins couldn't recognize her. Wherever they looked they saw massive vases full of cherry blossom flowers.

A typical Bel Air neighbour stepped in with her younger-looking husband holding her right arm as though he were another accessory, as if to ease her entry or the weight of her 10 Karat Harry Winston princess cut pink diamond ring. She looked lovely and elegant in miles of lavender layers and shiny high heels. Nevertheless

Ellie and Bernie were blinded by the strong glow of her ring. 'Definitely D-Flawless' Ellie whispered.

Bernie looked at the woman's left hand which was holding the Hermes Diamond Crocodile Birkin. It is what Maybach is to cars, Schloss Neuschwanstein is to castles, Monaco is to luxurious night-life, and Bozzi shoes to women!

Bernie looked closer at the Birkin and said 'Did you see the Birkin lock? It has at least 14 carats of pave diamonds on it'.

Bernie turned away rebelliously as if opposing to such over the top luxury spending.

However these Birkins were everywhere, on her left a woman in her fifties with an outstanding toned body walked by with a thirty-five centimeter matte poro croc Birkin in blue brighton without diamond hardware but with a gorgeously manicured fingers holding it tightly.

A tall blonde in Barbie pink Louboutins approached Ellie and Bernie, and while Fay and the blonde were exchanging social small talk, the Louboutins showed themselves to be young, well-mannered, slightly spoilt, but fine girl shoes.

'Sweet colour!' Ellie and Bernie complimented the Louboutins.

'Thank you! We are the Barbie edition this year.' They smiled at each other.

'Haven't you heard? Our master Christian Louboutin was commissioned to design three new Barbies to celebrate her fiftieth anniversary. Well, Master Louboutin decided to slim down Barbie and give her thinner legs, much to the chagrin of her fans. In addition to designing the dolls, he produced a hot-pink, human-sized Barbie shoe, which happens to be us.'

'Nice.' Ellie and Bernie both smiled and thought about just how much more the younger generation talked.

'Why do you think she had the need to tell us her life story?' Ellie asked as Fay walked away. 'We hadn't even asked.'

'Young ones are like that. They feel the need just to say everything about themselves. They think it makes them look more interesting for some reason. We were probably the same,' Bernie said, saddened by the realization that they were far from young.

Adam appeared from the back. He grabbed Fay's hand and took her with him towards the library room, where a very tall, older-looking man stood. 'Grandfather, Fay, my girlfriend!' he exclaimed.

The old man stared at her shoes. Then he slowly moved his head up and looked at her in amazement.

'Pleasure to meet you, Sir,' she said.

Ellie and Bernie felt his piercing eyes, and their heels started shaking. They recognized his familiar air, it was simply older and warmer. He now seemed like a nice old man, and he could be their Godfather, they thought.

The old man unhurriedly searched his pockets, took out his very stylish Tom Ford reading glasses and lowered his head to look closer at Ellie and Bernie. The twins dutifully stood still. His eyes starred in disbelief, and it were hard to understand whether he were furious or happily excited or simply confused.

'Where did you find them?' he asked gently, still examining the shoes. 'Your shoes, they are Balthazar Bozzis, if I'm not mistaken.' He gazed at the shoes again.

'Wow, Grandpa. I never knew you were a specialist in women's shoes,' Adam said in surprise.

Fay peacefully said 'My mother bought them in a vintage store.' 'They are one-of-a-kind, special order, handmade for some very important actress. That's as much as I know.' She smiled shyly.

Adam's grandfather's face transformed, his eyes sparkled with astonishing reminiscence, he silently whispered to Fay.

'They belonged to my good friend, Crystal, a Hollywood legend. And I know them since I was the one who placed the order,' recalled Adam's Grandfather.

'That is just phenomenal Grandpa! I am totally amazed this is a total bombshell' thrillingly said Adam.

'But I thought…I mean…' The old man winked his right eye as Fay understood. 'Wow, I am speechless. It's such a coincidence,' she said. This revelation was staggering, she realized that he was the very man who purchased Ellie and Bernie for the famous actress, Crystal Baron, and he was the grandfather of the guy she had a crush on for the past year. This was beyond ironic and bizarrely hilarious.

Adam stood stunned. 'Well, that wasn't the kind of introduction I was expecting, but I can't say that I don't like it!' He held Fay's hand more firmly.

To everyone's surprise, Mr Wesley hugged Fay and knelt down to take a closer look at the little Bozzis.

'Can you believe it, Ellie?' said Bernie. She couldn't believe it—the man she had hated for breaking Crystal's heart was right here and coming closer to them. And out of all people, Adam was his grandson.

'I'm totally amazed! He looks like a good old man. I even think he's nice,' Ellie said as her sister watched Marlon Wesley. Indeed, he had aged a lot since they last saw him. 'I guess age makes some people nicer,' Bernie admitted amazed of the revelation of Marlon Wesley and still confused how it all came to be the way it did.

The twins continued enjoying the attention they were receiving. All the other shoes could be heard buzzing and mumbling about the Bozzis, shoe gossip fly faster than a Peregrine-Falcon which is the world's fastest bird. In fact it is the fastest animal on the planet, when in its hunting dive, the stoop, in which it soars to a great height, then dives steeply at speeds of over 200 mph. Nevertheless our fellow shoes manage spread shoe highlight news much faster.

They obediently looked up to see Adam standing close and protectively by Fay who was suddenly the center of the attention of the whole reception.

'Fay is studying acting in New York. Isn't she wonderful?' Adam said, smiling and holding her by her waist.

'She is, indeed, and so are her shoes,' the old man said, smiling. 'I don't know if Adam told you, but I am currently working on my last movie about Crystal and her lucky Bozzis.' He beamed.

'Would you like me to give you the shoes? I have another pair. It would be an honour to have them in a movie, really,' said Fay.

Marlon Wesley old yet still a true charmer, placed his glasses back into his Loro Piana baby Cashmere light beige blazer took a sip of his favourite white dessert wine Chateau d'Yquem 1995.

'I just got a rather marvellous idea,' Marlon Wesley said. 'I am thinking that you could actually play Crystal's role. I mean, you do have the same shoe size, and you are slim just like she was. Everything else, makeup designers and hairdressers can pull off. Would you be interested, dear?' he asked in a very fatherly tone of voice that would make anyone at ease.

'I…I don't know what to say. It's the most important and greatest proposition of my life! I would love to! Oh, thank you so very much!' she said with so much happiness running through her veins that she wanted to cry out of all the thrill and joy that she had experienced and is still experiencing since a the past half hour or perhaps forty-five minutes, she had lost count of time.

'It's a great debut into the movie business too,' Adam added.

'Now you youngsters go and celebrate. And, Adam, make sure her feet are safe,' his grandfather teased placing his empty glass on one of the silver trays that were carried by the garcons caterers.

'I will,' Adam assured him, smiling.

The two lovers walked through the crowd, Ellie and Bernie striding right out.

'Hey Bozzis, come here, I wanna invite you for a dance' cried out a Da Vinci edition Berluti.

'And you'd think Berluti company who has been around since 1895 would have the best education and manners a shoe could wish for' supposed Bernie.

'They were created from a drawing of Leonardo Da Vinci a special edition pair of shoes and this is the way they behave like street shoes.' admitted Ellie 'did you see how he called us like we were some plastic dumb shoes' Ellie whispered.

The twins ignoring such pushy invitations to dance, were looking right up at Fay and Adam who seemed very at peace and happy like never before.

'Can you believe it? Did you see what just happened, or was it a dream?' she exclaimed to Adam, finding it hard to hide her bliss. Fay's exhilaration was beyond delight. Her heart was now pumping so strongly that it could jump out on that beautifully decorated dessert buffet table and land on the gloriously placed mille-feuille. She looked at Adam.

'You are one of a kind!' Adam said and then hugged and kissed her.

Ellie and Bernie, speechless, were now bumped into Adam's shoes. 'Hi,' whispered Biggie-Mo.

'Hey!' Ellie blushed, she was feeling her heel shiver nervously once again.

'Don't be shy. I'm not going to eat you. I just want to hug you,' said Biggie-Mo, smiling.

At these words, Ellie just gave in and let him embrace her. It lasted only a minute, perhaps two, but feeling his dark purple patent leather on her cheeks was worth every microsecond of it. She was peaceful and didn't want to be anywhere but right at that very spot.

'How was it?' Bernie's voice interrupted the feeling of paradise.

'What?' Ellie asked.

'How was the romance there? I was next to you all that time, you know. But you were on some other planet.' Bernie giggled.

Biggie and Bernie enjoyed watching their brother and sister fall instantly in love, or at least that's what they made it look like.

'In French it's called *coup de foudre*,' said Biggie.

Bernie added, Or *l'amour à premiere vue.*

'It was like you want it to last forever,' Ellie said, still in a daze.

'Wow, if I knew a hug could make someone this happy, I would totally hug all shoes that hit on me while we walk around.' Bernie laughed.

'You have to love the shoe as well; it's not that simple,' Ellie explained as they moved towards the dessert table.

'Love comes with time. If you keep on hugging a Havaianas for a year, you will get very attached. And suddenly you will declare that you cannot live without it and you are in love.' Bernie smirked.

'Didn't that happen to Lucy's silver sandals?' asked Ellie.

'Yes, exactly,' confirmed Bernie.

'They were just desperate. And could use the word *love* for *toilet paper*, I'm telling you,' snapped Ellie.

Adam went to see his mom, so Fay wandered around the reception, sipping on champagne and smiling. She couldn't believe her most impossible dream—playing in an A-list movie—was about to be true. She had a hard time believing it. It seemed like a fiction story, a movie, and an urban legend! She was living it, and it was the happiest, most fulfilling feeling ever.

As she continued thinking, everything suddenly seemed to fit. She was in LA in this gorgeous mansion with her boyfriend Adam, who happened to be the grandson of the very man who had about twenty years earlier made a special order to Balthazar Bozzi to order her little shoes.

She sat on the pistachio-coloured, sleek, satin lounger and observed Ellie and Bernie.

'You two are my luckiest shoes. I don't know what it is about you two, but I simply love you. I love you as though you were alive!' She gently wiped them with soft napkin that lay by the desserts.

'She's feeling us!' Bernie couldn't help but drop a few emotional tears.

'She is our angel.' Ellie hugged Bernie.

'Bernie, I think we are a great team, you and me, even though we think differently on certain aspects. We have lots of respect towards each other, and that is a great achievement,' Ellie declared.

While Ellie, Bernie, and Fay were having a moment of appreciation, a girl woke in the cloakroom floor downstairs. She hadn't a clue where she was or what she was doing on a pale pink floor; her first sight was a worn pair of what looked like Bozzi brown pumps.

She looked at the antique, gold-wood, carved mirror and screamed, 'Oh my!' Thankfully, no one heard, as the music was fairly loud and the noise from the numerous guests drowned out the sound of her.

She stood up at a snail's pace, fearing to stretch out her body in case she broke. She moved her arms bit by bit, then lifted her body, and finally stood on her feet. It was the most incredible feeling, like she had been born again. Daisy was a girl again. She didn't know what to do, to think, to say. All she knew was that she had to leave the cloakroom. She realized that she was wearing the J brands and the T-shirt and leather jacket, the same clothes she was wearing the day she and Isabelle entered the vintage store in Gramercy.

Life seemed so real, so good. She couldn't help but scream. She grabbed the shoe that was her dear friend Isabelle, still a shoe, and ran down the stairs.

She spotted Fay, but Fay just looked at the barefoot girl in blank surprise.

Daisy realized just how unreal her situation would seem to anyone in a normal state of mind, so she decided to leave the house. She didn't have a clue where she was rushing until she found her way to the main exit.

She screamed, 'Freedom!' and ran as fast as she could.

The security people of the Wesley home were somewhat confused and wondered if the old man who seemed so polite had been hiding the girl in the basement. Or was it some entertainment play that was held for the guests?

Daisy ran, not feeling her bare feet, only feeling the fresh spring breeze, the newly cut grass, and the sun. It was all real, and she was real. She was smiling, stretching her cheeks to the maximum, not caring about wrinkling her face, not caring about anything but being here and being alive.

She had finally realized what a great feeling it was to live to be alive and to run barefoot in Bel Air! Holding Isabelle firmly in her right hand, she stopped next to a magnificently tall palm tree and hugged it with all her might.

'Daisy! I cannot believe it! Why are you back and not me?' Isabelle was furious. She screamed her shoe voice out, but Daisy couldn't hear her.

At that very spot, Daisy made a promise to herself. She would never let go of what was left of her friend Isabelle, who had not been fortunate enough to wake up human. Daisy felt that there was still a chance, and she knew she would do whatever she could to ensure a happy life for Isabelle. She would take the shoe everywhere with her and never let her alone.

Isabelle was now even more depressed. She hated her situation and couldn't help but loathe Daisy for returning to her human body. Daisy had almost become accustomed to the whole shoe society and could have well stayed a shoe without much regret, Isabelle thought.

However, reality was different, and it seemed the incredible miracle had happened to Daisy because she had matured, changed her values, and most importantly become grateful for her life, even as a shoe.

Isabelle could not swallow her pride, and her anger took her over. She preferred to sleep as much as she could in order not to think.

Daisy continued to run until she was out of breath. She was dressed the same way she had been in the vintage store. She checked her pockets and was happily surprised to find her credit card in her right pocket. Everyone had always told her she would lose her card one day if she continued to put it there, but who could have ever known that a situation such this would present itself?

She hailed a cab, something almost impossible in Bel Air, as most people in the area had drivers or drove themselves, but it was a lucky day. A Beverly Hills blue and white taxi stopped at her feet. She ordered him to make a stop at Barneys, where she hurriedly got a pair of sandals. She then rushed back to the taxi and went straight to the airport. She purchased a ticket from Virgin America, direct to New York.

A few hours and three movies later, Daisy was finally back home. She realized that she had a deep fear of sleeping and was terrified of waking up as a shoe once again. But at some point her body couldn't handle being awake any longer, and she fell asleep on her couch while her house phone rang nonstop. The next morning she had to call her parents and friends and create stories and explanations for why she had been away for more than a month.

She decided a month of meditation in Tibet sounded the most appropriate. She told people, 'I had to get away from the New York buzz and get some real spiritual support.'

It sounded funny, but she had been meditating—maybe not in Tibet, but as someone's shoe she did lots of thinking about her life and resolving the conflicts within herself.

'Where were you? We missed you!' Her friends left voice messages.

She listened to them all. Then she placed Daisy on the window so she could enjoy the New York view and began to clean up her apartment. It was therapeutic and helped her to get her mind straight. She wrote a few emails to her family members, went down to Dean Deluca to buy some groceries had her coffee which tasted better than ever, and had long showers and rested in her comfortable bed that she had shipped from Europe, it was a Swedish brand that made the most comfortable beds at least for her taste. Surely a Hastens bed was better than the shoe box she got used to sleeping in since a few months.

As the days went by, she decided to start a charity action called "Shoes for Shoeless." Her friends loved the idea, and she began organizing her first event, where Isabelle would be the centrepiece. Daisy felt she had to lift herself to higher matters than her past life. She decided she would make a revolution for the shopaholic jet-setter people that surrounded her. She began with Facebook. She created a small group that ended up becoming almost nine hundred people.

She smiled to Isabelle and said, 'You'll see, my dear friend. You too will wake up being yourself. I believe it. Just try to be happy and find peace within yourself as a shoe. You will also, when you least expect it, wake up yourself!' She kissed the shoe and hugged it.

Isabelle watched her friend, and for the first time she had realized that she had to start working with her inner self that all this time she had been running away from reality instead of accepting it. Now for the first time, she tried to enjoy being a shoe, she focused on her gorgeously sleek shoe body and all the positive attention she gets from all the shoes around her. She began appreciating the little joys of being a shoe. Of course at first it was hard but slowly she begun to feel happier and slowly she felt she would achieve the ultimate contentment whether it will be in a human female body or a female shoe body.

* * *

LA: The Dream

Back in LA, Fay was living a fabulous life.

What can be greater than love? Fay, Adam, Biggie and Biggie-Mo, and Ellie and Bernie were now cruising in Malibu. LA was a dream world. The sun was shining, palms were everywhere, and stylish people in those Hollywood shirts and Ray-Bans walked the streets. Adam drove smoothly, while Fay let her hair free and danced to Empire of the Sun's "Walking on a Dream," which was perfect for her feelings.

'So, where are we going, Ellie?' Bernie asked.

'Don't question, Bernie. Fay will play in that movie, and then, who knows? We might be famous again!' Ellie exclaimed.

'What about Fay? I am really attached to her. What if we lose her just as we lost Crystal?' she asked.

'Bernie, stop right there. You are in LA! The dreamland! And everything is well. It can't be better, so just enjoy it, and as long as we are together, everything will be great!' Ellie assured her.

'Yes, you are right. It's just too good, and naturally I get scared that it may be jinxed.'

'Oh, trust me, we are not alone. Fay and Adam really seem like they are hitting it off, so we'll be a happy family, the family we never had.'

Ellie never thought of it before, but indeed, after Balthazar had made them, they were constantly living someone else's life, from Crystal to Fay and the horrible ten years in a dark box. This was the very first time they were living for themselves. They were being considered again, and thanks to them, Fay had gotten the main role in a movie. *Yes, shoe power!* Ellie thought.

And now it was "Cold Dust Girl" by Hey Champ playing, and life seemed better than ever again.

Adam brought Fay to that very same beach where, just a year ago, they had made out and then he had disappeared and never called her back. Ellie and Bernie got shivers from the déjà vu. They saw how much poor Fay suffered. However, they excused Adam, who seemed to have grown up since.

Everything was at peace now. No more fear, no more games. Fay and Adam cuddled in each other's arms and giggled from happiness. He was feeling much more comfortable with her presence. There was no more boyish awkwardness inside of him. And Fay was now a mature woman who felt fully satisfied with her life, her love, and most importantly her shoes.

Her shoes would give her a famous role in a Hollywood movie made by her boyfriend's grandfather, who was a major movie producer. It was more than a dream coming true, since she could have never even imagined something like that could be possible.

Ellie and Bernie wondered where Isabelle and Daisy were.

'Do you think they are still at the cloakroom?' asked Ellie.

'They should be,' reassured Bernie.

'Sister, we will be having the best experience ever in this movie,' said Bernie happily.

'I cannot wait! I'm so excited, Bernie!' cried Ellie joyfully.

Adam took her feet in her marvellous shoes on his lap and gently caressed them.

'I guess we could call the movie *The Incredible Story of Fay's Shoes*,' he said.

Fay smiled, looked at her little twin shoes and said, "Or *The Incredible Story of Crystal Barron's Unique, Most-Beautiful Pumps*."

They both laughed joyfully, and he gently smoothed both Ellie and Bernie. They felt the warmth of his hand, and it had been a long time since they had been caressed in such a fatherly way. They almost felt like babies born again, like that very first birthday when Balthazar was polishing them.

Adam's new I-Phone rang. 'Hello? Oh, Grandfather. Yes, we are together.' He paused looked at Fay. 'Sure, sure, I'll tell her. Okay, see you then.' He smiled and directly turned to Fay.

'Honey, I think your career just went to the top! You are to stay with us and work with the directors. The movie will be filmed in less than a month!' he said, checking for her reaction.

'Oh my God! In one month?' Fay cried in disbelief.

'May I accompany you on the red carpet when you win the Oscars?' asked Adam flirtatiously.

'I will think about it,' answered Fay, teasing.

'I think it's time for a little celebration at Trousdale. And perhaps a little dinner at Madeo?' he asked her knowing she loved Lobster spaghetti at the Italian hidden jewel Madeo restaurant.

'How could I say no to such a well thought out plan' she said obediently.

Ellie and Bernie smiled in relief; this was a new era, no more freaking out and worrying now they will live like new born shoes.

* * *

In a few months Ellie and Bernie were all over the cinemas. People loved the movie, where shoes were the main role. All Fay did was show off her nice legs.

At this year's International Shoe Society, all praised Ellie and Bernie for their grand success. The Bozzis were voted the shoes of the year and given a shoe medal of grand humanitarian help to the ISS.

The Bozzis' friends from the past all sat in the front row and waved at them: a blue suede low-heeled platform blue pump with two-tone rosette ornaments, Miss Violet Love; a multi-leather stiletto sandal with metallic napa piping named Kitty; a pair of beaded handmade Spanish sandals, Denis Jose Ignasio Pinto; and the handmade plastic-and-wire wings shoe prototype, Heather Paperstein. Ellie and Bernie looked out and saw all the speakers from the first ISS they had attended with Crystal. The twins were speechless. This was dreamlike; it was miraculous.

Then they saw their buddies from the vintage store: David and Gina, the Bourbon Street ankle boots, Jack and James, the Chelsea loafers, Alexandra from Rosebar, the vintage-style, purple stiletto. Bob and Rob were in the second row, clapping their refined John Lobb soles to greet the twins.

Lola and Lila, the red pumps from the Mercer hotel lunch, Kitty, Katy, Candy-pinkie, and Candy were all excited to see Ellie and Bernie at the tribune.

Violet and Allegri, along with Bee and Banu, were waving as well. Nora and Nola were back from their exile in India.

Bong-Chol and Ja-Hoon, the slippers from the private plane, were there as well, looking fresher than ever. And an exquisite Madame de Fleur didn't miss this social event; she waved with her elegant heels to the twins.

Biggie-Mo and Biggie were right next to Ellie and Bernie to give them moral support. From the back they could see someone very familiar.

'Of course, it is Hermeneus! The Hermes pantoufle!' cried Ellie in disbelief that even an old shoe had made an effort to come and congratulate them.

'Did you see Marla and Jasper from Harrods shoe department?' said Bernie, pointing at the two lovey-dovey shoes.

'Oh, my dears, it's wonderful to be here. We are so proud of you!' said Marla.

'Indeed, we came to New York for our honeymoon. What great timing, right?' Jasper said happily.

Ellie and Bernie enjoyed seeing Marla happy, and Jasper seemed really in love with her.

'When did you two get married?' asked Bernie, wondering how a male and female shoe could actually be at all times together.

'Oh, well, Jasper's master bought me for his fiancée and she loved me and my sister. Since then we are constantly together. No more Dior pump flirts for Jasper,' chortled Marla.

'That's great. We are so pleased,' said Ellie in relief for her friend's happiness.

Shoes were gathering up. There was hardly space for any more shoes, but they kept coming in. Soon the grand salon of the MET was filled with the most incredible shoes from all around the world.

Lady Dragon from the René Caovilla store had flown in from the Middle East to be the speaker at the ISS conference.

'Welcome to the tenth International Shoe Society conference. Today we are here to celebrate the grand achievement of Eleanora and Bernice Bozzi, who played in the first movie from the shoe perspective. The Bozzi sisters never forgot their shoe origins; they were always active in the shoe society and yearly meetings. They set a great example to the future shoe generations. Not only have they overcome the loss of their first mistress, who was Hollywood's legend of the 90s, but they also pushed themselves to promote the shoe life to newcomers who have been transformed into a shoe body. I declare on behalf of the International Shoe Society, Eleanora and Bernice are the shoes of the year! Have a wonderful year full of shoe health, shoe love, and a lot of pleasant and soft walking!' Lady Dragon swigged her heel in excitement and sent the twins a huge shoe kiss.

Ellie and Bernie walked up to the shoe tribune, but before they could say a word they suddenly saw a beautiful shoe. She was an elegantly mannered Bozzi who graciously marched right up towards them and even kissed them.

Surprised, the twins looked up and saw a transformed beauty-icon shoe, Isabelle Von Albrecht. She had her name printed on the back of her heel, which had become a few inches higher. Her rich, brown colour was now decorated with a Botox injected python décolleté. Her soles were freshly painted. But most importantly, her mood was ecstatically cheerful. She seemed delighted and content with life.

'I came here to thank you two for helping me out in my down days,' she said.

'I love my life as a shoe and would never go back into human form again. Daisy became human again, and she really is taking wonderful care of my life. Did you see my décolleté?' She pointed at her shoe chest. 'I had a few shoe surgeries. I'm finally taller, and my leather is smoother and shines. I found this new shoe spa. It's better than La Prairie clinic in Switzerland,' insisted Isabelle.

'You look stunning and joyful,' said Ellie.

'I'm so happy you love your shoe life,' Bernie added. 'In fact, I want you to say a few words. You shall be our star speaker!' commanded Bernie.

At the shoe tribune, the three Bozzis gazed at the shoe crowd that was almost a thousand pairs of shoes all looking at them and waiting for their speech.

'Thank you, dear shoe fellows. Your being here means the world to us!' spoke out Bernie.

'We love you and hope you will enjoy the upcoming movie. Our true achievement, however, is standing here with us,' said Ellie, smiling.

Ellie and Bernie were filled with indescribable joy their life had been like a dream fairy tale and it got better and better with each day. The twins sparkled from thrill to be on the tribune they looked at Isabelle and smiled.

'Her name is Isabelle Von Albrecht. She was a girl who had been transformed into a shoe. At first she was very much displeased and refused the way of life of a shoe. Ellie and I lost touch with her a few months ago. But we are pleased to see her with us tonight looking radiant and in high spirits. Ladies and Gentlemen shoes, I present you Isabelle Von Albrecht,' Bernie said loudly and went to stand by her sister.

Isabelle loved the attention as a shoe. She hadn't changed in that aspect. 'Dear shoes, indeed, like many of you here, I was a materialistic jet-setter for whom buying shoes, amongst many other things, was of paramount importance. My life revolved around shopping and having fun with my friends. One day, my friend and I awoke to be in Bozzi shoe bodies that, as you can see, I still am today. While my friend Daisy Sella di Cassolini had become human again, I decided for myself that I feel much happier as a shoe. Perhaps one day I will also be back to human, but I really hope it is not tomorrow!' She giggled.

The members of the audience smiled at her and waved their heels in anticipation of what she was going to say next. She felt wonderful being there and sharing this inner shoe happiness with the rest of the shoes.

She took a deep breath, looked up, and saw Daisy's silhouette. She watched her face look down at her and smile. Daisy wore Isabelle tonight. And Isabelle was immensely grateful to her friend for having created such a luxurious shoe life for her.

'Daisy has created a charity association called "Shoes for Shoeless." She is working hard on helping human beings and shoes. She also made my life a perfect vacation. I want to thank her, even though she cannot hear me. I also want to thank Ellie and Bernie, who have been so patient and sweet to me during my hardest moments. They showed me a great shoe life. Thank you Eleanora and Bernice Bozzi, for taking me on the most lovely and joyful journey of the incredible world of shoes.' Applauses were loud and harmonious. With colours of the rainbow coming through the labels of Andy Warhol Dom Perignon edition champagne bottles that were popping even more thunderously as the microphone was handed to a dazzling suede stiletto boot with chain laces and faux sock sung ecstatically 'Now dear shoes let's get the party started!'

The End

Acknowledgements

First and foremost I want to thank God for everything.

I wake each day thankful to have such a loving and supportive family.

Three people in particular must be thanked for being with me on this project: my dearest Mother and Father - I love you with all my heart. My one and only, best brother in the whole world Adil Bagirov - thank you for offering wise and spot-on advice on everything, thus making this a reality!

Thank you to my grandparents, who have always made me feel very special.

Special thanks to FMC and Bangoo B. - thank you for always being there for me and believing in me.

Professor David Roper thanks to whose assignment I have chosen to write about shoes.

Tatler Magazine London team - thank you for the wonderful learning experience during my internship.

I am lucky to have friends who were always there for me and in countless ways inspired my characters: Alicia Ferrero for having been a major inspirational friend, Iman Pasha for all her fashion tips and latest fashion news and invaluable advice, Nimet Ulubay for all the belief in me since school, Carolina Rodriguez-Larrain for her great energy and ever present enthusiasm, Toshimitsu Sagi for always being a great friend even far away in Japan, Marielle Hadid for the exciting insights of the LA girl, Isabelle Bschner for the wonderfully inspirational NY dinner parties. Thank you to Angelika Kolomoisky, Cristel Carissi, Camilla Ferrero, Azima K, and Dali A. Big thanks to my lovely cousins Leyla and Gunay Bagirova who were always supportive in my writings.

And lastly the biggest thanks to my readers! Thank you! I really hope you've enjoyed the book, and most importantly, the dear shoes.

Like us on Facebook: www.facebook.com/IAmAShoeAndYou